AKIRA TOKAI...
BY F...

"If all this is even close to the truth, we are looking at the biggest mystery...well, the Loch Ness monster sounds more believable than what I've learned, no, what I even suspect happened over Siberia."

"Wait a second. Suspect? I keep hearing 'craft' and 'hovering.' You're telling me," Kurtzman said in a voice gruff with disbelief, "that whatever the Russians shot down was flying on nuclear propulsion?"

Tokaido nodded. "A nuclear-powered aircraft could somehow drop onto Chicago or Los Angeles, resulting in a radioactive wasteland. Only, I'm thinking someone has taken a quantum leap into that particular danger zone. Someone...or some 'thing'?"

Kurtzman's mouth hung open. "What are you saying? That the Russians shot down a freaking UFO?"

DON PENDLETON'S
MACK BOLAN.
STONY MAN®

TACTICAL
RESPONSE

A GOLD EAGLE BOOK FROM
W◍RLDWIDE.

TORONTO • NEW YORK • LONDON
AMSTERDAM • PARIS • SYDNEY • HAMBURG
STOCKHOLM • ATHENS • TOKYO • MILAN
MADRID • WARSAW • BUDAPEST • AUCKLAND

First edition April 2001

ISBN 0-373-61936-7

Special thanks and acknowledgment to
Dan Schmidt for his contribution to this work.

TACTICAL RESPONSE

Printed in U.S.A.

TACTICAL RESPONSE

PROLOGUE

Siberia

Arkastk Tamalsty was grateful for small blessings. The world beyond the Ural Mountains could chase its madness for money and pleasure, and straight to the grave, as far as he was concerned. The gangsters and the corrupt politicians would consume this new post-glasnost motherland in their insatiable hunger for more money and power soon enough, but he might as well have been light-years from Moscow and Kiev, since even his own countrymen considered the Siberian frontier something like the far side of Mars. From all that he'd heard, the people of the cities had become like animals anyway, taking what they wanted with their violence, loving only money, worshiping only their desires. Even as he might pray for them, he wanted no part of this new Russia. Any man who lived a clean, quiet and honorable life would endure, even prevail after bad men choked on the vomit of their wickedness.

Or so he believed.

Tamalsty strolled on through the white-birch forest, his boots crunching in roughly two inches of snow coated by a thin layer of ice. Smiling, he tipped the bottle to his lips, stopped in a large clearing where a soft white sheen of starlight enveloped him, a shroud descending from nowhere out of the night. Enjoying the warm vodka buzz now singing in his ears, he took a moment to look up, wonder at it all. Stargazing, he shivered against the chill, but was touched by gratitude for the fur parka. The mane of black hair that touched his shoulders was a thick mat inside the hood, further protecting his head and neck against the cold. Swaying a little, he stared at the dark heavens. He found himself believing all the countless winking stars were smiling down on him, as if the spirits of his ancestors up there understood and sympathized with the hard life of a poor coal miner. Maybe the silent dead were simply reaffirming that a man needed only a loving family and friends to keep him happy, much less sane and strong in a world that wanted him to crawl.

Indeed.

They could have the cities and all the trappings of their ill-gotten wealth. They could even go on about their secret business in the military installation just north of his village without fear of a few coal miners getting curious and wandering in their direction. Why should he worry or care about men with guns? A man of peace and pure of heart feared not.

It was good to be alive, no secrets, no cravings to have or be more than a loving husband and father. Soon enough he would board the truck with his comrades and head out for the mine, where a ten-hour day would yield a handful of rubles to continue to feed his family. Now was his time to be alone, think his thoughts, feel blessed.

A belly warmed by 110-proof vodka always helped, of course, to stoke his gratitude and insulate his bones from Siberian wrath. If vodka was his one vice, surely the spirits in the sky would understand.

Tamalsty lifted his bottle. *"Dusha-dushe,"* he told the heavens. Soul to soul.

He thought about his wife, savoring the memory of their earlier lovemaking, then started to think about their five children and what the future might hold, when he suddenly spotted a strange dark object in the sky. A longer look and he thought the object shone, or maybe the stars were glinting off the object that hovered and was shaped like a—

A disk?

He blinked hard several times, rubbed his eyes, felt his heart skip a beat. He'd heard the stories lately from other villagers about strange lights in the sky, hovering craft the size of a city block that could move at incredible speeds, then vanish in the next few seconds. Looking north, he found the object still suspended. That was no helicopter, no scudding cloud, he decided, and no sound at all came from the craft that he could make out. He was vaguely aware of the bottle slipping from his fingers, felt his legs trembling so bad he thought he would collapse. Was he that stoned on vodka? Seeing something that wasn't there? What would he tell his family and friends? Who would believe him? They would dismiss his sighting—it was a UFO, he was absolutely positive—as the wild imaginings of a drunk.

Before he could further question what he saw, the

object darted sideways, moving faster than a shooting star as it flew east. Was "flying" even an accurate description? The craft had no wings, no tail.

He was sure it would disappear a moment later, leaving him to question his own sanity, when ten, perhaps twenty, slender objects began to shoot across the sky on tails of fire. The first series of explosions shattered the silence in crunching peals of thunder. They were firing surface-to-air rockets, he knew, at the strange craft, attempting to blanket the sky with one volley of missiles after another in hope one would score and blow the thing out of the sky. Incredibly, the craft stopped in midair, abruptly, then streaked west and began to ascend.

The entire sky erupted in a blinding wall of white fire so brilliant, in a hellish roar so deafening Tamalsty cried out loud, shielded his eyes from a glare that felt as if it scorched him to the bones, cleaved his brain in two. He heard himself screaming as what felt like a wave of fire washed over him, forcing him to his knees.

He feared the worst—hearing the angry crackle of fire all around him—and then found it.

Opening his eyes, he discovered the trees around him were being eaten up by a rolling sea of fire.

Terrified, he attempted to run, but only heard his boots squishing, as the ground felt as if it wanted to suck him into the earth. He cried out in alarm, staring at the ground. Where snow had covered the floor of the forest, there was now nothing but a quagmire of mud.

And the white fire kept screaming around him, threatening to burn him alive unless...

He slogged through the mud, running best he could, a lumbering jaunt that seemed to go on forever. If he could reach the tundra edged up against the forest, he would clear the firestorm, save himself from certain death. But something was terribly wrong with his body; even his bones felt as if they'd been set on fire. He fought down an awful sickness bubbling in his gut, his skin feeling singed as if he'd been held over greedy flames by starving hunters, like some rabbit on a skewer. He forged on, grunting from exertion, grateful that adrenaline, at least, was clearing out the vodka cobwebs. A new light was shining ahead, he saw, and as he closed on the edge of the forest, he heard the bleating of helicopter blades, the grind of truck engines straining as they hauled themselves over what clearly now looked to be a marshland out there, more snow melted into a sea of muddy goo. No explosion he had ever seen or heard about could set trees on fire, turn vast tundra into a lake of mud. What was he now witness to?

Was this simply some drunken hallucination?

Tamalsty crouched at the forest's edge, unsure of everything. A half mile or so across the tundra, four large transport helicopters were hovering over a pile of wreckage. Shadows in spacesuits, some armed with assault rifles, some holding slender poles with disk-shaped objects fixed to the end, were lumbering around the mound of glowing debris.

Tamalsty heard his labored breathing, glimpsed the air pluming from his mouth in white clouds, afraid the simple act of exhaling would betray his position to the spacesuits. Hunkering down in a copse of trees, he watched as two of the helicopters scissored back and forth over the wreckage, their searchlights sweeping the black tundra floor. Looking for what? Or whom?—the pilot or pilots of the flying saucer?

More spacesuits were now disgorging from large transport trucks. A steel cable was lowered from two of the choppers, spacesuits lifting large shiny sheets of the UFO, crating them up. The spacesuits moved the flat giant pieces, longer than his cabin, as if they weighed nothing more than sheets of paper. Was it possible? he wondered. Had they shot down a spacecraft from another world? Or was it an enemy craft? He had heard about the Americans' stealth aircraft.

The village! His family! In his fear and curiosity he'd forgotten all about his own people. He was up and trudging east, steering well clear of the firestorm behind him. At least a mile or so to the village, he figured, his mind racing as he feared the fire in the sky had...no, he told himself. Just get back home. They were all safe, alive.

He churned his legs, sloshing through the mud. It was strange, he found, what adrenaline could do, how fear could push a man like he could never dream, as he cut the distance to his village by half in less than two minutes. Then he heard the shouting and the screaming in the distance, followed by long rattling bursts of weapons fire. He cried out loud, gripped by sudden panic.

"Oh, no, no, no!" he shouted, aware of what was happening even as his mind failed to grasp the reason for what he knew was going on.

And what he would find.

He saw the spacesuits beyond the clearing, hauling men, women and children from the log cabins. Several of the cabins were ablaze in the same white fire that was eating up the forest. Forget that their homes were burning—Tamalsty found himself witnessing a sudden and unexplained mass execution. Assault rifles were blazing, bullets chopping up his people without warning. Beyond the outer limits of the glaring searchlight of the chopper hovering over the village, he even saw Natasha and his children gunned down, their bullet-riddled bodies collapsing on one another, his wife clutching their small bodies, her back to the killers, as if she could shield them from the barrage of lead.

This was utter madness. How could this be happening? Why?

Fighting off the sickness in his belly, Tamalsty pitched to the ground just as he was steeled to wade straight into the murderers, kill as many of them as he could with his bare hands before they sent him on to the next world to be with his family. Then he pulled his hands out of the mud, froze and choked down the scream at the sight of hands covered in oozing sores. Staring at the mass of raw, blistered flesh, he realized his skin had been burned, and nearly right off the bone. He felt a cold wind next, blown over him by rotor wash. A probe of his head, touching his skull, and the vomit gushed out.

Just one brush with his ruined hands, and he realized the hood had been burned off his head. Where there had been hair, there was now nothing but seared craters, gaping sores that burned like acid to the touch.

Dazed, drenched in vomit, Tamalsty stood. He

trudged on through the forest, willing his legs to move somehow, skirting the perimeter of the village, weaving, sucking wind. The weapons fire abruptly ended, but the echo of his people pleading for their lives hung somewhere in the roar of fire in his ears.

A voice in his head cried out for God, for deliverance, some comprehension of this insanity.

Some explanation for the unexplainable.

Again he stared at his hands just before his legs gave out. Mind numbed by horror, he rolled down an embankment, oblivious to the white beam sweeping past him, then the bleating faded, leaving him alone with another dying wail of the nightmare in his head.

Tamalsty stood, kept walking for what felt like hours, felt tears like fire burning up behind his eyes as he staggered on. He wanted to curse himself, a coward for not committing suicide against the spacesuits. Oh, God, no, his wife, his children were dead, gone, butchered like cattle.

Why?

Ahead the shadow rolled out of nowhere, blocked his shuffling march. Tamalsty saw the spacesuit, glimpsed the large pistol lifting in a gloved hand and heard, *"Stoi!"*

He cursed the spacesuit, felt his hands clenching up into claws. Reason somehow filtered through the rage in his heart. If the spacesuit was going to kill him, he would already be dead. So he stared at the dark visor hiding the face in the helmet, pondered what to do, heard the snarling voice muffled inside the bubbled cocoon.

"Kuda ty yedish?"

Tamalsty laughed bitterly. Where was he going? What a stupid thing to ask.

The spaceman paused, the silence between them tapped into by the distant crackle of fire. "Do you speak English?"

An American? Tamalsty nodded, felt himself shaking from head to toe, the fear and the horror threatening to break him down into a blubbering mass of tears. "Some. Yes." Another long silence and he wondered if the spaceman was staring at his burned scalp and face, repulsed by what he saw. "What...has happened? What has happened to me?"

"I'm afraid...you've been exposed."

"To what?"

"High levels of radiation."

Another wave of nausea, and Tamalsty struggled to stand, swaying, before the spaceman reached out and grabbed his arm. "Are you saying...I'm dying?" The spaceman said nothing. "Answer me!"

"Yes," the spaceman said. "A day or two, three, maybe four...knowing what I know...but eventually...yes, you will die."

Tamalsty gagged on his vomit. This wasn't happening. A UFO, blown out of the sky. A forest on fire. A tundra melted beneath his feet. Spacesuits swarming his village, butchering everyone like sick cattle. His strangled voice, as he wiped bile off his chin, could have cried out from the surface of the moon. "Why? What is happening?"

"The end of world, my Russian friend," the spaceman answered. "Ours, for starters, if we don't leave here now."

Bekaa Valley

THE EXCAVATION SITE threatened to expose them. It didn't matter in his mind if one man's terrorist was another man's freedom fighter; something drastic had to be done, and soon, or Muhmad Nabaj knew the Israeli-American archaeological team would stumble across their cache of weapons and explosives.

"There is nothing in those catacombs but mummies, cobwebs and dust! Why here? Why now?"

The longer Nabaj knelt on the hilltop, watching the archaeologists through his high-powered Russian field glasses, as they wandered around pillars chipped and cracked by time and nature, the dozen or so men and women stringing out their thin ropes, brushing this and that, fingering their maps or whatever, the deeper his agitation burned, and the more his fear of discovery built.

Well, curiosity was about to get the best of the infidel snoopers. But how to do it, quick and quiet? The next problem was how to load up the trucks, make their way through the Anti-Lebanon Mountains and cross the border safely into Syria? That alone could prove a logistical nightmare, what with Israeli F-15s periodically swarming the skies. Getting spread across half the Bekaa Valley by a 20 mm Vulcan Gatling cannon or a Sidewinder missile, unable to cap off the first AK round in anger at the infidels' flying demons, probably wouldn't land him on the short list of martyr greats in the eyes of God.

Nabaj watched as Ali Zamadh adjusted the headphones to a parabolic mike and twisted the knob on the monitor, which was the same shape and size as a laptop. Zamadh lifted a finger to signal for silence. "Strange. He rambles from one subject—"

"What? What is he saying?"

"Shh. A Roman general named Calibus, who conquered Syria...64 A.D., putting it under Roman rule. He says Calibus fell out of such favor with Herod for some sexual indiscretion with one of his mistresses...the Jew is saying this is the Roman version of the American tomb of the unknown soldier in Arlington, Virginia. Herod erased the name and all memory of General Calibus, and anyone who even uttered his name was fed to the lions. Calibus is Herod's disgraced and unknown soldier, even though history states it was the Roman General Pompey who took Phoenicia, which, you know, is present-day Lebanon."

"Yes, I know my history of the region!"

Zamadh, oblivious to the sharp defensive tone, went on. "This site, he says, has been excavated in the past, unsuccessfully, but he saw this site in a vision...seven visions...claims this is where...the missing papyrus scroll of the Seventh Seal is located? In their Bible this is where the final battle between good and evil will be waged." Pause. "What? EBEs—or extraterrestrial biological entities—in Nevada? Says he has seen things..."

"What?"

"Something about autopsies...he calls them...very strange..."

Zamadh became silent, then shook his head, stoking the anger in Nabaj as he let the field glasses drop from his face. "What?"

"The Others. He refers to them as the Others, or the Ancients, or the Elders. Says they have been here since before the dawn of human history. Says they helped in writing...the Bible... Now...shh...space-time continuum, how he perfected $E=mc^2$ when he worked as an aerospace engineer for the American NASA, says that mass can give way to energy if enough energy is created, no, he says mass can be reshaped by energy that makes possible travel at the speed of light. Now he rambles on to the soldier, the big one with the gray hair he calls Colonel David. The prophet the Jews call Jesus?''

Zamadh chuckled, but Nabaj found something like grim curiosity in the eyes and voice of his brother freedom fighter, as if he were fascinated by what he heard with his spying. ''He says Jesus was created...by alien genetic engineering?''

''What? Is he mad? Is he smoking cannabis or is he just senile? That old fool is saying their so-called Messiah was an alien?''

''There's more—and the Jews, as you know, believe Jesus was simply a prophet.''

''I know that already! What is this babble?''

''Now he says the end times will be marked by strange lights in the sky, unexplained disk-shaped aircraft, so-called UFO sightings and abductions that were, uh, prophesied by this St. John the Divine whose life and death were pretty much unaccounted for. He calls the unexplained years of this John...missing time.''

Nabaj shook his head angrily, fought down the impulse to rip off the kaffiyeh and fling it down the slope as he felt the cold sweat trickling down his neck, plastering shoulder-length black curly hair to his flesh. The waiting and worrying was over. It was time to turn his sweat into their blood.

"What is all this nonsense?" Nabaj rasped, then waved a hand. "Never mind. Have they found the entrance to the catacombs?"

"They believe they are close. They have found the pyramid tomb inside the ring of columns...he is comparing to Stonehenge...the Mayan and Egyptian pyramids...these are the columns he saw in his vision...they are an astronomical calendar...and a landing guide for the Elders...but...he talks on again about EBEs."

Nabaj cursed. What was this fantastic rambling that even had Zamadh so enraptured? He was dealing with lunatic archaeologists who saw spacemen and visions of the end of the world in the Bekaa Valley. And they called him a fanatic?

Nabaj took in this stretch of the Bekaa, tracing a route down and then out when they had taken care of these infidel nuts. The two of them had taken up their surveillance position in a copse of cedars. The distance to the Roman ruins was roughly a thousand meters, he figured, and with the sun rising over the Anti-Lebanon Mountains, the first rays were striking the snow-coated peaks of the Lebanon mountains on the other side of the Bekaa, a sharp glaze of white light washing over the arid steppe below. Hopefully, between the cedars and the rising sun, they would remain undetected, unless, of course, one of the hired guns decided he needed to take a look around the valley.

Mentally, he tabbed up the numbers. Since they first began watching the archaeologists yesterday the numbers had stayed the same: three soldiers, toting

Galil assault rifles, their grim and wary manner betraying them as either current or former Israel Defense Forces soldiers, maybe Mossad. Hired guns, he figured, there to watch the fourteen men and women digging through the ruins, men guarding the children at play. The infidels had set up tents, their half-dozen four-wheel-drive vehicles having hauled in the team and their gear from Israel to the south. At first, Nabaj had considered them just a curious nuisance. Now they were dangerous, if not ignorant, intruders, snakes that had slithered into his home away from home.

Heaving a breath, adjusting his white head cloth, Nabaj looked down and behind at their Volkswagen van, parked at the bottom of the hill. Inside, Turaj was monitoring the state-of-the-art Russian radar. Just beyond the van's drapes he made out the insectlike bristling of the antenna of the battlefield surveillance radar. Nabaj wasn't taking any chances a few F-15s were on the way, ready to blow them off the valley floor, gone to Paradise without striking some massive blow at the Great Satan. Working on the Doppler principle, the radar picked up only moving objects, its range reaching as far away as twenty kilometers. Any change of tone over the headphones, and Turaj would come running. The problem was, Nabaj had left behind in the stone hovel several kilometers to the east any weapons to defend themselves against a sudden Israeli strike. They were supposed to look nothing more than simple bedouin, not the most-wanted Syrian freedom fighters to ever cross over into Lebanon, with a track record of sniping off Israeli soldiers or blowing up IDF or Mossad outposts in suicide-bomb runs. Naturally, the right amount of money was passed off every few days to Colonel Qaadafal, the greedy buzzard who also took money from the PLO and Hezbollah.

Perhaps it was time to pack it up in Lebanon anyway, march off into the haven of Syria, simply leave behind the dead bodies of more of his hated enemies.

"We have what?" Nabaj said. "Three hundred AK-47s down there. RPGs. We have a dozen Sagger AT-3 antitank guided missile launchers. We have SAM-7s. Grenades and land mines. Surveillance equipment. A fortune in hardware we paid the Russians for to carry on our jihad, and now it could all be discovered. I will not sit by and wait for Israeli tanks to roll in and seize the cache. Listen to me carefully, Ali, this is what we are going to do. Take off the headphones!" he barked, his rage growing the more Zamadh wore that stupid mesmerized look, the man now muttering something about the Vatican, how it jealously guarded in a vault a message in writing delivered by the Virgin Mary to some children at Fatima naming the date of the Christian so-called Armageddon.

Once he had Zamadh's undivided attention, Nabaj began laying out the plan to deliver his own version of Armageddon to the infidels. Nothing mystical about it, a bullet to the head, he explained, made everything far more real than some vision of a spaceman in a dream.

The end of the infidel world was on the way, all right, and the last vision they would see, as far as he was concerned, was the Prophet Muhammad paving the way for their own Messiah, the Mahdi.

Or so he explained to Zamadh. It was time to go down there, and set the unbelievers right.

DAVID HATOVOR KNEW the Bekaa was an archaeologist's treasure trove, but he had been paid to stay vigilant, armed and ready to kill. Sight-seeing and indulging in flights of fantasy about a missing scroll—allegedly naming the date and events unleashing the beginning of the end of the world—weren't part of his job description when he'd been hired by the curator of the Eretz Israel Museum in Tel Aviv. A man's job, though, could define his very existence, and on that count Hatovor always gave due respect, even if he disagreed with those he was paid to protect. Like now, as he found himself silently at odds with most of what he heard from the wizened, stoop-shouldered ex-NASA aerospace engineer.

A former colonel in the Israel Defense Forces, Hatovor was a soldier, first and last. After retiring from the IDF he was considered one of the top terrorist hunters in the world. His scorecard of confirmed kills in Lebanon was impressive, and he knew he had saved Israel unimagined grief by waxing some of the most vicious terrorists in the Middle East. These days he hired himself out as security for archaeological excavations, or tour groups of foreigners with more curiosity than good sense.

As an educated man, despite his firsthand knowledge of the region as a spawning ground for murderers, he found himself captivated by Benjamin Feinstein. Man was history, and history was man. Or was it?

For the sake of practicality, Hatovor always researched the background of those he was paid to protect. Feinstein was a Jewish American transplanted to Israel. Several years ago his career at NASA had ended abruptly. Some inquiring by Hatovor with his American intelligence contacts revealed the man had been forced into early retirement. That was as much as his overseas spook buddies would say about Feinstein's NASA stint. Beyond NASA, his life was public record. He lectured at the universities in Israel, mostly on biblical history and Middle East archaeology. He wrote papers espousing his own theory of relativity, antigravity, space travel at the speed of light. Whether physics or fantasy, it was all as alien to Hatovor as one of the little gray man Feinstein seemed to believe he'd seen at a classified military installation in the American southwest.

What did Feinstein really know? he wondered, and stared at him, the thin wisps of white hair fanning down from his liver-spotted bald skull, those blue eyes full of a sincerity, some grim determination that made Hatovor wonder if the former NASA aerospace engineer was even in the world, so locked into his own world that other human beings didn't really even exist. People were simply there to confirm his rumored genius as the man who had discovered the mystery of the atom.

"I see I have not made you a believer, Colonel David. Perhaps you think me mad? Or just some old fool?"

Hatovor began feeling the weight of the Galil assault rifle slung around his shoulder. There was something in the air beyond the ring of columns, but he couldn't begin to define what was disturbing him. He checked the flat plain that edged up to the foothills flanking the ruins. It was damn quiet, so still out there. That they hadn't seen the first sign of life since setting up camp yesterday was perhaps reason enough for concern. Instinct wanted to warn him they were being watched, but he decided to keep his fears to himself.

And Feinstein hardly looked troubled by the idea of Muslim terrorists lurking around the valley, armed to the teeth, hearts full of hate for anything that didn't bow to Mecca.

"I have seen this place before."

Not wishing to get baited into some long philosophical discussion, Hatovor silently watched as Feinstein stood between two columns. The old man looked from his compass, to the foothills to the east, his eyes lighting up with childlike glee as the first rays of sunshine struck a column, casting a long shadow over a row of unmarked tombs directly behind him.

"Just as I saw it in the vision, yes, Colonel David, the sunlight breaking through these two columns. It was almost as if St. John spoke to me, guided me here. Yes, I know. You have difficulty believing John would leave the missing scroll of the seventh seal in a Roman tomb, the same Romans who persecuted him and exiled him to Patmos. Perhaps, in his moments of divine inspiration, when his disciple Prochorus wrote John's words, John told Prochorus where to take and hide the missing scroll."

Was that a shadow up there in the cedars?

"The one that holds the date and the events that will signal the beginning of the end of the world."

Hatovor immediately regretted saying that, as Feinstein regarded him with an angry look. "The voice told me the tube can be broken, but if the scroll is unraveled by a man who is not pure of heart, then he will burst into spontaneous human combustion. Thus take the secrets of the Apocalypse with him to the next world. Now you have kindly but skeptically told me there is no evidence John ever set foot in the Bekaa. I have seen otherwise in the visions.''

Hatovor heard Shaibla's voice crackle over the handheld radio and broke the old man's intense stare. ''Colonel, we have company, sir.''

There was a sudden flurry of activity near some rubble at the deep north corner of the ruins. Hatovor plucked the radio off his belt and watched as two of the American archaeologists ran for Feinstein. They were hopped up with excitement, flapping their arms, telling the old man that after clearing the brush and boulders, they had found the entranceway to the catacombs exactly where he had told them to look. Their giddy report went on to state they had also found a stone tube, Hebrew writing on it. As Feinstein broke into a sprint, Hatovor was gripped by the sight of the old man running fast as a jackrabbit.

''Sir, are you there?''

''What do you have, Shaibla?'' Hatovor asked, walking between columns, striding toward the row of tents.

''Could be nothing, sir. Two bedouin, coming this way on camelback.''

''I'll be the judge of what's nothing. You and Hertzl get in here and watch our people. I'll go have a word with the nomads. There's some commotion at the north side. They think they've found something.''

Hatovor slipped the Galil off his shoulder, cut Shaibla's voice off just as the man confirmed the order. Something was wrong; Hatovor felt it in his bones.

As Hatovor closed on the tents and Shaibla and Hertzl swept past him, he spotted the two bedouin, noted the traditional Arab garb, no weapons he could see, not even the traditional *jambiya* sheathed inside their black sashes. They were riding in slowly from the east and didn't look like any threat, but Hatovor hadn't lived as long as he had by trusting appearances. He was about to call out a greeting in Arabic.

The sudden racket of autofire and screaming jarred Hatovor. It was enough to cause him to twist his head, spot a group of armed shadows charging between the east columns. AK-47s barked in unison, and they cut Shaibla and Hertzl down with long sustained bursts. The head-clothed shadows surged on and mowed down the first few archaeologists they came across, burning up full clips on one or two victims as if they had hundreds of rounds to spare. It was overkill, no doubt, but it clearly told Hatovor these ancient ruins would claim still more ghosts. It was too late to curse himself for letting his guard down, allowing his mind to wander and wonder while the small army of killers had moved in. He had let himself get talked, and to death.

They said, he thought, that not even God could change the past. So he did the only thing left to do in the present.

Hatovor wheeled, triggered off a few rounds from his assault rifle, nailed one of the camel riders and sent him flying. The other bedouin was already rapid-firing a pistol he could have pulled out of thin air. Even as he adjusted his aim, Hatovor knew he'd never make it, figuring the least he could do for himself was die on his feet. A microsecond later his fear was confirmed, and the lights went out.

New York City

BOB KACHIK WAS old school. Second-generation Hungarian, born and raised in Queens, he believed in family and friends, hard work, discipline, loyalty and honor. He was also the special FBI agent in charge of a baby-sitting detail that right then pushed to the limits everything in life he truly held near and dear.

Like basic right and wrong, human decency and common sense for starters. Just what the hell was wrong with a world that wanted to coddle, schmooze and suck up to the biggest crime boss New York, not to mention the whole U.S.A., had ever seen bloody up its city streets?

The slim, dark-haired FBI SAC shook his head at the mass of blubber stretched on the couch of the two-bedroom apartment, then looked around the so-called safehouse on the twilight zone boundary between Brooklyn Heights and Cobble Hill, a little slice of hell he suspected wasn't so safe anymore.

The snoring whale in question was Yuri Mosnivoc. A chain saw buzzing on would have been preferable to what Kachik was forced to listen from a gaping mouth that made such a loud, hideous noise, he imagined the sound alone could peel paint.

In the dead of night, six antsy agents cluttered up the apartment, pacing, worried about the death threats issued by the Mosnivoc Family. They were forced to hold the hand of the biggest Russian Mob boss to ever come down the pike, give the guy anything he wanted, including the FBI hauling around a television set, hooked up to cable and VCR, as they moved the guy all over town from safehouse to safehouse.

Kachik was ordered—by way of an implied threat the world was watching and his job and pension were on the line—to treat the crime boss like he was visiting royalty, or even maybe the Second Coming descending in a blinding light from the polluted sky over Brooklyn.

That came, almost verbatim, straight from the State Department, which, Kachik heard, was taking in the face the proverbial crap rolling downhill, and all the way from the Oval Office.

A cell phone trilled, and a moment later Kachik found Agent O'Malley grimacing, holding the thing out like some poisonous snake ready to bite. "It's, uh, Carlington again, sir."

Great. The golden boy from the State Department, he knew, the schmuck who'd been running interference between Moscow and Washington ever since Mosnivoc had been snatched up in a joint FBI and Justice Department sting in Brighton Beach. There was more flak flying around these days between Russia and America since the whale's arraignment at the U.S. Criminal Courthouse in Brooklyn—well, Kachik imagined it would be easier if both sides just started lobbing ICBMs at each other.

Kachik rolled across the living room, snatched the cell phone from O'Malley. "What?"

"I'm not sure I care for your tone of voice, Agent Kachik."

"What can I say? I'm under a lot of stress."

"Aren't we all? I'll get right to it, then. I understand from the director that you're moving him again."

"That's right. It's a little thing called security."

"I thought we had an understanding he was to remain in a suite in the best hotel in Brooklyn, and not some crack flophouse. Hello?... I'm speaking to you."

"I'm here."

"I understand you haven't allowed him to speak with his lawyers or visit with the envoy that flew all the way from Moscow yesterday. Are you looking to commit career suicide, Agent Kachik? Do you understand what is happening between our country and Russia because some of our cowboys up there felt a sudden urge for career advancement and decided that a simple Russian businessman was the biggest criminal since Capone? Do you understand that myself, even the President of the United States is walking on a diplomatic tightrope? That this entire mess is threatening to throw both countries back into the cold war years?"

Kachik squeezed his eyes shut, ground his teeth, heard the blood pressure roar into his ears. The State Department eunuch whined on about diplomatic relations, how the FBI had damn well better have all the evidence they claimed they had that Yuri Mosnivoc, a former KGB agent, had at one time supplied valuable intelligence to the CIA. Otherwise,

want his fatasski in court so bad, I'm prepared to die for it.''

"I demand to know what is going on! And who you call asshole!''

"Shut your hole!'' Kachik roared over his shoulder. Something was going down; he was sure of it. Hurley and Peters were out of the play. Kachik wouldn't let their blood go unavenged, silently urging the goons to show themselves.

He could damn near feel them, close, and looking to seal them in a pincer strike.

Whatever, they'd been made, and that was enough. Mosnivoc's goons were ready to make good on their threats. Kachik was betting his life on it.

Kachik opened the door. Crouched, M-16 poised to fire, he surged out into the long, dimly lit hallway. Nothing in either direction.

"Let's shake a leg!''

They were forcing Mosnivoc out the doorway, a human shield shuffling him along, when Kachik saw the big shadow burst into the hallway, his massive shotgun outlined for a split second by the light spilling over the fire escape from the west end. Kachik held back on the M-16's trigger, heard the shotgun roar, glimpsed three more goons surge behind the shotgunner. Fire raced up his side, deep jabbing invisible torches telling him he'd been hit. He was going down, tasting the blood on his lips. Fair enough. He wasn't about to go quiet.

"Get Mosnivoc the fuck outta here!'' Kachik roared, landing on his back, sweeping the assault rifle back and forth.

One shadow dropped under his barrage, but six,

maybe seven more grim shooters were pouring into the hallway, shotguns roaring, machine guns chattering. Bob Kachik knew right then he was going to die, but if he was checking out he only hoped Mosnivoc made it out of there in one piece.

And live long enough to hear the gavel pound and the jury drop at least five hundred years in prison on his murdering head.

CHAPTER ONE

Stony Man Farm, Virginia

Barbara Price punched in her access code. Getting the green light, she was cleared for entry into perhaps the most secret vault of intelligence gathering on the face of the planet. Long legs then carried the tall blond woman into the room after the steel door opened on a soft pneumatic hiss, then shut behind her with all the sound of a falling leaf. She was two strides deep in the nerve center of Stony Man Farm when she sensed the tension right away, read grim looks that could have been set in stone. Intense stares fixed on the screens of their computers, four individuals were hunched at their respective workstations, fingers flying over keyboards to steal data out of cyberspace as easily as professional pickpockets would lift wallets bulging with cash and credit cards. Only here thievery saved innocent lives.

Three men, one stunning redhead, they were the cyber wizards of the Farm, the best of the best at what they did, she knew. In short, they were the brains behind the brawn of the Stony Man warriors—Able

Team, Phoenix Force and, of course, Mack Bolan, also known as the Executioner.

And these cyber wizards never failed to amaze Barbara Price.

If any of them noticed the Farm's mission controller watching them work over their shoulders, none showed it. They were consumed by what they were doing, and she knew enough to let them have at it. It wasn't rudeness or disrespect that they left her standing, ungreeted, unacknowledged. It was simply genius hard at work, driven to find answers and clues to three separate situations she had earlier alerted them to. She had earlier been briefed by Hal Brognola, the director of the Justice Department's Sensitive Operations Group, who also doubled up as the liaison to the President of the United States. Two out of three of the incidents causing all the concern here had already made world headlines. The third situation, however, was being kept hushed up, as if it never happened. Why? Well, that was just one of several big questions of the hour.

She watched on, felt her respect, a subtle sense of awe deepen for the wizards. They could have been four Einsteins on the verge of discovering how to split the atom. Hell, they could have been sitting right in the middle of a hurricane, oblivious to everything but the task at hand. She knew she could learn more in the next few minutes by just listening.

"This is all very strange, I mean I'm talking damn near spooky."

Aaron "the Bear" Kurtzman shifted his bulk in his wheelchair, sipped the sludge he passed off as coffee and scowled across the room at Akira Tokaido.

"What's spooky is that unholy racket you have cranked up loud enough to... Hello? What is that noise from hell anyway?"

Akira Tokaido was the youngest member of the cyber team. He wore blue jeans, a concert T-shirt and a denim jacket, and loved rock and roll, playing it constantly on the CD player with headphones meant to drive the heavy metal into his own brain. Only today Price could clearly hear the pounding thunder, knew the screeching guitar riffs were grating on Kurtzman's nerves. Respectfully, and no less gratefully for all concerned, Tokaido killed the volume. "Sorry."

"No sweat. So, other than your taste in music, what's so spooky?"

Kurtzman, one of Price's closest friends, struck her as being edged out or tired. Perhaps, she decided, it was just his mind racing more than usual, since the man was looking to shake it up, uncover some truth in cyberspace he was sure was there but couldn't quite grab.

Tokaido was shaking his head at his computer screen. "Weird. If my data from the NASA and NORAD satellites isn't a smoke-and-mirrors job, well, they picked up the craft in question over the Arctic Ocean, roughly seven hundred miles due north of Khatanga. The craft looks to have appeared out of nowhere, according to their tracking, over Severnaya Zemlya. This craft was tracked for roughly a thousand miles, on an arrow straight due southwest course, where it came to a hovering position near the Ural Mountains. We have already determined, from a little hacking into the backdoor mainframes of our friends over at the CIA and the NSA, that this is an area where a major Russian military installation, housing more than a few ICBMs, is located. Now here's the punchline, sports fans, and don't everybody laugh at once. The time recorder at the bottom of my screen shows the craft was tracked flying from point A to point B in under ten seconds."

The moment of silence was deafening before Kurtzman said, "Impossible. A thousand miles in ten seconds? Nothing can fly that fast."

"Nothing...that we know of," Tokaido muttered, turning his attention back to his screen.

"What was that? Listen, it must be some mistake, Akira. Check it again. You're seeing a meteor on the screen, a shooting star, that's all."

"I'm getting the same read as Akira, Aaron," Huntington "Hunt" Wethers said. The black ex-professor of cybernetics from Berkeley looked so baffled to Price, she thought she could almost see some more gray sprouting around his temples as his brilliant mind tried to fathom whatever it was he'd discovered. It was rare indeed that she ever saw them so bewildered.

"The new Terra satellite," Wethers continued, "was placed into a stationary hold over the Central Siberian Plain when it intercepted Russian radar and satellite readings and tracking for the same craft in question. With all due respect, Aaron, I don't think a shooting star can stop on a dime, hover, then take off at a forty-five-degree angle, abruptly stop again and resume a flight path in the opposite direction, flying at around one hundred miles per second."

"What the... You're serious, aren't you, Hunt?"

"Dead. Now I also hacked into the backdoor mainframe at Houston, which, as you know, is NASA's flickering shadow in comparison to our intelligence-gathering operations here. Houston confirmed the craft was indeed being tracked by the Russians. Unfortunately, Center Houston realized they had a thief in their cyberspace." Wethers shrugged. "I tried to stay in, but I was forced to use our lockout program before they tracked us back here. The good news is they think it's the SVR attempting the cyber burglary, so they believe Russian intelligence is sweating out what we know about the craft and their tracking of it that they don't."

"As we all know, the craft was shot down by the Russians. But watch," Tokaido said, "the computer graphic I re-created of the explosion. This was measured by Terra thermal imagining."

Price watched, wondering where it was all leading, as Tokaido hit a few keys on his console. A line of curved blocks flashed on the screen, then a brilliant simulated light flared, quickly roiling into a mushroom cloud. At the top of the screen she read "Effects of a ten-megaton blast." She felt her breath sucked down into her lungs, quickly aware of what Tokaido was about to show them. The fire-cloud graphic boiled out on a line across the screen. A graphic of a crater, smoking and glowing. At the marked-off five-mile zone from ground zero, "Complete destruction" flashed onto the screen. At ten miles was "Lethal winds." At fifteen miles she saw "Ignition of fabrics." Between fifteen and twenty miles there was light damage, power outages, electromagnetic chaos.

And finally, at twenty miles and beyond was "Blistering burns."

"That is the effect of a ten-megaton thermonuclear explosion," Tokaido announced as the firewall faded from the screen. "If I'm right, and the craft exploded about four miles up, not only did they probably see the blast all the way to Moscow, but we are looking at a radioactive hotbed east of the Urals that would make Chernobyl nothing more than a flaring match in the night. I might even be wrong on the blast radius, meaning the blast could have reached as high as twenty megatons. You see, a typical nuclear explosion yields energy as fifty percent blast, thirty-five percent heat, fifteen percent radiation. What we just saw exceeds that by as much as twenty percent down the line. My thinking is that kind of explosive force may tend to throw off the most sophisticated satellite imaging, maybe since the heat is so intense the digital imaging cameras want to wink out."

Tokaido heaved a breath, appeared unnerved for a moment by what he'd discovered. "I can outline a hot zone on the computer, gauging winds, mountain buffers, but I'm telling you in the months to come you'll see thousands of cases of leukemia, cancer and other illnesses for hundreds of miles in all directions of the blast site from fallout. So if what we also discovered about burning villages and whole forests set afire from the initial CIA and NSA station chiefs' reports out of Moscow, and factor in the tight-lipped blanket denials between the CIA and the SVR about a major nuclear explosion over the skies of Siberia...well, the Loch Ness Monster sounds more believable than what I've learned—no, what I even suspect happened—over Siberia.''

"Wait a second. Suspect? I keep hearing 'craft' and 'hovering.' I'm getting a little uncomfortable hearing all this, and it's not my coffee kicking in. You're telling me," Kurtzman said in a gruff voice of disbelief, "that whatever the Russians shot down was flying on nuclear propulsion?"

Tokaido nodded. "That's what I'm saying, Aaron. Hey, if it can be done with submarines, ask yourself why can't a plane, a satellite, whatever, fly or orbit and likewise be powered by a nuclear reactor?"

"Real simple..."

Tokaido forged on, holding up his hand to Kurtzman. "I know, the conventional thinking is the earth is covered by three-fourths water, yes, I understand that. And a nuclear-powered aircraft could somehow end up dropping into Chicago or Los Angeles, the result being a radioactive wasteland where only armed spacesuits dwell. Inherent risk factor, too great to put one in the air. Only I'm thinking someone somewhere has taken the quantum leap beyond this particular danger zone. Someone...or 'some' thing?"

Kurtzman's mouth hung open. "What are we saying here, folks? That the Russians shot down a freaking UFO?" He paused, looked around the room, then stared at the Farm's mission controller. "Barbara? Please, tell us we're not crazy. Tell me we're not chasing phantom aircraft in the sky. Tell me we're not scripting an *X-Files* episode."

Tokaido cracked a wry but nervous grin, obviously shooting to break the grim mood all around. "If she asks for a cup of your coffee, she's the one I'll worry about."

Kurtzman cocked an eyebrow at Tokaido. "That swill has made many a man the warrior that he is today, young grasshopper."

"I'm not sure what we have concerning the Siberian situation," Price quickly said, feeling herself falling into the same somber and puzzled mood she'd walked into. "Why don't we move on to the other two incidents for the time being."

"Right," Kurtzman said. "Let's stick to the facts. Carmen? You've been mighty quiet."

All eyes turned to the redhead at her workstation. Carmen Delahunt's lips were pursed, her brow creased, but the taut expression took nothing away from her beauty. "Well, Aaron, I've been using your new CONTACT program to try and tie in the three separate situations, inserting the three names you gave me into the program, which, I must say, is a work of genius."

Under different circumstances Kurtzman might have smiled, thanked her, but today he simply acknowledged the compliment with a respectful nod.

"It allows me to type in any three letters or the name of any military, intelligence or law-enforcement agency in the world and I have instant data. CONTACT literally does all the work for you. Anyway, I did an extensive background search on the three subjects in question, but I'm coming up empty. There's nothing in the plus columns. No equal signs anywhere. No bingo, no grand slam."

Kurtzman frowned. "Meaning no connections between the hit on the FBI team in Brooklyn, the slaughter of the Israeli-American archaeology team in the Bekaa Valley and our ten-megaton fireworks show over Siberia?''

Delahunt shook her head. ''I didn't say that. I get the feeling the program is trying to tell me something, but I think I need more information, maybe from Katz about the situation in Lebanon. He said he'd have more within the hour once he touched base again with some of his Mossad contacts in Israel, one of which was first on the scene when the tanks rolled into the Bekaa. Israeli fighter jets, as I'm sure you know, make frequent flyovers of the valley.''

''Hoping to blow a few bad guys back into Syria,'' Tokaido said.

''Exactly,'' Delahunt replied. ''Only the bad guys won this round, vanished into thin air, it would seem. The F-15s found the bodies in some Roman ruins. Eighteen dead, including three Americans and three former Israeli soldiers who were hired as security detail.''

Price saw Kurtzman look her way. Yakov Katzennelenbogen, the former leader of Phoenix Force, was the Farm's tactical advisor. Given the fact that prominent Israeli citizens had been murdered by what was most likely an Islamic terrorist group, Katz was pulling no punches to get a lead on the killers. With his extensive background of former service to the Israeli army, then later serving as intelligence chief and aide to Moshe Dayan, Katz would come through with some answers. More than a few people in that part of the world owed Katz, and even with their lives.

''Katz gave us the name of a Syrian terrorist he thinks could be responsible for the massacre,'' Kurtzman told Price. "A man by the name of Muhmad Nabaj. He had been waging jihad on Israeli military outposts in southern Lebanon, then switched to raids on settlements in northern Israel. He's known to also recruit teenage Palestinians for 'martyrdom.' Meaning he has them strap on a backpack full of dynamite and set themselves off in the middle of crowded Tel Aviv streets. Mossad says his MO is that he always leaves the dirty work to someone else while claiming his sick glory from a distant hilltop. He'd rather live to see someone else kill for him another day than put his own head on the chopping block."

"Sounds like the world would be a little kinder and gentler place without him," Price said.

"Yeah, a slice of heaven even, to give it the good old classic understatement. What about the FBI fiasco, Carmen?" he asked.

"Five agents dead. Three critically wounded. Shooters went down, DOA. No ID, nothing to tell us who they were, although your first two guesses don't count. My read on it tells me the FBI wanted to keep it out of the papers, but the egg on their faces was all over front page across the country this morning."

"A leak," Wethers said. "Or someone on the home team jumped to the other side of the tracks."

Anger flashed through Delahunt's eyes as she glanced at her screen. "I'm getting a definite bad feeling about the whole mess, Hunt. First, there's been death threats hurled every day at not only agents assigned to guard this Yuri Mosnivoc, but their families, as well. Second, the State Department, according to Hal's report, which came to him via the FBI, wants to coddle Mosnivoc. Says his arrest is questionable, maybe even illegal. I think we can all add two and two here. State is worried this will set back relations with Russia forty years or more.''

"Just what the Russian Mafia needs," Kurtzman growled. "Politicians and dipos making a poster child out of this Mosnivoc like he's some New Age messiah come to save his unemployed, starving countrymen."

"That pretty much sums it up, Aaron," Delahunt said, "how State is spinning out the damage control. But from what I've learned, Mosnivoc is clearly what the FBI claims he is, which is the biggest Russian Mafia boss to ever land on the shores of Brighton Beach. They have him nailed, dead to rights. Wiretaps, video surveillance, physical evidence, informants in his own organization, which is extremely unusual to see Russian gangsters singing against their own. Whatever, his trial begins tomorrow at the U.S. Criminal Courthouse in Brooklyn. You can only imagine the logistical nightmare, the security migraines the FBI now faces." She paused, shook her head.

"What?" Kurtzman asked.

"Hal's report from his FBI contacts," Delahunt went on.

Price listened with mounting concern as she stated two agents were on the street, waiting with the vehicle that was to transport Mosnivoc to another location, when they were attacked, allegedly from behind, but received only minor head wounds.

Wethers spoke her thoughts. "I smell inside job."

Kurtzman again looked Price in the eye. "Barbara, not to change the subject, but there's something else

I turned up when I was poring over the sat pics. Thing is, I can't even look at it again without wearing sunglasses or feel my heart lurch into my throat." He paused, then said, "I came across an area just over the border in Syria where the archaeologists and their security detail were slaughtered. It's clearly some sort of complex, but thermal imaging turned up so much heat radiating from this site that I damn near thought I was going to be blinded."

Price matched Kurtzman's worried look. "You're saying you've discovered the Syrians have built a nuclear-waste reprocessing plant?"

Kurtzman nodded. "It sure looks that way. Now, you want to talk about strained international relations? If the Israelis get a look at this... I don't think I need to tell anyone here the Israelis have a track record of blowing places like this off the map so bad, you don't even have a Stone Age left after the smoke clears."

Another long moment of silence, grim stares passed all around.

"If I may add one more thing," Delahunt said. "It's about the man who headed up the archaeological team in the Bekaa." She tapped some keys on her console. "This is where CONTACT stumbles some, and where I feel it wants to tell me something important, if not critical."

Price watched as Carmen hit the return key, scrolling up what looked a manuscript, but the pages were riddled with black boxes, emblazoned with *Delete* in white lettering. Her eyes shone with an intense curiosity. "Benjamin Feinstein was a former NASA aerospace engineer. He was with NASA for fifteen years.

It took some detective work, but I've found that he worked on several classified joint NASA-military projects, all of them with names that sound like something a ufology buff would come up with. What I'm showing you here is his letter of resignation CONTACT conveniently borrowed for me from NASA's personnel department. Feinstein quit, or rather I'm thinking he was quietly put out to pasture by NASA, after hitting the talk-show circuit. He started telling the talking heads he was assigned specifically to work on 'reverse engineering' of alien craft. He's written articles for respected science journals about particle reactors that bombard an alien element he calls 'Number 116.' Of course, you all know there are only 109 known elements on Earth. Genius or fanatic—who can say? But Feinstein said the photons hit the nucleus of this Element 116, eventually generating gravity waves beyond the perimeter of the atom. Energy is amplified to distort time and space. He also claimed to have converted mass to energy, that he can warp space and time between two points. If that's possible, he said man can travel at the speed of light. Then you have gravity breakdown into three electromagnetic waves…well, there's a lot more, but I think you know where I might want to head with this.''

Kurtzman observed, ''What I'm hearing, we're throwing a lot of mud on the wall, hoping something sticks, but my gut's telling me there's some connection somewhere.''

''Carmen, I want to know more about Feinstein,'' Price said, and was beginning to get the same feeling as Kurtzman. But what connection could there be between a slain former NASA aerospace engineer, the nuclear explosion of a mysterious craft over Siberia, much less a tie-in with a Russian Mob boss?

"You've got it," Delahunt said.

"Is there a mission in the near future?" Kurtzman asked Price.

"I don't know—yet. Let's wrap this up for the time being. Get your thoughts, facts and figures together. We're going to the War Room." Price checked her watch. "I originally came in here to tell you Hal's already being choppered in. He should be landing anytime. He didn't say anything about Phoenix Force or Striker, but he ordered Able Team here, since they were already in the Washington area. Gadgets and Rosario are on the premises as we speak," she said, referring to Rosario Blancanales and Hermann Schwarz, then added that she'd recalled Carl Lyons, the leader of Able Team, from R and R, six hours ago.

"Please, tell me that Hal has something more on all of this than guesswork, theories and suspicions," Kurtzman said.

"We'll find out soon enough if some of the mud sticks."

CHAPTER TWO

Carl Lyons was in a foul mood when he stepped off the Bell JetRanger. The leader of Able Team was hungover, sunburned, bone tired, aching and itching from head to toe. Despite the aloha shirt, white silk slacks and alligator shoes, he knew he looked like crap on a stick.

So much for vacations, so long paradise.

Right then, Miami was a giant sore of an ugly memory, and the slightest movement sent jolts of pain through his whole frame. Even with his dark Blues Brothers shades, it hurt to see sunlight blazing down over the Shenandoah Valley, unless he squinted hard enough to drive blue eyes deep into their sockets. The bottom line was, he felt mean enough to bite the hooded head off a cobra.

There were reasons for his righteous anger, and despite his best effort to forget, he still gave it some fleeting recall, maybe trying to fathom what just went wrong and where, as if it really mattered now.

She had sure looked sweet and innocent enough, a creamy young blonde who had dripped charm and schmooze, complete with big-daddy talk, all over him. Of course, it always helped a man get plenty of female attention in a gentlemen's club when he carried a wad of cash fat enough to choke a rhino. He should have known better, drinking and carousing, but once in a while he owed it to himself to cut loose. His life was spent on the firing line, and the former LAPD cop never knew when his next day would be his last.

Well, maybe he'd had too many shots and beers under the belt when the lady in question spun her web. Maybe he shouldn't have fallen dead asleep after their long romp in his hotel suite, where Lila—if that was even her real name—came on like one big love goddess, making him feel younger than he really had any right to feel. Maybe he should have kept one eye open, and she wouldn't have lifted almost four grand in cash out of his pants pocket, sashayed off, disappearing like...well, yes, the proverbial thief in the night. It was certainly out of character for him to allow himself to get sandbagged that way. Hell, he was Ironman, after all, and getting ripped off by anybody, man, woman or street punk, was the kind of thing supposed to happen to the average platinum-plastic-carrying Joe.

Screw it, chalk it up to bad experience. R and R was over, duty called and soon enough he'd be back in action. Some good old-fashioned kicking of bad-guy butt, he hoped, would cure what ailed him.

Lyons found a reception committee of four black-suits waiting for him as he stepped beyond the chopper's rotor wash. The whole picture inside and beyond the Farm's helipad looked tranquil enough, but it always struck him that way, this little slice of paradise planted in the Shenandoah. It could have all been a large farmstead with main house, barns, equipment sheds and various and sundry outbuildings. They could have been growing apples here, tilling the land, one big happy farmer and his family. That was unless a man knew the whole truth about this place. And the reality was the postcard scenery housed the country's most top secret covert command and control center, where warriors came and went to do battle with a whole range of thugs, terrorists, madmen and anybody else who posed a threat to the United States, her allies or any group of poor unfortunates around the globe who—regardless of race, color or creed— found themselves under the hammer of a tyrant.

Appearances were, indeed, deceptive in this case. There were hidden antiaircraft batteries, an armory, a workshop where the best in firepower was not only stored but created by a weapon smith named John "Cowboy" Kissinger. There were more sensors, cameras and other surveillance equipment spread around, not even the smallest of rodents would go undetected. Every entrance had a coded access not even the best in high-tech B-and-E gear could crack. There were false windows, bulletproof, of course, with armor plating running down the garrets. Last, but not least, farmers didn't carry HK MP-5 submachine guns to pick apples, much less greet new arrivals on their land.

There he was, ready and itching to get back out there and kick ass and take names, so maybe his own anger would provide motivation enough to do whatever it was that would be asked of him. So his Miami party had been cut short by two days when Barbara Price had raised him on his secured cell phone, informed him a DEA Gulfstream had been scrambled to Miami International Airport take him to Dulles, where a chopper was on standby to fly him to the Farm. No sweat.

It was time to pull it together.

Lyons let the blacksuits put him through the standard drill. A small black box came out, and Lyons put his thumb on the pad. The green light told the blacksuits he was who he was supposed to be, even though the blacksuit flyboy had radioed ahead and told the reception crew Able One was en route, ETA, the works. They didn't take chances here.

Security protocol out of the way, Lyons strode on. When he spotted the real welcoming committee near the main house, he shook his head, then clenched his jaw as pain shot through his skull. Dead ahead, they were all grins and chuckles. Here we go, he thought as he scowled at Hermann Schwarz and Rosario Blancanales, the commandos who rounded out the other two-thirds of Able Team.

"You look like shit," Schwarz cracked. "You look like you've aged ten years since I last saw you. No, on second thought, you look like some hundred-year-old lounge lizard doing hungover renditions of old Sinatra tunes."

"I look how I feel," Lyons growled. "And lounge lizard's not even close. More like a hungry, angry croc. Stow the wisecracks, guys."

Blancanales's grin widened. "You know, after you called us at our posh accommodations in Arlington—a one-star fleabag, but hey, we're not big-time Miami kind of guys—I got to thinking about what you told me happened to you down there."

"What another big fat mistake that was."

Blancanales forged on. "So I thought you might need us front and center to hold your hand. You know, I even thought about making up one of those placards, the kind you see a chauffeur or long-lost aunt holding up at the airport. Something like Welcome Home, Ironman. We Missed You, Nice Of You To Survive Miami Without Your Pals."

Lyons rolled up, stopped in front of the comedians. "I'm not in the mood," he said, and meant it, but saw right away they weren't about to let it go so easy. What the hell, maybe he'd earned some ribbing.

Blancanales kept grinning. "I'm glad you didn't ask me to wire you some money, or we might have never seen you again."

"You should choose your lady friends a little more carefully from now on, don't you think, Ironman?" Schwarz posed, matching Blancanales grin for grin. "Maybe next time use some of your *shotokan* karate moves instead of trying to come across like the greatest lover since Errol Flynn. What's with you and Grimaldi and Miami anyway?" he said, referring to Jack Grimaldi, Stony Man's ace pilot.

"It must be all in the beaches and the mint juleps," Lyons rasped.

Schwarz chuckled. "Every time one of you guys goes down there, you get yourselves in a jam, come back, broke, pissed off at your buddies even. If you like, Pol and me can break out the violins, but I don't think that jackhammer in your brain could take it."

"Hey, but Gadgets, I can see Carl spent some time at least working on his tan," Blancanales cracked. "I think I can dig up something for that sunburn. Man, that must hurt.''

''Are you clowns through?''

''We just had to tell you how missed you were,'' Schwarz said, the wisecracking tone gone from his voice. ''We worry about our fearless leader when he's out of our sight too long.''

''I'm touched. Now, does anybody have any idea what may be coming down our way? I'm feeling this sudden urge to kick ass.''

''Have you had a chance to read today's paper?'' Schwarz asked.

''Somehow I must have missed the newsstand at MIA.''

''I can only imagine. Well, while you were working on your tan and being relieved of your hard-earned money, Hal had us do some background digging on a few FBI agents,'' Blancanales said. ''He thinks there might be a problem.''

''In what way?''

''There's this particular Russian Mob boss who's being sat on by the FBI in Brooklyn,'' Schwarz told him. ''Supposedly no one but the home team knew the location of the safehouse. Well, a few goonskis tried to free him last night in a Wild West show that would have made the OK Corral look like some kids picking off soda cans with slingshots.''

Blancanales picked it up from there, turning as dead serious as Schwarz. ''Major shootout between the FBI and some unidentified thugs, none of whom will any longer drink vodka and eat caviar, I'm happy to report. Sad to report that more than a few good guys went down and all the way out to make sure the boss stayed in one piece. The good news is the guy is still under the FBI's umbrella.''

Lyons saw where this might be headed and groaned. ''Don't tell me. We're going to be assigned to a baby-sitting detail because the FBI may have a snake or two under the bed?''

Blancanales shrugged. ''I have to believe that's why Hal's here. You flew in about five minutes behind him.''

''I didn't see his chopper.''

Schwarz pointed past Lyons to a second Bell JetRanger that was grounded about forty yards beyond his own ferry ride, and Lyons looked in that direction. ''In the shape you're in, I'd be surprised if you could even find—''

''All right, all right.''

Blancanales clapped Lyons on the shoulder as the three men headed toward the main house. ''It's really good to see you, Carl. But next time you go on R and R, how about considering your buddies here? Gadgets and I haven't seen even a day of your brand of R and R in over a year.''

''I'll give it some serious thought. Right now, I think I could use a cup of coffee—even if it's Bear's swill.''

HAL BROGNOLA WAS a blunt and direct man. The other party never had to wonder whether he or she was getting straight talk. This was especially true when it came to addressing the Stony Man support staff about national security, and the big Fed didn't disappoint Barbara Price this time out, either.

''I'll get right to it, people. At around 1600 hours

eastern standard time yesterday there was a reported but verified UFO sighting over Siberia, east of the Ural Mountains. Our satellites, as I'm sure most of you now know, monitored the whole incident. There was a subsequent explosion in the range of fifteen megatons that was—I'm told by a reliable contact at the Pentagon—seen all the way to Moscow. We now know the Russians shot this something down. The something they shot down was a wingless, disk-shaped prototype U.S. spy plane with nuclear-warhead-delivery capability, classified as a black project code-named Centurion X. In a nutshell, people, it was our UFO they shot down. The Russians are now in possession of pieces of our flying saucer.''

Price saw no one move, not even draw a breath. She couldn't help but glance at their faces. Clearly reading their expressions, the Farm's mission controller knew Brognola had everyone's undivided attention.

The four cyber wizards were present, along with Able Team and Yakov Katzenelenbogen. Katz had his prosthetic arm resting on his own intel packet, and Price would have sworn the device jumped a little from some nervous impulse sparking from his shoulder, his mind trying to grasp what Brognola had just dumped on them.

"What was that?" Katz asked, and now Price was certain of his disbelief. "Did I just hear you right, Hal?"

"You heard me right. Now, we have a lot of ground to cover. I'll begin to lay it out, but feel free to cut in at any time."

Price listened, on the edge of her seat, like all present, as Brognola put it to them. She had no doubt the information he came by was legit. The big Fed tapped a manila folder, explained there was some sketchy intel inside relating to Centurion X, most of it loose pieces, but with a few key names attached, one of which was Benjamin Feinstein. He informed Kurtzman and the other cyber wizards they were to pore over what he'd brought, make headway toward the location where this craft was built, any other pertinent information they could dig up that might help them all understand what in the world exactly they were dealing with regarding the craft itself and its builders.

"Well, if what we've discovered so far about this craft is to be believed," Tokaido said, "we're looking at a technological advance that would make the United States look as if it just invented the wheel, or the light bulb, with the rest of the planet still on foot and living in the Dark Ages."

Wethers added his thoughts. "Indeed. Now that Hal has stated it has nuclear-delivery capacity...well, here's the problem the way I see it. Say, just for argument's sake, we've used some sort of reverse engineering, that is if you believe the stories coming out of Area 51 are true. If we did it, the Russians can do it now that they are in possession of parts of the craft. Another problem is they may have even captured its pilot or pilots, will pick their brains about this craft, perhaps have their own flying saucer with nukes in the skies by year's end. Incredible as it all sounds, we think this craft can fly three, maybe four or five times the speed of sound."

"Come on, you're kidding me, Hunt," Schwarz said. "No flying machine I ever heard of can go that fast. The speed of sound in air is what—about 750 miles per hour?"

"Or 350 meters per second," Wethers said.

"G-force alone would kill a man," Schwarz commented.

"Unless the craft was, say, outfitted with an alloy that we—meaning all of us here—have never heard of."

"If this plane, or craft, or whatever," Lyons said, "is such a hot commodity, how did the Russians manage to shoot it down so easy?"

"We're looking into that," Brognola answered. "My guess is pretty much backed up by first reports from my contact at the Pentagon. The Russians simply blanketed the sky with surface-to-air-missiles."

"Spray and pray," Lyons said.

Brognola went on to state the Russians were denying they had shot down the craft in question. The pilot, he said, had apparently jettisoned, might be on the run inside Siberia, his GPS module equipped with reverse tracking, but that he could only be monitored during an American satellite passover.

"It's questionable, however, if the pilot is still even alive," Brognola said. "If he jettisoned just as their rockets slammed into the craft, a fifteen-megaton blast would have incinerated him, needless to say.

"The problem is indeed with the Russians. But it's more on our home front at the moment than over there, at least from a public viewpoint. Here's where it gets messy, here's where the coincidence between a Russian Mob boss and our UFO wants me to toss caution to the wind and send out our troops." He quickly reviewed the Mosnivoc situation, the FBI fiasco of the previous night, the State Department's jumpy nerves over diplomatic relations with Moscow. "The Russians have demanded that Mosnivoc be returned to them, unmolested, every stain the FBI has smeared over his good name removed. Their own diplomatic corps has even made a few veiled threats that if Comrade Yuri isn't released immediately there will be 'repercussions and consequences.' They claim he is a legitimate businessman being framed by the FBI. We, of course, know otherwise. Mosnivoc goes on trial tomorrow for a list of crimes too long to get into. Between the threats the FBI has received, the fact that they've bounced Mosnivoc all over Brooklyn and have still had security breached in the worst way imaginable leads me to believe the FBI has a Judas under its nose."

Lyons scowled into his coffee cup, but sipped anyway, then cleared his throat. "Is, uh, this where we come in, Hal?"

"More on you guys in a minute, but I'll tell you now, yes, you're going to Brooklyn. Now I don't want to get sidetracked on this craft and UFO talk. You're maybe wondering if there's a mission, if anyone is about to drop into Siberia to recover pieces of this craft or scoop up the pilot. All I can tell you is I've been in touch with the President, and he wants this UFO situation 'resolved,' to use his words, before it somehow goes public. The problem is he doesn't quite know how to go about it. Meaning we're not sanctioned for a covert foray into Russia—yet. I'm working on it, but again, the problem is the Mosnivoc situation, which I personally consider nothing more than a fly on the back of a tiger. We have the don, they now have our UFO. All things considered, it's straining relations with our Russian allies to a point that I can't even say what the hell may or may not happen."

Brognola suddenly looked at Kurtzman, studied his troubled expression. "Bear, you look as if you've got your own bomb to drop."

"Since you've indicated Able is paying the FBI a visit in Brooklyn, I'll move on from there. All I'll add on that score is that Mosnivoc is as dirty as the day is long. A background check on the don has turned up he provided the CIA some information on KGB activities in the East Bloc countries during the cold war."

When Kurtzman paused, Delahunt added, "My own background check would indicate Mosnivoc played our side like a fiddle during those years, sending the CIA on the proverbial wild-goose chase. I would strongly urge Able to watch their backs when they go to Brooklyn like they've never done before. More than a bad Fed or two could be behind last night's hit."

"My whole point. I couldn't agree more with Carmen," Kurtzman said. "Moving on...while poring over sat pics of the Bekaa and Syria, I turned up what clearly looks like a nuclear-waste reprocessing plant just inside the Syrian border. There's my bomb."

Brognola's gaze narrowed, his expression dark. "You what? That's new to me."

"I've confirmed it with Israeli intelligence," Katz said. "I've also confirmed my suspicions that Mossad believes it was Nabaj who murdered the archaeology team. There is a definite storm building inside the

Israeli military machine. And I think everyone present knows how I feel about murdering fanatics. My sources tell me Nabaj most likely skipped off into Syria, but I would like nothing more than to see him and his butchering cronies found, and shot up so much there wouldn't be enough for the buzzards left to eat.''

"Amen to that," Kurtzman added.

Brognola looked from Katz to Kurtzman, then back to Katz. "Hold on a second here. What's this storm talk? Katz, I hope you're not implying that maybe you've learned the Israelis are set to blow this reprocessing plant off the map?"

"Let's just say they're in conference," Katz said.

"The President needs to know this, and like five minutes ago," Brognola said, looking set to bite his cigar in two.

"You're saying we'll have another mission?" Kurtzman asked.

"Barbara, where's Phoenix Force?"

"They were flown by a C-130 to the Aviano air base in Italy after wrapping up their mission in Senegal. They're standing down."

"They're now on standby. Get hold of McCarter ASAP," Brognola said. "I want you and Katz to put together all the logistics to get them into Syria and have a look at this reprocessing plant. If it is what you say it is, Bear, and I don't doubt you're right, it will be shut down."

"You realize," Katz stated, "we may have to work with Mossad and Israeli commandos if we get the green light from the President."

"I want you to pick the brains of your contacts

over there," Brognola said. "I want a full report on their plans, their intentions, even their thoughts on the Syrian situation every hour on the hour."

"You'll have it."

Brognola paused, looking as if he'd aged five years in five minutes. "Okay, let's give and take a few more minutes, then I need to get in touch with the Man."

"If this Syrian situation blows," Kurtzman said, "we're going to need all the help we can get. By the way, speaking of major help, anybody know where Striker is?"

"He's in Hawaii," Brognola said, answering Kurtzman's question about Bolan's whereabouts.

Price happened to glance at Lyons, who was suddenly scowling at Blancanales and Schwarz. "No, guys, not the time or place. Don't say it, don't even grin."

"No," Brognola said, a wry twist to the corner of his mouth as he looked at Able Team, "Striker isn't on vacation. I'll tell you what. Whatever is ahead, whatever mission or missions there are, if we come out the other side I'll guarantee the three of you a weeklong rock-and-roll party in Miami like you couldn't imagine."

Price saw Blancanales and Schwarz perk up at that.

Grim as hell, the man from Justice told Able Team, "I'll even pay for it out of my own pocket."

CHAPTER THREE

Hawaii

"Looks like paradise has turned ugly. Not nearly as grand as the view from your balcony."

"What the hell's that supposed to mean, Belasko?"

"Means you won't find these in any travel brochures for the islands."

Mack Bolan slipped the dozen eight-by-eleven colored blowups back into the manila envelope and held out a hand. One glance was plenty enough of the guy in various entanglements with brown-skinned beauties. The Executioner pretty much knew the score here if he was to head out from there with a shopping list of bad guys. When the man in dire straits snatched the packet away, Bolan glimpsed the scowl out of the corner of his eye.

"What is this? Hal Brognola sends some wiseass who wants to stand there and judge me in my darkest hour?"

Maybe it was the grim twist to Bolan's mouth that set off Special Agent Mark Rivers, flaring up all kinds of resentment and indignation in the Executioner's face. Or maybe it was the hole that this Justice Department agent had dug for himself, and now the guy was simply looking for the first available target to vent his woes. Whatever, Bolan had a job to do. Specifically, though, this was a favor for Hal Brognola.

But this was no mercy call. The more he saw and heard from Rivers, the more Bolan knew there were poisonous snakes slithering all over paradise.

"Just so we're clear, others take care of the judging part for me," the Executioner said.

"Whatever you say, Mr. Fucking Clean."

While the slim, gray-haired Rivers stood and stared and boiled in his own anger, the soldier took a moment to both enjoy the scenery while giving the situation some brief mental replay, wanting to determine how he might put two and two together and come up with a mission.

The balcony ran halfway around the special agent's renovated split-level, offering a bird's-eye view of both green-carpeted foothills and pristine white sandy beaches. The wood beneath Bolan's wingtips was teak, damn near spit shined. The whole place, in fact, was bright and gleaming with teak or mahogany, polished glass and brass, lush tropical vegetation all around. Rivers's slice of Nirvana was nestled close to the beaches of the north shore of Oahu, where the glistening gem of the Kauai Channel separated the fiftieth state's most populated island from Kauai. If Bolan rounded the corner he could gaze at miles of beaches loosely packed with surfers, sun worshipers and parasailors and anybody else who flocked here to escaped the maddening tourist crush of Honolulu and Waikiki on the other end of the island.

Adjusting his dark aviator shades, Bolan, who

came to Rivers under his cover as Special Agent Michael Belasko of the Justice Department, watched a rainbow of colored birds flapping around the mushroom caps of prehistoric-looking treetops. There was even a waterfall down there, a silver spring that glinted like a bed of diamonds against a blazing sun.

The Garden of Eden, right, but paradise all ended with the view. There was, indeed, the soldier thought, something to be said that if it all looked too good to be true...well, watch your ass, or a man could kiss it goodbye.

Mark Rivers had all but kissed it to hell.

Even still, the soldier believed the guy was only one piece in a larger, more ominous puzzle. Hal Brognola, Bolan reflected, had sent him to Oahu to find out the truth behind why a longtime friend of his had murdered his wife and three children, then turned the shotgun on himself. More troubling, peep show blowups of Brognola's friend were found at the crime scene. A family man who had an impeccable service record, John Pritchett had been tasked to organized crime like Rivers, working the Yakuza and Triad beat on the islands. Somebody had bagged Pritchett in his weakness, extorted him, and it didn't take Sherlock Holmes, Bolan knew, to see it had pushed him over the edge. Well, Brognola had run the background on the name of a fat-cat Japanese mobster for the Executioner, the same Yakuza boss in question that Rivers claimed was behind the sex scam, but Bolan needed a few more facts before he marched off for his own brand of island touring.

The soldier saw Rivers raking him up and down with a suspicious look, his gaze settling on the bulge on Bolan's hip where the .44 Magnum Desert Eagle was holstered. The aloha shirt was baggy, flowing down, and Bolan also had the white windbreaker hanging over the big piece, but a trained eye would know the hand cannon wasn't standard-issue hardware for any G-man. The warrior's Beretta 93-R was also snug in its usual place, stowed in shoulder holster, and once again the wary eye could tell Bolan was no tourist suffering jet lag and out for a good time. Heavier firepower, along with the rest of his gear—battle and otherwise—was housed in his war bag, which now sat in the Bell JetRanger, the chopper that had ferried him from Wheeler Air Force Base and was now parked out front of Rivers's posh mini-estate.

Rivers heaved a breath, lost some of the edge in his voice. "Look, Belasko, I called Brognola and pretty much laid it out, not to mention I dumped my career on the chopping block."

"You want points for coming clean, you'll have to look somewhere else."

Rivers ignored Bolan's remark. "I know Pritchett was a friend of Brognola's. Hell, he was my friend, too—we worked together on a major Triad case a few years back, the man even took a bullet for me."

"Pritchett's why I'm here."

"Because he was Brognola's friend. Okay, so I figure you care more about getting to who is behind this than telling me I'm finished with the department."

Bolan felt his mouth tighten in a grimace. "I hear plea bargain. If you're asking for career salvation, it's not my call, but a betting man would mark you down as a sure loser."

Rivers scowled. "I have a wife and two kids, Belasko. I sent my family to California until this mess is somehow sorted out. Okay, I made my own bed. I read you, loud and clear. If I'm fired, fair enough, but I don't want to lose my family. They're all I have left, and the last thing I want is for my wife to find out the truth."

Bolan looked over his shoulder. "Looks like you've done pretty good for a guy living off a G-man's salary. I'm sure you'll survive."

"Hey, I resent the hell out of that. You look into my background, you'll find my wife inherited very nicely from her parents."

"Maybe so."

"Maybe nothing. If you're looking for some offshore account, you won't find it with me."

Bolan hadn't intended to get sidetracked by the guy's bitter stand. It was enough the soldier had thrown some bait out there, feel Rivers out, see if he was set to play ball. Time to cut to the chase.

"How did it happen with you?" the Executioner asked.

Rivers grunted, and the anger came back. "Yakamu 'Benny' Fugasami is what happened to me."

"I have a file on the man."

"I bet you do. Then you know he *is* the Yakuza on the islands. I mean this guy and his horde are like something straight out of the old code of Bushido, long and short swords, death before dishonor, the whole nine yards of samurai nonsense. I even know of three of his guys who let him down sticking the short swords in their own bellies, committing traditional seppuku. These guys are maniacs."

"And Benny has you by the shorts."

"Benny has a lot of guys by the shorts. As for me, it was a few drinks, a back room with a hidden camera, a twenty-year-old island girl looked like she could have been sent straight from heaven...I don't know what came over me. Boredom, a middle-aged guy looking for a little excitement, something else, something different."

Bolan had the picture, but he wasn't about to cut the fallen Justice man any slack for regret and stupidity. "You mentioned something about Fugasami having a full plate of problems. Meaning what?"

"The word on the street is a Chinese Triad is trying to cut in on Benny's turf, so now Benny's feeling the pinch, which means the man could be more dangerous than ever. And believe me, paranoia won't destroy him."

"He's looking at a war with the Triad?"

"Word is it could start anytime. Huan Chengdu has an army that can match Fugasami's samurai, gun for gun or sword for sword."

Bolan filed that away, mentally saw a plan of sorts shaping up. Getting caught in the cross fire of a turf war was nothing new to the soldier. In fact, there were times in the past when he'd initiated a war between competing Mafia families, then stood on the sidelines while they savaged each other, shaved the numbers down for him so he could step up to the plate and swing for the fences.

"What else about this extortion angle?"

"Well, what you may not know is that there have been a few other murders and suicides on the islands, thanks to Benny, no doubt, tightening the thumb-screws on some law and military VIPs.''

"I already know that. A DEA agent killed his young wife, then himself two weeks ago. There was a Navy captain found hanging from the rafters of his home, a suicide note and more blackmail pics scattered around the scene. Another Navy man who specialized in nuclear fusion walked into Benny's so-called Golden Geisha Palace three days ago, sat down, ordered a beer, then blew his brains out all over the waitress. I'm taking it Benny's gentlemen's club in Waikiki is where all the backroom shenanigans take place."

"The Golden Palace is nothing more than a huge whore warehouse by the beach. Marines, Navy SEALS, hotshot fighter pilots, they go there to let their hair down, running for a night of bliss from all over the island. Schofield Barracks, Wheeler and Bellows Air Force Base, Hickam and Pearl. You have the cash, Benny has the room and Miss Island Doll Baby of your choice."

"You're telling me you don't know how many soldiers, sailors or officers might have Benny's net dropped over them?"

"This thing could be bigger than Godzilla, Belasko, if some of what I've learned is true. Listen to this. There's a classified military compound on Molokai where they post armed guards around the perimeter, and beyond. It appears so classified, buried so deep, it doesn't turn up on any files we have on current military operations or projects on the islands. You even got signs all over that state they are authorized to use deadly force against the curious. Now, once a week a few of the big shots from this compound fly up to savor some of Benny's finest doll babies. What goes on down there on Molokai, I couldn't tell you. I do know that this compound has been in place almost six years. But you ask around, schmooze some top brass who has a few martinis under the belt and may be inclined to some loose talk, nobody knows a thing about it. Other words, you get the stonewall treatment.''

A dark look fell over Rivers's face. "I can tell you ever since the compound has been there, a lot of folks around here claim to be seeing strange lights—hold the laughter here—and flying disks in the sky at night. I'm not much on UFO fantasy, and I believe that what they see in Nevada around Area 51 at night is nothing more than classified military aircraft, but I've seen hovering and shooting balls of light over the Kaiwi Channel I can't explain. And I've watched with my own eyes, stunned as hell, things that fly at speeds I've never seen, disks that can stop in midair, then shoot off at a vertical leap and vanish.''

"Fugasami doesn't strike me as an *X-Files* fan. What's the light show have to do with the Yakuza anyway?''

"Benny's asked me personally about what I think goes on down there.''

"So the island hoppers from Molokai are on Benny's short grooming list.''

Rivers nodded. "That would be my guess. Benny's looking to expand his VIP clientele. They say knowledge is power, and it's already looking like Benny knows most of what goes on around the islands. DEA.

Justice operations. Now he's looking, I suspect, to dig his claws into classified U.S. military projects.''

"Maybe he already has.''

"Maybe. So, what now, Belasko?''

"Exactly what do you give Benny to keep your wife from pulling a Bobbitt number on you?''

"You know, you're all heart, Belasko.'' A grunt, the guy wincing at some mental picture he could have done without, then Rivers said, "Money. I give him a cash payoff every week. But the last couple of weeks he's putting some fire to my feet, saying he wants more.''

"Knowledge about Justice operations being mounted against him.''

"Right. I can't do that. I can stand going down by myself, but the idea of betraying my own people, maybe getting them killed…that would push me over the edge and into the abyss. Despite what you've seen and heard, I believe I can somehow redeem myself.''

Bolan let that go, knowing time would tell and actions would speak. "How do you get the payoffs to him?''

"I take it to a bald King Kong with a Fu Manchu name of Barzama. I arrange to meet at the man's suite at one of the resort hotels Benny owns.''

"Make a call and tell this Barzama you're sending along someone who has an offer to make to Benny.''

"Like the one he can't refuse?''

"Like the one he won't. This is what I want you to do,'' the soldier said, and laid out Rivers's part in what Bolan knew would only be the first phase of a new campaign. The Executioner wasn't much for detective work, hated mysteries, in fact, and he sus-

pected he was about to step into some insidious plan
that went a long way beyond simple sexual blackmail.

Rivers peered at Bolan. "What the hell do you plan
on doing anyway, Belasko?"

The Executioner turned away from Rivers. "I'm
going on a little tour of the island."

Rivers glanced at the bulge of the Desert Eagle.
"How come I get the impression the tour package
doesn't come with any of the usual sight-seeing
rounds?"

The Executioner showed Rivers a grim smile.
"Let's just say there's a few fallen angels about to
get kicked out of paradise, and leave it at that."

Russia

MOTHER RUSSIA, he knew, had always lived in a state
of paranoia and xenophobia, always would. The largest landmass on the planet, with a history as brutal
and unforgiving as the terrain itself, he thought.
Something like close to a hundred different ethnic or
religious peoples staking claim to various independent
enclaves now called republics. Terrorism and organized crime now threatening to hurl Russia into a
state of anarchy that would turn the clock back to the
days of the czars in order to violently reverse chaos
to order through military rule. In the final analysis,
the black cloud of fear forever hanging over his country was very understandable.

And now Major Pavel Zherkovsky was looking at
the unexplained which could only brand Russia with
a new kind of fear. If nothing else, he was certainly
left wondering exactly what it was their SAM missile

barrage had luckily blown out of the sky. What secretly unnerved him was the thought that they had indeed bagged some alien spacecraft.

Dressed in his army uniform, the major stood before the reinforced glass partition that had just been hermetically sealed to keep out the radiation still emanating from what he had come to think of as "the thing," whatever it was. He glimpsed his square face, the bristles of his buzz cut in the reflection of the glass as the biohazard team below turned on three flamethrowers, began spraying brilliant tongues of white fire over the wreckage. The team hosed down the debris for a full minute with superheated thermite fire that might have melted a pillar of steel. There was no smoke, no sign of burning or meltdown he could detect. When the flames retreated back into their nozzles, other members of the biohazard unit stepped up with AK-47s, unleashed long volleys of autofire. From his viewpoint above the testing area—the hangar used to ground their choppers now cleared except for the wreckage and the suited men—he witnessed something he found even more strange. The bullets appeared to skim off the white-orange coating like stones some boy sent skipping off the surface of a pond, the volley of lead winging in screaming ricochets off the hangar wall below. The autofire ceased when some of the biohazard team starting yelling and flapping their arms at the shooters, everyone realizing they would more likely end up shooting themselves than drilling the first dent in the thing. Someone examined the assaulted surface, then looked up, shaking his helmeted head. They took sledgehammers, pounded the wreckage. They used knives to try to scar the outer layer. More helmet shaking.

If Zherkovsky didn't understand the method to this madness, he knew it would all look like some bad slapstick comedy. He watched as a grenade was placed beneath one of the inch-thin sheets of wreckage, the team lumbering back as the steel egg detonated, sent the debris soaring straight up where it hovered, then floated down, looking as if it weighed no more than a feather. Not the first sign of a hole, not even a sawtooth edge on the wreckage. Incredibly, despite the fact they had blown the thing out of the sky, the edges of at least some of the wreckage should have been jagged, Zherkovsky thought, since the missiles had ripped the thing apart, and any aircraft he'd ever seen blown to hell showed clear signs of mutilation. Except the perimeters of the debris were still round, as smooth as glass. Not only that, but the thing should have been vaporized initially, given the force of the explosion that had boiled across the sky earlier, and in a nuclear firecloud, no less. That alone left several questions hanging in his mind. Had the thing been carrying nuclear weapons, touched off by his surface-to-air missiles? Had it been flown by nuclear propulsion, some sort of small reactor loaded with uranium or plutonium?

What was this thing? he wondered. Then, as if to mock or stretch his disbelief even more, he watched as two biohazard-suited men lifted a piece of wreckage, released it and stepped back. The hunk of debris actually remained suspended in the air for several seconds, then slowly floated to the hangar floor, not the slightest sound as it touched down. A whispering voice from the next room would have made more noise.

"It has to be some sort of alloy that generates gravity waves, perhaps antigravity. That is the only explanation."

Zherkovsky turned, somehow kept the startled expression off his face as the SVR agent walked down the narrow steel-walled corridor. When the agent stopped beside him and stared down at the team, Zherkovsky said, "Did you see what they did to it?"

"Yes. It is fantastic."

"No dent, no scarring, not a scratch. What is it, Comrade Denkov? Titanium? Some sort of fabricated aluminum we have never seen?"

"I cannot say. I can say Moscow has already scrambled our top aerospace engineers, physicists and other specialists. They will be landing here I would say within the hour. What we need to discuss, Major, is a series of problems this may create for our country. First, we must continue to execute any civilians within a hundred miles of the explosion. We cannot afford any witnesses in the hot zone who may pack up and flee to the cities and tell wild tales about UFOs being blown out of the sky."

"I disagree with the order I was given. We are murdering our own countrymen. These are good and simple and honest people in the Siberian frontier. Coal miners, not soldiers and secret agents worried about national security."

Denkov clenched his jaw. "Your compassion for peasants is duly noted, but listen to me very carefully. Things have changed. However, feel free, Comrade Major, to contact Moscow and explain your distress.

If you have any qualms about your orders, I am sure they will be glad to relieve you of your command here."

"You said yourself the amount of radioactive fallout will kill off any villagers within this hot zone in a matter of days, weeks at the outside."

"The problem," Denkov said, "is that the Americans know about the explosion. We now believe that the aircraft was carrying a load of nuclear weapons, or perhaps it was flying on some sort of nuclear-propulsion guidance system. The American CIA station chief is allied with a few of my fellow agents in Moscow who seem to not have the backbone necessary to hold their tongues in the interest of national security. Glasnost has had many unfortunate drawbacks, one of which is our own intelligence agency has this unexplained impulse to trade information with the CIA."

"Their satellites will pick up the execution sites, the mass graves my soldiers are now digging. Satellite imagery, I'm sure you know, is so advanced now it can read the license plate off a car. What if the American satellites find my soldiers piling up bodies in trenches dug out by bulldozers?"

"I am hoping in time it can all be explained away."

Zherkovsky grunted at that. The man had all the answers, but the major sensed the SVR agent was holding something back. "Really? And how do you intend to do that?"

"That is not your concern. Now, here is the problem, the way Moscow sees it, which is your concern. We will call it the panic factor among the masses, the calm before the storm of an outbreak of hysteria that must be stopped here and now in these parts before it can spread. Yes, we know over the past few years there have been numerous UFO sightings, especially in Siberia, with a few alleged sightings over Moscow and Saint Petersburg even.

"Up to now, we can explain it away as the gibberish of some drunk. That was then. Now we have in our possession something we clearly cannot explain away. If the masses believe not even their own government can protect them from unexplained flying objects, ones that could be capable of dropping out of the sky before our radar even discovers they are there, capable of unleashing nuclear missiles on our cities, there could very well be an uprising, out of sheer panic if nothing else."

"You do not give these 'masses,' as you call them, enough credit."

Denkov's gaze narrowed over his piggish black eyes. "You know what Compound ZX545 here houses in its silos. You know this is one of the largest installations of nuclear weapons in our country. Some basic facts quickly. SALT is all bullshit. The Americans think we are under twenty thousand nuclear weapons, when, in fact, we are just over thirty thousand strong. Here you have nearly three thousand missiles alone that could easily vaporize the continental United States—or China, for that matter. We have MRBMs, ICBMs, IRBMs. We have multiple warheads in SS-20s, 17s...."

"Your point?"

"Obviously, you miss it. We cannot have the Americans follow the trail of the wreckage back to here. They would cry foul, that we have not complied with the nuclear disarmament agreements, just for one thing. But there's more, things which you do not know.''

When the SVR man paused as if for some dramatic effect, Zherkovsky growled, "I don't have time for games. What?"

"There is a situation in America perhaps you are aware of, involving a certain Russian citizen being held prisoner and about to stand trial in their country.''

"You're speaking of Mosnivoc?"

"Yes. He is former KGB, which, you know, was the predecessor to the SVR. No one is concerned about what he did or did not do years ago. We are concerned because the man has knowledge, was in fact instrumental in some dealings I know of, matters that involve the sale of certain nuclear materiel to some people to the south.''

"Kindly stop speaking in riddles. I know certain facilities were dismantled under the disarmament treaty with the Americans, that this matériel has left the country.''

"And where did the U-235, the plutonium, parts of missiles and reactors go?"

"You're telling me something I already know. Mosnivoc, most likely, sold them to some terrorists.''

"Not just any terrorists." Denkov cleared his throat. "I will say no more at this time. The Mosnivoc situation is being taken care of.''

"Why tell me this?"

Zherkovsky watched Denkov stare down at the test

area as Geiger counters and other instruments were waved over the wreckage.

"Do you know anything about Roswell, New Mexico, Comrade Zherkovsky?"

Zherkovsky shook his head. More spook games. "Late forties it supposedly happened, yes, I know something of it. An alleged UFO crash-landed. The wreckage and supposed bodies of little gray men were recovered and hidden, again supposedly, at some classified U.S. military installation. Supposedly, there was an elaborate cover-up...." Zherkovsky stopped when he felt something like icicles jab at his nape. "What...what are you saying? You're saying we have found bodies of little—"

Denkov chuckled, waving a hand. "No, no. Nothing so fantastic, although we have already discussed the possibility a pilot or pilots ejected from this craft and are now on the run somewhere in Siberia. If that is the case, we will find him, or them..."

"Or 'something'?"

"Do not let your imagination run so wild. The reason I mentioned Roswell was because...well, say the stories are true. Say the Americans used reverse engineering and perhaps duplicated some alien spacecraft."

Zherkovsky scowled when Denkov stood there, grinning as if he were the jealous guardian of some universal secret.

"I take it you are eager to tell me something."

"Am I now?" Denkov said.

"If you know something I do not, comrade, I remind you I am the commanding officer here and you will show me due respect."

Denkov nodded, turned and began to walk away. The SVR agent stopped and pointed toward the test area. "This is what I know. That UFO? It was built by the Americans. Yes, I see the look of disbelief in your eyes. Feel free to call Moscow. They will confirm that what we are now in possession of is the debris of an American flying saucer. Think what could happen if the Americans decide to mount some covert operation to retrieve what is down there. Imagine the consequences. Need I say it?"

Major Zherkovsky felt his jaw go slack. He didn't know what to believe, but when Denkov strode off he found himself staring back down into the test area, his mind racing with a dozen questions and twice as many worst-case scenarios. If what the man told him was the truth, and American commandos attempted to storm the installation...

He didn't want to think it, didn't dare, but he couldn't help but wonder if Mother Russia was on the eve of World War III.

CHAPTER FOUR

Stony Man Farm, Virginia

It was all Hal Brognola could do to keep the anguish off his face, but he knew he was still falling short of keeping up appearances. Somehow he fought back the wet fire building behind his eyes, even as he felt his teeth grind together so hard he pumped a loud ringing in his ears. Telling himself to pull it together, he sucked in a breath, but it was air that felt like super-heated wind going into his lungs. Somewhere in the corners of his narrowed gaze he saw Kurtzman, Weth-ers, Delahunt and Tokaido look away, focus their own heavy expressions on the monitors of their computers, allowing the big director of the Sensitive Operations Group of Stony Man his moment of silence.

"I'm sorry, Hal."

It was rare, if ever, Mack Bolan issued those words, and when he said them he damn well meant it.

Brognola straightened, squaring his shoulders. "So am I."

"Hal, just so I didn't have to rely on Rivers's ver-sion, I paid a visit to an Inspector Maiki who headed up the investigation of your friend's death. The case is officially closed. If I find out it was anything other than what it looked like, I'll handle it on my end.''

Even though he read Bolan's message, loud and clear, that someone could have disguised an execution as a murder-suicide, Brognola scowled, felt the acid churning in his belly. ''We were good friends. Came up through the Justice Department together in the old days after my service with the marshals...before he joined the organized crime division in Oahu. Said Hawaii sounded like a good place, a clean place to raise a family. Sounds like Oahu is crawling with all manner of temptation. He caved. Dammit! I thought I knew the man. My wife and I would spend a week or so every couple of years with the man and his family, all things permitting. I lost touch with him. I guess he lost touch somehow with himself.''

Bolan's voice was level, but the note of compassion was clear enough. ''Don't beat yourself up over it.''

''Understood. What's done is done.''

Brognola was listening to Bolan's voice over the satcom, the connecting speakerphone on so all present in the Computer Room could catch Striker's update, give the warrior some of their own facts and findings in return.

''Far as I can tell,'' Bolan went on, ''our suspicions about the extortion angle are panning out. Benny Fugasami has opened the proverbial Pandora's box. I intend to shut that box, and in his face.''

''And Rivers?'' Brognola asked, feeling fired up with renewed anger over the whole treacherous mess of Feds gone bad over a little extramarital romper room. "What's his squawking been all about? He want a deal?"

"He knows he's finished as far as the department goes."

"He's got that right. He's so finished he might as well tie on one and take a long swim out into the channel after slashing open a few bloody gashes on his arms and legs."

"Well, he's keeping some remote hope alive he doesn't have to turn himself into shark chum."

"How remote?"

"A happy home, see his kids through college, marriage intact, like that."

"I wish him luck. He'll be lucky if he's not facing three lifetimes' worth of a paid vacation in Leavenworth. He'll know some real hell on earth if that happens. What else did he tell you?"

"That Fugasami is looking to grab up a few big fish Rivers says fly up from a classified military operation that's been on Molokai for around six years. Now Rivers pays the Yakuza boss cash, only Benny wants full knowledge of any and all ongoing Justice operations that may be closing in, wants to know everything, law and military, happening on the islands."

"Tightening the noose on Rivers, looking to squeeze him for information on the good guys," Brognola rasped.

"Exactly. The boss wants more than just money from our fallen Fed, but so far Rivers is unwilling to give up his own."

"That's mighty decent of him," Brognola growled.

"He's in deep, that much I know, and I'm about to go swimming myself in some dangerous waters.

The way Rivers makes it sound, and I haven't discounted anything yet, Benny Fugasami sounds like something that just stepped out of feudal samurai Japan. To stay in the game as long as he has, I can be sure he has the clout in his circle and beyond to keep him in power and climbing his own version of a ladder to success."

Brognola watched as the cyber wizards tapped keys. Kurtzman and Tokaido were busy printing out some more background information he had just asked for on Fugasami.

"Striker," Kurtzman said, scanning his intel sheet, "it would look like Rivers may be right about our boy Benny being the shogun of the new millennium. Get this. His father, Tenjiki Fugasami, is believed to be the father of the modern-day Yakuza, although given how rich Japanese history is in folklore, it's hard to tell where the line between fact and fiction blurs. One fact we know is the old man was a Japanese soldier who took to selling the local geisha beauties to GIs after the war. Went on to extortion when his countrymen got back on their feet and opened up a few small businesses in and around Tokyo. One son, and young Yakamu apparently wasn't much on education unless it had to do with the martial arts. Champion kickboxer, fifth-degree black belt, and that's not touching his expertise in swordsmanship, judo, *shotokan,* and the list goes on and on."

"So, other than being the ultimate samurai, Benny inherited the kingdom," Bolan stated.

"Made some big bucks, so says this Justice Department report," Kurtzman went on, "allegedly through the export of Japanese software. His father committed ritual seppuku for which I don't have the details. Anyway, after his dad's hara-kiri, Yakamu moved to Oahu, late eighties, where he started a chain of sushi restaurants, then somehow turned entrepreneur with a few five-star hotels in Honolulu and Waikiki. Now he's the proud owner of two gentlemen's clubs, where, I gather, all the hanky-panky happens.''

"You gather right," Bolan said. "And the 'somehow' you mentioned is the backbone behind the legit mask."

"Narcotics, prostitution, gambling, extortion, the usual sins of your big-time gangster," Kurtzman said.

"It probably goes without saying," Tokaido put in from his workstation, "that the local PD is bowing and scraping before this would-be shogun for big Yankee dollars. In other words, Striker, watch your gaijin assets. I'm looking at a list of murders here, tied to Fugasami, but never proved, of course, that could turn one of his resort hotels into a giant mausoleum."

Brognola took a packet of antacid tablets and popped three, washing them down with Bear's muddy brew. "I probably shouldn't bother to ask, but what's your plan for Benny?"

They listened while Bolan told them he was paying Benny's extortion front man a visit, courtesy of a phone call from Rivers, who dumped the cash payoff to the bad guy in question, only Mike Belasko was standing in for the Fed gone wrong. That was that. Well, Brognola could fill in the blanks from there. The Executioner was going hunting, about to put some heat to Benny's butt, make him squirm, look over his shoulder, while squeezing any information out of any of these modern-day samurai that Rivers had neglected to mention or simply didn't know. Things were about to get very hot and ugly, Brognola thought, in paradise.

"Striker," Brognola said, "there's a lot happening on our end, none of it good, all of it shrouded in riddle. Before I get to that, tell me some more about this classified military base Rivers mentioned."

As Bolan related Rivers's tale of the strange light show over the Kaiwi Channel, the alleged sighting of flying disks, how this compound was patrolled by armed soldiers and signs were posted how they were authorized to use deadly force, Brognola noted the keen interest lighting up the eyes of his cyber wizards. When Bolan finished his report, the Computer Room was dead silent for several moments.

"I know I didn't put anyone to sleep," Bolan said.

"Quite the opposite, Striker." Quickly, Brognola told Bolan about the UFO incident in Siberia and the Russian shoot-down of what Stony Man now knew was an American aircraft, wingless, nuke or laser propelled or whatever, no one could say for sure. Then the murders of an Israeli-American archaeological team in the Bekaa Valley by what Mossad believed were Syrian terrorists who had vanished over the border, the Israelis believed, next door to their homeland. Next the suspected discovery of a Syrian nuclear-waste reprocessing plant, finally relating events and suspicions about the Russian don about to stand trial in Brooklyn.

"You're looking for a connection, a mission for Able and Phoenix?" Bolan said.

Kurtzman brought Bolan up to the minute on Able Team.

"You're looking for Feds gone wrong in Brooklyn," Bolan said, an edge of disgust in his voice.

"If there's a snake under the FBI bed in Brooklyn," Kurtzman said, "we can all be sure they'll find it, and trample it all to hell."

"Bottom line, Striker, we're not sure what we have exactly. A number of loose ends look like they want to tie together, and we think we're getting close to having a mission for Phoenix," Brognola said. "A major problem we face is that the Israelis know about the Syrian reprocessing site. I don't have to spell out the potential for disaster in the Middle East if the Israelis blow the place clear back into the Bekaa."

"Has the Man sanctioned a mission against the site?"

"Not yet. He says he's weighing options, but I'm pitching hard to get Phoenix into the game. I was about to have Barbara put them on alert, but I've told her to wait until we have a viable plan of attack in place and the Man, of course, gives us the thumbs-up. Katz is calling in some favors now from some of his old buddies in the Israeli military and intelligence circles, trying to keep the Israelis from doing something that would prove disastrous to any ongoing peace process over there."

"Disastrous would be a classic understatement," Bolan said.

"Indeed. I want to handle this the quiet, covert way, but I need the green light."

"And the long pause I rode out was everyone thinking there's some connection on my end?"

Brognola sipped his coffee. "Suggesting?"

"Our side has somehow created a prototype classified aircraft, whatever it may be. And the Russians have pieces of it."

"And the secret is on Molokai?" Kurtzman asked.

"It has been called the Forbidden Isle, am I right?"

"That was because it was a leper colony during the late 1800s," Hunt Wethers said.

"Gotcha, Hunt," Bolan said. "Not because it's a UFO launching pad."

Brognola heard his mind racing with a slew of new questions.

Bolan filled in the silence. "The pause I hear is you telling me there's a lot of work to do on your end. One other thing. There's some bad blood on the island between Benny and a local Triad. The big sword for the Chinese is named Huan Chengdu. Word is war is about to break out between Benny and Chengdu. I need background on Chengdu, places of business, hangouts and so on."

"Thirty minutes, keep your fax on," Kurtzman said. "You'll have your shopping list for Chengdu."

"Striker, for the time being," Brognola said, "you have my blessing to give Fugasami and his samurai all the taste of hell you can dish out. But this thing isn't just about some simple extortion angle. He's after something, maybe even already has it. Information, key military personnel quaking in their wingtips, I don't know. But find out before you carry out my blessing. I need answers on our end. You might even consider taking a little trip down to Molokai while you're out there."

"It's being strongly considered. First Benny. I'll be in touch."

"As much and often as possible. Something tells me your plate has only just begun to fill up."

"You'll know something soon, one way or another."

"Stay frosty."

"Always."

When Bolan signed off, Brognola found himself staring at a new round of dark questioning looks. Then he saw Carmen Delahunt holding out what looked like some sat pictures.

"Hal, guys, I think you might want to take a look at these. I came across them while going through the Pentagon's back door on our UFO problem."

Brognola took the pictures. One look at the armed spacesuits, the sprawled bodies and the digging equipment and the big Fed felt a fresh knot of acid in his gut. Stunned, he passed them to Kurtzman.

"It's been pinned down as a village called Obstk," Delahunt said as Kurtzman perused the satellite imagery. "It was the closest village to the explosion site. Not only would it look like the entire area east of the Urals is irradiated..."

She lapsed into hard silence that Kurtzman finally broke. "These are pictures of bodies being buried in a mass grave."

"And those images clearly show," Delahunt said, "bodies traumatized by wounds inflicted by bullets."

Brognola stared at each of them in turn, his jaw gaping. "What the hell is going on over there? The Russian military is now murdering their own people who may have witnessed what they believe is the downing of a UFO?''

Grim, Kurtzman handed the pictures to Wethers. "That's exactly what they're doing."

Hawaii

YAKAMU FUGASAMI considered himself shogun of the islands. His climb to the top of the Yakuza had begun nearly fifty years ago when he was a wild urchin running in the bombed-out, fire-gutted rubble of Tokyo, hustling their own women for the gaijin. When he thought about it, he felt terrible shame over having had to hand over their own women like common whores—mothers, sisters, daughters—to a bunch of barbarians for money. He was no mere pimp, far from it, but it had been a necessary evil back then if he was to survive in postwar Japan, see himself rise up and someday slay the dragon that had nearly destroyed his country.

More than half a century later, and he was on the threshold of doing just that.

At the moment his eyes were shut to the world of his penthouse suite, the two Chinese thugs kneeling before him on the thick plastic sheet.

Fugasami was samurai.

For whatever reason, though, his enemies had begun calling him "Benny." The disrespect was clear, duly noted. There was the Triad, and always the American law enforcement, running around and smearing his image and reputation as warrior with Benny this, Benny that. Over the years he had given them Benny, all right, shown them the foolishness of their disrespect. Funny how one swipe of his long sword could change a man's impression of him, and forever.

That was then and this was now, of course, but it was still good to remember the old days, when he had nothing, when his father had warned him that the Americans would forever keep warrior Japan a slave to them after the war. In the years to follow, after they had dropped their atomic bombs and Japan had arisen from the ashes to eventually become an economic giant, Fugasami was ashamed that his own countrymen had become the pleasure-seeking, money-worshiping pigs like the West. What his father had said had come to pass in the worst way. Japan was that slave to America, even if his own countrymen didn't see the chains shackling them because they were fat in their wealth and creature comforts. The Japanese, once strong and invincible in the code of Bushido, had fallen victim, he thought, to an old American cliché.

If you can't beat them, join them.

Fugasami joined no man, would gladly accept his own death before being cowed into submission by those who believed they wielded power over him, or sought to control him, or backstab inroads into his empire. His rise to Yakuza boss roared volumes of clear testament to an iron resolve to die standing on his feet as samurai. Yes, he had left behind the countless headless or disemboweled or dismembered bodies of competing Yakuza families, his reputation cemented in the blood of those rivals. He had driven the Vietnamese and Thai gangsters out of Hawaii even, sent the few lucky survivors back to their respective countries quaking in terror and spreading the name of Yakamu Fugasami as samurai, his name something to be dreaded, if not honored.

Now it was time to show the Chinese that Oahu wasn't big enough for them, either.

Fugasami opened his eyes, glanced at his four samurai, whose dark gazes were fixed on the Chinese. In private he insisted his samurai address him as Lord Fugasami. Failure to do so, and they were offered the short sword to disembowel themselves in seppuku. It had happened before, one time only, and never again.

As the short, slender Fugasami stood before the two Chinese Triad thugs, he wondered if he should force the issue of even his enemies honoring him as Lord Fugasami, but one look at the defiance and hatred in their dark almond eyes told him it would simply be a waste of time. He had more-urgent business to attend to.

He reached behind his head, tugged at the gold-braided ponytail, then drew the long sword from his scabbard, which was secured inside the black sash around the waist of his dark silk slacks. Chang and Wuhan knew the moment of truth had arrived. The only question in Fugasami's mind was, which one.

Fugasami indulged several more seconds of silence before he began. This was ritual execution, and he was about to send a message. Why not drag the drama out a little, let the dogs taste their fear?

He glanced around the suite of his penthouse, breathing in the smell of fear from the Chinese. The top floor of his Golden Samurai Hotel overlooked Ala Moana Beach, but the spectacular view of Mamala

Bay was shut out by the drape drawn over the balcony window behind him. All was bathed in shadow.

He was ready. It was time to do it.

"One of you must decide who will be the message I send to your boss," Fugasami began.

Wuhan spit on the plastic.

"I see."

The sword leaped up as if it had a life of its own. The razor-sharp steel, tempered, honed in weekly ritual by his own hand, slashed into the side of Wuhan's neck with a wet thud, swept through flesh, bone and gristle with all the ease of scissors cutting paper. In less than a heartbeat it was over. Wuhan's head dropped to the plastic under a thick rain of crimson, rolled up and stopped, a pair of bulging eyes staring up at Chang. As if electric charges were surging through the corpse's body, arms twitched, thick fingers of blood jetting over the plastic. Chang looked set to vomit as he stared at the headless corpse, which did a slow-motion topple to the side.

Fugasami, careful not to get any blood on his Italian leather wingtips, stepped up beside Chang, fisted up his shirt, used it like a rag to wipe the blood off the blade. Sheathing the sword, he barked, "Gamiki-san."

His samurai moved across the room and dumped a small black duffel bag beside Chang.

Fugasami nodded at Wuhan's head. "Take it."

Shaking, Chang took the head by the hair, held it away, then settled it into the bag as if it were some cursed object.

"Before you run, dog, listen to me! Tell your master that Yakamu Fugasami is shogun. Your master has shown great disrespect and utter disregard for his own life by attempting to curry favor with my distributors. He wants to offer them a bigger cut of my narcotics trade? He tries to buy my own whores out from under me? He goes to my own policemen and offers them more money to work for him?'' Fugasami chuckled. ''Tell him if it's war he wants, it will be war unlike anything he will ever know. His vaunted ninja are no match for my samurai. Show him your friend there, and explain that if Chengdu does not leave the island I will send his head back to China to any other Triad who believe they can come to my island to do anything other than pay me homage. Go!''

Chang didn't have to be told to leave again. Fugasami resisted the sudden urge to chase the dog down and slay him for cowardice alone, the Chinese thug practically running out the front door, grateful only that he was still alive.

Despicable. If Chengdu's men were all like that, Fugasami decided any war that erupted would be a one-sided slaughter.

The cell phone trilled, and Fugasami watched as Gamiki strode his way, holding out the instrument. ''It is the Russians again, Lord.''

Fugasami waved him off. The Russians again. He was getting sick and tired of their nagging. ''Tell them I will have what they want by tonight. Tell them they had better have the necessary funds promised. I will arrange a meeting at my convenience.''

Gamiki bowed his head slightly, wheeled and walked away to relay the message.

Fugasami moved for the balcony as his samurai began rolling up the plastic around the headless corpse. He needed to think, put together a war plan, aware he would have to go on the offensive now that his errand dog would deliver the warning. He caught a whiff of Wuhan, the Chinese having released himself in the moment of truth. Disgraceful.

Fugasami wanted some fresh air while viewing some of the beauty of his island kingdom, before he showed the Chinese that he would always be shogun.

THE DINNER CROWD was revved up and partying hard by the time the Executioner walked through the outdoor cabana of the Kahuna Hotel. Two callbacks, and Rivers had arranged for Bolan to meet the front-line extortionist but at a place of the thug's choosing.

No problem.

It was beautiful out there on Waikiki Beach, the diamond waters lit up to glistening aqua sheets by the setting sun, sailboaters still out in force, with bikinis marching in an endless parade of tanned nubile flesh all up and down the white sand. Bolan couldn't resist one more look back before striding into the lounge. Damn shame, he thought, but death had come to more than likely scar up paradise forever.

Such was life when savages sought to devour the garden.

On the chopper ride to Fort DeRussy Military Reservation, Bolan had received the necessary intel on Chengdu from Kurtzman. A black Ford sedan had been on hand when he disembarked, the wheels arranged for Bolan by some quick logistical magic performed by Brognola. War bag loaded up in the trunk, the soldier was good to go.

Show time.

According to Kurtzman's intel, Chengdu was no Fugasami, as far as money, power, assets went. He owned a restaurant in Honolulu, a warehouse along the harbor. Bolan's Triad shopping list was complete with the addresses of Chengdu's top thugs, cronies and other associates. The soldier would pay a few of them a call in due time.

Chengdu didn't know it yet, but he was as finished as the man he was looking to dethrone.

Huan Chengdu might not have all the ill-gotten prestige and clout Fugasami carried on the islands, but the Triad boss was a former colonel in the Red Army, which meant more than likely he had contacts and muscle back on mainland China, not to mention the possibility Chengdu could have eyes and ears all over Oahu. Chengdu was on the backburner for the moment, but Bolan was about to give the ex-Red Army colonel center stage spotlight.

The soldier rolled through the dining crowd, tuxedoed waiters weaving their way carefully past the big man in dark shades. Bolan felt a few indignant looks shot his way when he disregarded the serving crowd fighting to get to tables with trays loaded to the edges with plates. The Executioner was laser focused, and he spotted Barzama in what appeared a private little dining room beyond the packed bar.

Rivers's description of the Japanese thug was on the dime. The Executioner found the bald giant sitting at a round table heaped with plates of crab legs, fruit, oysters, lobster. Barzama didn't even look up as Bolan entered the room, the thug acting as if he didn't have a care in the world other than gorging himself as if Waikiki were about to go down in history as the next Sodom and Gomorrah. Sizing him up, the soldier noted the man was all shaved skull, as smooth as a cue ball, with hanging wisps of black mustache. At the moment, Barzama, bulging biceps rippling beneath a short-sleeved white silk shirt, was busy chomping on filet running damn near red to raw. Standing nearby, two Yakuza flunkies in dinner jackets watched Bolan from behind dark shades with something close to contempt. One of the thugs opened his jacket, displaying the hilt of a sheathed samurai sword.

Rivers was right again, the soldier decided, but was hardly in the mood to give the guy any points for accurate detail. Just the same, Bolan noted they took their samurai gig serious.

The Executioner was no stranger to the code of Bushido.

Barzama finally glanced up at Bolan, the thug slobbering around a chunk of dripping meat, as the warrior stopped in front of the table.

"That doesn't look like Japanese cuisine to me," Bolan said. "Where's the sushi?"

Barzama looked at his flunkies, snorted. "You're very observant, gaijin. At least you're not Russian. I'm tired of Russians."

Russians? Bolan masked his surprise, but filed a mental note to ask Barzama about that in a few short moments.

"So, what's this offer, gaijin? I hope Rivers grew a brain instead of something else for a change. First, I want his payment. I have some pressing bills to pay."

"That's no longer part of the deal."

Barzama stopped chomping. He looked at Bolan, eyeballed him up and down as if seeing him for the first time, which, in fact, he was. He said something in Japanese, thinking a mere gaijin wouldn't understand the language. The Executioner knew enough to get the gist. Barzama gave the order for the four of them to be left alone, which one of the flunkies relayed by handheld radio to someone out front. Barzama had the word passed on there might be a little noise, some gaijin screams, nothing to worry about, but they were not to be disturbed. As soon as the flunky was off the cellular, Bolan heard the door to the private dining room click shut, muting out all the laughter and merriment of the dining crowd. The Executioner also caught the next order, Barzama telling his samurai to disarm the gaijin.

"I wouldn't do that," the Executioner warned, as the thugs stepped his way. "The hardware stays."

Barzama laughed. "You understand Japanese. Very good, we should get along very well, then, in the next few minutes, no failures to communicate."

Bolan held his ground, waiting as their smug faces came closer. Flunky One with the sword was about to draw the weapon when the Executioner pivoted, drilled a snap kick into his jaw.

The private party was under way.

CHAPTER FIVE

New York

Special Agent Karl Lemon, aka Carl Lyons, couldn't believe his eyes. In fact, Lyons found himself so stunned he was speechless for the first time he could recall. He glanced from the FBI special agent in charge to the Buddha-like mass sitting at the kitchen table in the dining-room alcove. A slab of stuffed veal chop, about the size of a T-rex thigh, Lyons figured, was being devoured by the biggest, deadliest, most powerful Russian mobster to ever land on American soil. Had he just been picked up by the mothership, Lyons wondered, and whisked off to some other dimension? Given what Stony Man had dropped on him back at the Farm—UFOs getting shot down over Russia, nuclear fireclouds vaporizing great chunks of real estate in Siberia—he half expected to blink his eyes and find a room full of little gray men instead of the FBI.

"Can you believe this? Look at that, will ya."

"I'm looking," Lyons growled, "and, no, I don't believe it."

Lyons glanced at FBI Special Agent in Charge

Masterson, caught the tall, lean, mustachioed Fed shaking his head in disbelief, then again observed the object of their disgust and angry confusion. And what Lyons saw was, in fact, so unbelievable he had to look around the large living room of the brownstone just for a reality check.

Okay, five FBI guys in dark suits, wireless earplugs in place, all packing Glocks M-16s, cocked and locked, in the general vicinity. He blinked, moved and opened his own war bag. Okay, SPAS-12 and the squat little send-off gift from John Kissinger still there, zip it up.

He walked to the door, opened it and found two more dark suits out front, grim faces with eyes shielded by sunglasses watching the brownstones, the apartment buildings, the shops and businesses that packed this part of Flatbush. On either end of the street were dark sedans, with the ground troops monitoring the action. He glanced across the street, up three stories to the one-way window, behind which Schwarz and Blancanales were doing their own surveillance gig, having installed the special glass themselves before hunkering down to be his eyes and ears.

That done, Lyons felt a cold ball of rage lodge in his gut. He was on planet Earth, all right, even if it was the teeming, bellowing madness of grimy brownstoned, redbricked Flatbush.

Lyons marched back into the brownstone, found Mosnivoc pouring a glass of chilled vodka while wiping some dripping mozzarella cheese and prosciutto ham off his chin. The Russian gangster palmed a remote control and started flicking through the cable channels. The TV had been set up on the table for his easy viewing.

"I ask for Playboy channel. No Playboy channel. My man at State will hear of this, be sure, comrades!"

Lyons stared at Masterson. "How many guys you lose so far?"

"Five, and we've got two more barely hanging on."

"And who's jerking our chains down at State?"

"Some asshole name of Carlington."

Lyons chuckled grimly and rubbed his face. "Let me get this straight. That tub of lard over there *is* what they say he is, right?"

"Right. No question."

"Five dead FBI men because of him, and we're supposed to let State order up room service and the Playboy channel and maybe bring in some naked dancing girls and we're more or less told by Washington to kiss his ass or else."

"That's pretty much the size of it."

"Well, watch this. I'm about to size it all down where it should be."

"I need *machorka* in minute, comrades. I ask for Cuban cigar, but I take *machorka*. Someone go to liquor store, I need more vodka soon."

Enough was enough.

Lyons marched into the dining alcove. He knew this was a make-or-break moment, could even bring the wrath of State down on his head, the proverbial feces hitting the fan, flying all the way to land on Brognola's desk. Well, he didn't care about anything right then other than making a personal statement to the boss. He was angry as hell over this outrageous and insane spectacle, not to mention still tired, hungover some and still steaming about Miami. Worse, he hated like hell the idea of even being attached to this baby-sitting detail, but would ride it out as the dutiful Stony Man warrior he was.

Because he was itching, hoping for some action at some point soon, hungry only to dish out some serious payback on some goons who were part of a criminal organization that had already wasted five good men. Why not, he figured, get the ball rolling right now, make some noise and see who came running to the rescue?

The Russian boss was chomping away, filling his glass when Lyons rolled over him, ripped the chop out of his mouth. Mosnivoc stared at his empty hands, his wet mouth gaping, and started to bellow, "What is the—"

And Lyons slapped him in the mouth with the chop, cheese and flecks of Italian ham spraying the Russian's silk robe. "Shut your fat mouth!"

The Russian tried to stand, but Lyons pounded the chop in his face, driving him back into his seat. Three, four, five vicious wet-sounding slaps just to let the Russian know who was the real boss here. Was that a chuckle he heard out there in the living room? Whatever, Lyons finished up, slamming the mangled slab off the Russian's head with another mushy-sounding but loud whap. It was such an outrageous display of contempt and disrespect, something Mosnivoc would have never dreamed possible in his worst nightmare, that he sat in utter shock, took it. The horrified look, though, quickly faded from the Russian's

bulging stare, defiance and outrage filtering into eyes
that burned up at Lyons.

With a casual flip, Lyons tossed the brutalized chop
across the room, scored a two-pointer as it disappeared into the trash can. "There's a new boss in
town, asshole, and you're looking at him. Far as
you're concerned, I'm the wrath of God, your worst
nightmare, a never-ending seizure in your Stoli-
soaked brain, the hemorrhoid you'll never get rid of.
You will not, I repeat, you will not even take a leak
unless I say it's okay. From here on you eat ham-and-
cheese sandwiches and drink coffee just like the rest
of us." Lyons grabbed up the Stolichnaya bottle,
hammered it to splinters off the table, spraying slivers
and liquid over Mosnivoc.

The Russian gangster quivered with rage. "You are
making very big mistake."

"It wouldn't be the first time," Lyons told the Russian. "Probably not the last."

"Carlington will hear of this. I will see you so fired
you will be beggar in street!"

Lyons pointed to the cell phone in the living room,
fighting down the impulse to haul out the .357 Colt
Python shoulder-holstered beneath his windbreaker and
pump one in that fat smug face. "So call him. He can
make my day, too."

"You are dead man."

It was all in the look, the tone that flared up Lyons's gut instinct the Russian knew another plan was
in the works to set him free.

"For a guy running a billion-dollar empire, you're
not too smart. You just told me you have an ace up
the sleeve."

Mosnivoc blinked, his expression melting to neutral.

Turning away, Lyons marched back to the living room. The grim twist to Masterson's mouth matched a few other looks Lyons found watching him. He heard that low chuckling now from somewhere in the audience. If he didn't know better, he would have sworn the FBI men were on the verge of giving him a standing O.

"Hold the applause, guys," Lyons told his audience.

Masterson stared at Special Agent Lemon as if he'd just found the hero in life he'd always been looking for. "You know, I wouldn't have missed that for the world. You realize the little windbag at State hears about this…"

"Right. I'm finished with the Justice Department."

Masterson chuckled. "I can hear Bob Kachik laughing from the other side."

"What little I heard about the man, sounds like he was my kinda guy." Time to get down to the business of the plan Lyons had shaped in his head since flying from the Farm. On his order before leaving the Farm, contacting the FBI field office in New York, Lyons made sure Hurley and Peters were reassigned to street surveillance. "I just worked up a big appetite, guys. How about you call Hurley and Peters in here," Lyons told Masterson. "I'm sending them out for pizzas. I want the works. Extra cheese, sauce, all the toppings. I want to see pies dripping with all the trimmings or I'll send them back."

Masterson nodded, kept on gazing at his new idol.

"Let me guess. You're going to send the bill to the State Department for reimbursement?"

"Carlington hasn't even begun to know the meaning of reimbursement." Lyons jerked a thumb over his shoulder. "By the way, pie heaven is for us. The don's already had lunch."

BLANCANALES LOWERED the field glasses, caught the grin on Schwarz's face.

"Sounds like Ironman's back to the guy we both know and love," Schwarz said as he adjusted the volume on the monitor box connected to the parabolic mike. "I wish this thing could see through walls instead of just listen."

Blancanales wished he could have seen that show himself, Ironman slapping around the biggest Russian gangster since God knew when with his own lunch. "If this Carlington's as big a butt-kisser to Moscow as we think, our 'hero' could get us all yanked off this detail."

"Don't sweat it. Hal will pull us through any storm the State Department blows our way."

Blancanales shook his head, hoping that was true. Their part of the detail was every bit as important as Lyons holding down the fort from the inside. For their end of the assignment, Brognola had found them a vacant room in an apartment complex on an angle nearly a block south of the brownstone. They were the eyes and ears for Lyons, their presence unknown to the FBI. If something looked hinky down there on the street, they would alert Lyons, go running in, guns blazing, if the action called for that. If they had to travel around Brooklyn, their black Ford Taurus was parked out behind the apartment building in the residential lot.

"Hey, I can't have my wife finding out about us, you unnerstan? Hell's wrong wich you, calling me at home last night?"

"I'm gettin' sick of this, Donny, all this hiding and lying when you said you were leaving her!"

"Dammit, Carly, you don't get it, do you? I'm married, I got three kids, a good job, money in the bank. She finds out about us, I'm out in the street, homeless, penniless for..."

Blancanales looked at Gadgets, who was panning the mike on its swivel mount. He had the mike aimed at a parked dark blue Cadillac near Flatbush Avenue.

"What the hell are you doing, Gadgets?"

"Just checking out my toy. You know, gauging the range for the digital amplifying system I installed on this puppy. The laser sensor I installed works so good, I could probably hear through a thin wall, although I may be dreaming since I have to focus the mike on glass."

"I know all that, you've told me four times already. My problem is I would have never figured you for a Peeping Tom."

"Just having a little fun, Pol, killing some boredom, that's all. Relax. Have another doughnut." Grinning, Schwarz panned on, settling the mike on two salty-looking characters engaged in what looked like an argument about two blocks to the other end of the street.

"You'se into me for two large, Frankie. You'se a sick fuck, you got a problem, ya know dat? Don't know when to say enough, that you'se a freaking loser, can't pick a winner God come down through the ceiling and tell you'se...."

Blancanales knew Gadgets loved his techno toys, but this was pushing it toward obsession, the way he saw it. "Hey, come on, Gadgets..." Blancanales was about to pursue his point when he spotted their two FBI marks walking into the brownstone. "Get serious, Hermann, our suspect rats just went inside."

Schwarz aimed the mike back where it should be. Adjusting the dial on the monitor, they heard Lyons telling Hurley and Peters to go out and pick up three large pizzas, all the trimmings. The two agents didn't protest, but Blancanales guessed they were grateful to go do something other than sit in their car and twiddle their thumbs.

Only Ironman, he knew, was the man with the plan. If Lyons's hunch played out, the FBI duo would attempt to make contact with some goons, hand over the location where the don was being sat on, steer gunners their way. The conversation inside the brownstone was short, with Lyons playing the big spender and dipping into the war budget Brognola allotted. No sooner were Hurley and Peters coming out the door than the handheld radio beside Blancanales crackled, Lyons speaking in a low voice.

"Pol, pick up."

Blancanales grabbed up the radio. "What do you have? And why are you whispering? Why do you have the radio on? I can barely hear you."

"I'm in the bedroom, alone. Figure it out, you're such a people-oriented kinda guy."

"All right, you don't want to clue in Masterson you think—"

"Listen up. I'm sending those two for pizzas, corner deli," Lyons said, and gave out the name and exact location for the lunch pickup. "I told them to walk, so you won't have to worry about losing them in traffic. If I'm right, those two will try and make contact with some very ugly Ivans."

"I hope you're right. Surveillance detail is like watching paint dry. I need some action beyond sitting here, listening in on all the crack deals on this street. By the way, if it goes south, who gets the pies?"

"Tell him we're tired of eating stale doughnuts," Schwarz piped in. "Tell him this Flatbush coffee even makes Bear's poison—"

"Stow the comedy," Lyons said, his voice edging up a notch with impatience. "Gadgets, you stay put. Pol, grab your hardware and move out now."

Blancanales was up and moving. He looked down into his opened war bag, couldn't resist hauling out his present from Kissinger. Schwarz turned, watching as Blancanales examined the squat, stainless-steel multiround grenade launcher.

"What did Cowboy call this? Little Bulldozer?"

"Yeah," Schwarz said. "Eight chambers, next to no recoil. Pumps out 40 mm rounds, HE, incendiary, smoke, flash-stun. Scaled down, upgraded version of the MM-1 Multiround Projectile Launcher. Cowboy gave you six of those spherical reloaders."

"Showed us to just hold the reloader over the chambers, thumb the release and eight more bombs-away drop right into place. A trigger-happy guy could probably take out a whole city block with this thing."

"Right. Instant killzone, war made easy. I'm not

sure how smart it was to give Carl one of those, given how bent out of shape he still is about Miami.''

''What do you mean?''

''Remember what Cowboy said? He told Carl specifically if he has to use it, try to restrain himself from blowing up half of Brooklyn.''

Blancanales cocked a wry grin as he stowed Little Bulldozer beside the M-16/M-203 combo, zipped up and headed for the door. ''Oh, I'm sure, Gadgets, if we find ourselves staring down twenty or so Russian shooters, Carl will do his best to honor Cowboy's request.''

He heard his teammate chuckle, then caught Schwarz zeroing back on the feuding lovebirds.

Hawaii

SAMURAI NUMBER ONE flew back, all flailing arms and jaw so shattered he'd be lucky to find himself on a liquid diet for months to come. That was, of course, if he survived.

Number Two was about to pull his sword when Bolan bored ahead, hammered a head butt that turned the thug's nose into red mud. The soldier heard Barzama snarling something in Japanese, the shaved-head thug frozen in the corner of Bolan's sight by this lightning attack, long enough for the warrior to grab Nosebleeder by the lapels of his jacket. Whirling like some human tornado, Bolan spun the would-be swordsman, relieved him of his sword on the way and at the same instant hurled him over Barzama's spread. Plates and food followed the flying samurai as he slammed into Barzama. As they crumpled in a heap of rage, washed by hot melted butter and whatever else came off the table, Bolan drew the Beretta 93-R. The weapon already threaded with the sound suppressor, the Executioner dumped near silent death on Barzama's swordsmen. A soft chug, and Number One took a 9 mm Parabellum round between the eyes, his feet whipping out from under him just as he was trying to stand and get back into the action.

Growling, Barzama was shoving Number Two away, reaching a paw beneath the table, when Bolan cored another round, scoring a head shot. Blood and little gobs of gray matter burst out the back of Number Two's shattered skull, sent him twitching and falling back to drape over Barzama, effectively pinning the big man to the floor. The gaijin hurricane that was Bolan rolled ahead, threw the sword out. Barzama hissed, a sound somewhere between a cry of fear or angry resignation, as the blade flew his way.

The edge of the blade rested against the shaved-head thug's throat.

Bolan stowed the Beretta. Reaching under the table, he found the holstered pistol attached to the underside. He came back with a stainless-steel .45 Colt, tucked it away in his waistband. Barzama's nostrils flared, the rasp of angry air filling the silence, as he sat there, his shirt doused and stained with a good portion of his dinner.

"Rivers decided he doesn't want to play ball with Benny," the Executioner told Barzama. "Your boy's packed up his toys and gone home."

"Then we'll find him and convince him otherwise."

Bolan felt his mouth tighten in a grim smile. What

Barzama didn't know was that Rivers had been whisked to a safehouse in Makiki Heights where a team of Justice Department agents had the fallen Fed under twenty-four-hour watch until Bolan was ready to ship him back to the mainland and into Brognola's not-so-gentle care.

"You will be found," Barzama said.

"I'm counting on it." Bolan decided to throw a little more confusion into the play. It was a long shot, and he already suspected Barzama more than likely wouldn't bite as he said, "Chengdu has brought in some outside help."

"You?"

"Me, maybe."

"The Chinese would never let a mere gaijin anywhere near their Triad."

"Maybe Chengdu's had a change of heart. What can I say? This is war, right? Huan wants Benny off the island, wants to cut him up for shark chum. Maybe using 'gaijin' is Chengdu's way of sneaking up on your backside, you not seeing something that's there until it's too late. The ninja way of doing business."

"Kill me now."

"No, I'm going to let Benny see he might be overpaying his samurai." Bolan saw Barzama considering something. "I see you. You're thinking maybe Rivers went to Huan and sold his soul to the other side."

The soldier could tell Barzama didn't know what to believe. Whatever, he was finished here, had sown the seed of doubt. Time to move on.

Stepping back, the Executioner raised the sword, then drove it down, impaling the edge of tempered steel into the side of Barzama's table. Watching Barzama, the soldier backstepped across the room. There was no obvious change in the volume of dining merriment beyond the door. With any luck, Bolan would quietly make it out of there, and on to his next stop.

"They say red meat can dull a man's reaction time," Bolan told Barzama, turned and took the doorknob.

Barzama was all defiance as he slowly hauled himself to his feet.

Bolan opened the door. "Enjoy your dinner. When Benny hears about this, it could be what you might call your last supper."

New York

BINGO.

The guy was on the first pay phone he found near the pizzeria. Blancanales averted Hurley's roving watch as the FBI man looked up and down the crowded sidewalk, checked the way across the street, touching his sunglasses with fingers that clearly trembled. He was dropping change, punching numbers with what struck Blancanales as urgency bordering on panic, when the Able Team warrior decided to make his move.

Peters had just disappeared inside the pizzeria, and Blancanales knew he had only a few moments to make the snatch. Then what? Well, he'd figure that out on the way back, raise Lyons, put a plan together, even if it was something done on the spur of the moment.

It was time to do something, anything to up the ante and hopefully flush a few snakes out of hiding.

The FBI man was dirty; Blancanales was sure of it. It was a whiff of corruption that grew stronger in his nose the closer he moved to Hurley. Despite the blaring horns, the bellow of the lunchtime crowd surging all around him, the hordes of Brooklynites filling the delis, bodegas and restaurants, vendors barking and hawking, Blancanales picked up some of Hurley's conversation.

"It's me. I don't have much time. I have a feeling I'm being watched. Yeah, yeah, right, I'm being paranoid. First, you have my money?"

Blancanales lugged his war bag ahead but he didn't need the heavy stuff at the moment, or so he hoped. He was reaching inside his windbreaker for the Beretta 92-F, when Hurley turned his way and picked him out of the crowd. Two last charging steps, and Blancanales thrust the muzzle of the Beretta into Hurley's ribs.

"Take the bag," he whispered in the FBI man's free ear. "Do it, and now, or I'll shoot you where you stand."

When Hurley left him a free hand, Blancanales lifted a finger to his mouth, plucked the receiver for himself. With the Beretta snugged tight between their bodies, Blancanales felt reasonably safe that no passersby could see the weapon. And, if they had, he figured they would have cried out by now. But this was Brooklyn, he knew, where the Mafia still ruled, more or less, and folks still tended to mind their own business when they saw guns.

Something good to be said about apathy for a change, he thought.

Blancanales glanced at the pizzeria, spotted Peters forced to wait behind a few patrons before he could place Ironman's pie feast. He heard the voice on the other end squawking. He was no voice expert, but it sure sounded like a Russian tongue to him. Holding the receiver against his leg, he told Hurley, "Tell him you have to go, that you spotted what you think is that tail. You'll call him back later."

Blancanales put some pressure on the muzzle as Hurley took the phone, relayed the message and hung up. As quick and as casual as possible, Blancanales relieved Hurley of his weapon, dropping it in the pocket of his windbreaker.

"Who are you?"

"Just some guy pissed off I won't get a slice of all that pizza."

"You with the Justice Department?"

Blancanales hid the Beretta beneath his windbreaker, muzzle aimed at Hurley. "Move it. Stay beside me. Nice and easy. Run, scream, and I'll shoot you down like the dog you are."

One look at the fear on Hurley's face, and Blancanales figured the dirty Fed would go with the program. If not, an idea was forming in his head to show Hurley there were indeed fates worse than death.

CHAPTER SIX

Stony Man Farm, Virginia

If the road to hell was indeed paved with good intentions, then Hal Brognola was quite possibly staring down a short walk that could soon enough dead-end over the abyss. Of course, he would have changed the path before it was too late, but it wasn't his call.

"Yes, sir, I understand the political ramifications, the position yourself and the Israeli prime minister are in. But time is running out, the way we see it. Give me an hour, and we will have a viable plan on your desk. Yes, sir, I understand. I'll get back to you ASAP."

Brognola put the phone with its secured line to the White House down on the table. Alone in the War Room, he felt a nagging sense of foreboding. Belay that, hell, he saw a dark future headed his way. If he didn't get Phoenix Force into the act, and soon...

He wasn't much on diplomacy or political maneuvering, but he understood the thin ice on which the President of the United States now stood. An attack on a sovereign nation, even if it was a known haven and breeding ground for terrorists such as Syria, was something that had to be planned, thought out with extreme care to detail, with every contingency shored up. Not to mention the attackers able to practically walk, or in this case fly, off into the sunset, no one the wiser as to who did the dirty deed. The Man was concerned about Syrian retribution in the Middle East if the least little clue was left behind when the Syrians found themselves staring down the ashes of their reprocessing compound. The Israelis were also concerned about renewed terrorist attacks, since all fingers would point their way when the smoke cleared. But the Israelis wanted something done, and soon. They were pretty much telling the American political machine they could take care of the Syrian problem themselves, then put their country on high alert against any terrorist retaliation. Meaning they were on the verge of shooting first, damn the fallout and the consequences.

Brognola was no dreamer, no doomsayer, but just like that, he saw nuclear fireclouds on the distant horizon. Panned on in his imagination, saw Yakuza gangsters bringing down good men through extortion, laughing all the way to their offshore accounts. Next viewed in his mind's eye Syrian terrorists running amok in Lebanon, shooting up the innocent in the name of some jihad. Missiles, armed with nukes or otherwise, flying all over the Middle East, vaporizing whole city blocks. He saw an armada of Israeli F-16s laying waste to half of Syria while small armies of fanatics swept across the Lebanese-Israeli border in suicidal martyrdom for the bombing of the nuclear-waste reprocessing plant. No doubt, he was sitting on a time bomb about to blow in his face.

Looking into the future, yes, and seeing a world on fire.

He didn't want to think about Pritchett, but couldn't help but briefly wonder where it had gone wrong for his friend. Funny, he thought, how a man never really knew another man, even a close friend, could never spot that dark corner of his heart until after the fact when that darkness was brought to the spotlight. And this was a guy he'd gone through more than a few front doors with, no less, both of them laying it on the line for each other when they'd been Justice agents in the field. Clenching a fist so hard the knuckles popped, he found himself clinging to some remote hope the big guy would find that the murder-suicide was staged by Yakuza executioners.

Remote, yes, and fading fast.

The intercom buzzed with Kurtzman's voice.

"Hal, a couple of matters you need to know about."

"We're on the verge of looking at the eleventh hour. Tell me you have some answers, Aaron."

"I have something, but we're not sure what. Hunt was plowing through the Justice organized-crime files in Oahu. Get this. There's a long and detailed report about the presence of known Russian gangsters on the island."

"What?"

"Specifically, they have been linked to Mosnivoc's organization. And they have been sighted in the company of Fugasami."

Wethers came on. "Two guesses who wrote up this report, and the first two don't count."

Brognola snorted. "Rivers."

"I wonder if he bothered to mention this to Striker," Kurtzman said.

"Striker's update would never miss that kind of detail."

"In other words," Kurtzman said, "Rivers conveniently neglected to mention he was having Russian Mafia sightings all over the island. But why?"

Indeed, Brognola thought. "As soon as Striker touches base again, you tell him he may be looking down some Russian guns. Once Striker starts kicking ass and taking names, you can bet he'll find out what the Russian angle is."

"Hal, I've been thinking about our Syrian problem. Let me lay this out. First, looking at these sat images of the compound, it's clear to us—the camo netting, the armed soldiers, antiaircraft batteries, jeeps with mounted machine guns, not to mention the stacks that jut out of the ground that would release some of the heat from reactors below—the Syrians are hard at work trying to build maybe at least a warhead that could be fitted on an SA-5 or SS-22. Who, over the years, has dumped off billions of dollars' worth of weapons to the Syrians?"

"The Russians."

"Right. Everything from MiGs to one of those SS-22s in question. The problem is the Syrians reneged on their end of the mutual-defense pact with Moscow about ten years back."

"Meaning the Syrians owe Moscow a bunch of money."

"But the Russians have never cut the Syrians off. It's business as usual, but there's been an added twist to the funneling of weapons into Syria. The stakes are getting higher these days, and there's more money to be made on the nuclear end of things. Now, ask yourself where any U-235, U-238 or P-239 may have come from. And where could a country known to sponsor terrorism, whose army practically controls the Bekaa Valley, get the technology to build missile delivery systems?''

''Something tells me you're going to say the Russian Mafia?''

''Exactly where I was headed. But the picture gets even darker with the next whopper I'm going to lay on you. As a KGB agent, Yuri Mosnivoc had the keys to the kingdom of a major silo slash nuclear facility near Moscow. Supposedly, this was one of the nuclear facilities that was dismantled under the arms reduction treaty, only no one seems to know where a lot of the matériel went. Now Mosnivoc bought out a chunk of Aeroflot a few years back, but the details of the whole deal are a little sketchy. My guess is the don made an offer someone couldn't refuse. At any rate, it took some digging, but the CIA kept some record of flights made by Aeroflot that were never logged. Namely flights from Moscow to Damascus. At least ten that are showing up here on my monitor.''

''Despite the way it's looking, Aaron, good work. Pass that on to the others. That little piece of dark news may or not have the Man give Phoenix the green light, but it's definitely a cannon shot. Where's Katz?''

''He's with Barbara in her office.''

''Keep me posted.'' Brognola raised Price. ''Barbara, Katz, I just touched base with the Man. We're still waiting in the wings, political considerations on his end, a few bruised egos over at the Pentagon that want into the act, that sort of thing.''

"Speaking of egos," Katz said, "I've been doing a serious tap dance through the minefield with my Israeli contacts. To say they're nervous about the Syrian situation doesn't even begin to touch the reality of it. I may have bought us a day, day and a half tops, but the Israelis are putting together a surgical strike as we speak.'' A pause, a new edge to Katz's grim tone. "Hal, we have major problems as far as the Israelis go.''

"How come I don't like the sound of that, Katz?"

Price said, "Hal, Katz has learned that the Israelis are mounting an operation to go into Syria, unlike anything they've ever done. It's about as serious as it gets.''

"How bad?"

There was another pause on the other end, then Katz said, "They're fitting up a few F-16s with nuclear-strike capability.''

Brognola froze, cursed, aware a moment later the cigar had fallen from his hand. "I'm on the way.''

Hawaii

THE SIGN ANNOUNCED the place as Chengdu Ltd.

Forget all the six-figure pleasure craft bobbing around in the harbor, Mamala Bay beyond. No time to indulge viewing one of the most beautiful sunsets on the planet. A grim-faced Bolan walked right up to the front gate, looked at the guard in his booth, then drew the Beretta 93-R with attached sound suppressor. The guard gaped, balked, but Bolan told him to

open up or he was dead in the next second, and if he
didn't understand English he was really out of luck.
What the guard couldn't do, a grenade or quick stitch
of 9 mm lead could do on the gate.

The soldier's intent at Chengdu's warehouse was
plain, pure and simple. Kick ass, burn the place down
and in the process maybe grab up a tour guide for
other Triad haunts. For round two Bolan had a war
satchel slung around his shoulder, the nylon bag
chock full of HE and thermite grenades, spare clips
for the mini-Uzi in special shoulder rigging beneath
his windbreaker, Beretta and .44 Magnum Desert Eagle. To whip up some wholesale destruction, the Executioner had brought along an M-79 grenade
launcher.

There was plenty to do, all right, and a load of
unanswered questions, the least of which concerned
the Russian angle. He had skipped grilling Barzama
on that note, having seen any lengthy interrogation of
the thug would have been a waste of time. Unless he
missed his guess, Benny would soon be handing Barzama a short sword anyway for ritual suicide in the
face of dishonor.

The guard's knowledge of the English language
saved his life. The gate opened, and Bolan rolled in.
Three strides and the soldier slammed a short right
pile driver off the guy's jaw, sent him sailing back
into his booth, slumped out for a long nap. A previous
drive-by of the warehouse grounds had revealed a
team of men loading an eighteen-wheeler with crates,
both large and small. A handful of Chengdu's goons
were on-site, supervising the loading, openly displaying holstered side arms or toting around compact

subguns. The soldier could reason well enough this was Chengdu's storing house for drugs, weapons, cash and whatever else he might hold near and dear.

They were still in the process of loading the eighteen-wheeler near the open bay door when Bolan got the show started.

The warehouse itself was one of those wooden jobs that dated back to World War II. With any luck at all, Bolan figured a few well-placed thermite bombs would have Chengdu searching for other real estate to store his contraband.

Only the Executioner didn't intend for Chengdu to live to see the next sunrise.

War was descending over paradise.

By now the gunmen were gawking Bolan's way, reaching for hardware when the soldier let a 40 mm incendiary round fly. Streaking on, the hellbomb tore into the big rig's engine housing. A whoosh of white fire, guys nosediving this way and that, metal shrapnel flying all over the loading dock, and the gas tank caught fire. A second fireball erupted to end their day's work, all but vaporize whatever it was they had loaded.

Bolan was cracking open the shotgun-style launcher, feeding another 40 mm firebomb into the breech, when the Chinese thugs got it together. Slipping the launcher around his shoulder as it rained debris and angry fire sent a lot of the work force running for their lives, the Executioner hauled out the mini-Uzi. Three Triad goons were picking themselves up, brandishing weapons, when Bolan hosed them down with a burst of 9 mm doom, raking them left to right, human dominoes tumbling with brief screams of agony hitting the open grounds. He figured five hardmen around the tractor trailer, and saw the other two thugs come staggering next through the raining trash. Two more stuttering bursts, and Bolan zipped them off their feet.

By now they were charging through the open bay door, Bolan adjusted his aim, waxing two more sub-gun-wielding thugs. He found two workers holding their arms up, masks of pure terror seeking out the big invader as Bolan angled for the loading dock.

Beyond the door, he could see guys scrambling all over the warehouse, shouting in Chinese, trying like hell to make themselves scarce. The Executioner checked his flanks and rear, a visual compass that told him he was clear and free to pick it up a notch.

He did. A few quick moves, and he dumped three thermite charges into the warehouse, then put the M-79 back around a shoulder.

Something other than smoking metal was dropping around Bolan. A glance to his side and he found the featherlike falling of blackened paper. Another search of the area, and the soldier indulged a grim smile.

It was raining Yankee dollars.

The warrior settled his look on one of the workers. "You speak English?"

A shaky nod, eyes popping with fear and the Chinese man said, "Yes. Why?"

"You're coming with me," the soldier told him, stepped up and ordered him to put his hands together. Once the man complied, Bolan snapped on the plastic cuffs.

"Why?"

"I need a tour guide. Looks like this is your lucky day."

Mini-Uzi fanning the dock, Bolan found no more takers. A shimmering wave of white fire was raging through the warehouse, thick clouds of black smoke boiling out the bay door. The Executioner took his tour guide by the shoulder and hustled out of there. Chengdu's world was burning, but as far as Bolan was concerned, this was only the beginning.

The worst for Huan Chengdu was yet to come.

Brooklyn

"YOU ARE in a world of shit, my friend."

Carl Lyons repeated that, staring down at Hurley, who looked as if he wished he could disappear through the floor. When Blancanales had informed him of the snatch, Lyons put together a plan by the seat of his pants. After filling in Masterson, it was agreed that Peters would be told his partner had been pulled off the detail for a family emergency. Of course, that might not stick if Peters decided to make a few calls, but Lyons was hoping jumpy nerves would send Peters running to the Russians. Masterson was all too willing to go with whatever play Agent Lemon wanted, since the worst thing in the world to the FBI SAC was a dirty cop.

Roughly thirty minutes ago, Lyons had left Masterson with Mosnivoc, then gone on a long three-block jaunt, finally circling in behind the apartment complex to join his teammates. The whole time running he couldn't wait to get there and see what a traitor looked like in the flesh. It now took every bit of self-control for Lyons to keep from ripping one of Hurley's arms off and beating him half to death with it.

Schwarz picked up the ball, hacking away on his computer. "Looks like you've been running up quite the tab on your Russian buddies. Look at all these credit-card invoices. I mean when you eat out you go first-class, nothing but the best for you. Look at these bank accounts." He whistled. "What is this? You own a place in Southampton?"

Lyons leaned down and put his hands on the table, his face inches from Hurley. "You want to tell me how a G-man making what, forty, fifty tops a year, can even set foot in Long Island without walking around in a monkey suit with a tray of martinis and serving up the smoked salmon?"

"You're screwed to the royal gills here, Hurley," Schwarz said. "Your life's an open book, and the plot sickens. I can tell you any and everything you've done, possessed, obsessed over for the past ten years. You know, a Social Security number, even a simple phone bill makes detective work on the Internet so easy you've got ten-year-olds can recite a person's life, chapter and verse."

"What he's saying, is, don't bullshit us."

Hurley got defiant, pointed at Blancanales, who was sitting in a chair by the window. "The quiet one, he must be the good cop."

Lyons chuckled, but it was a sound that put the fear back in Hurley's eyes. "I start slapping you in the mouth, you'll see just what bad cop-good cop is all about."

"What do you want from me?"

"That's better," Lyons growled. "For starters, why?"

"Money."

"That's it," Schwarz rasped. "You gave up five FBI men for dead for a few bucks?"

"As simple as that."

"Oh, you rotten bastard." Lyons barely restrained himself from busting the guy up. "Masterson knows, Hurley. And Peters, I'm thinking, will go running to the Russians and steer them our way. Fact is, I hope he does just that. My guys hate this surveillance duty anyway. I'm saying they're edgy, might just shoot you for the hell of it and save the FBI a major headache in dealing you to the courts. You'll beg to go to Riker's if I cut them loose on you."

"I see three men here, and how many others back at the safehouse? You know how many shooters just flew in from Moscow?"

"I have this feeling you're going to tell me," Lyons said.

"At last count, I saw thirty."

Those were big odds, Lyons thought, and the good guys were holding on to the short end of the stick.

Lyons looked at Blancanales. "Pol, you said this guy was phoning home when you grabbed him."

"That's right. He was in the middle of giving up the safehouse for another Russian siege."

"Gadgets, can you rig me up a trace?"

"Can do, Ironman. Give me a couple of minutes."

Lyons watched as Schwarz went about hooking up a monitor to the phone, then settled his grim look back on Hurley. "You're going to finish that call.

Keep it simple. Just tell your Russian friends everything is fine. But keep him talking.''

"About what?''

Lyons stepped back before he started tearing into the guy. "How about your money for starters.''

CONSTANTIN BYLOKIV stared at the phone, read something into the FBI man's voice he didn't trust. "You sound funny,'' the big ex-KGB officer told Hurley.

"I think I'm just coming down with a cold, nothing to get concerned about.''

"Your health is the least of my concerns.''

"Right, right. Say, anyway, we need to talk about my money, we didn't get a chance to finish our talk.''

"Yes, that was most strange.''

It became even more odd to Bylokiv when Hurley started rambling about his woes, his paranoia that the other FBI men were looking at him funny. Rushing his words together, not letting Bylokiv respond.

Bylokiv cut the man off in midsentence, dumped the phone on the kitchen table. He looked around the Brighton Beach house that was one of Mosnivoc's properties, but one that was under another name, of course. "Boris, you say you have a number to reach Peters?''

The lean, shaved-head Kyricik nodded, his long fingers caressing the stock of the AK-47 he looked eager to use. "Yes. Problems?''

"I am not sure. We can no longer stay here. Something feels wrong. We'll leave now, get a few of the others from the hotel. I will call Peters from a pay phone. I need to meet with the man.''

"Dangerous. I get feeling not even their own people trust those two. Could be followed."

"There is no other way. Our orders are clear. If we cannot free Comrade Yuri, then we are to kill him along with the other FBI men. Even if it means our own deaths."

LYONS READ the frustration on his teammate's face. Schwarz shook his head. "Not enough time. But I can run the number down through the phone company. We can have the location within the hour."

"He got spooked, didn't he?" Lyons growled at Hurley.

When Hurley didn't answer, Lyons watched as Blancanales stepped up.

"Allow me," Blancanales said.

Lyons knew this was where Pol, short for Politician, tried to work a little psych ops, going for the heart, a kinder, gentler way in to get an enemy to come around.

"You know," Blancanales began, "I don't believe you're all that bad a guy. Life is tough, it's full of problems and worries, disappointments, broken dreams. Hey, I know something about problems. I know we all have problems, money, family, job. Basic stress of life. A man doesn't feel appreciated or respected maybe. Maybe you saw your golden years weren't going to be so golden, so you went for yourself. It's understandable in a way. Maybe your wife doesn't love you anymore—I don't know."

Lyons couldn't believe it. Hurley averted Blancanales's gaze for a moment, and he would have sworn a nerve had been touched. The bad Fed damn near looked choked up.

Blancanales cleared his throat, gave Hurley a gentle pat on the back. "What I'm saying, is if you work with me and my friends, maybe, just maybe I can put in a good word for you when this is over, and I believe you do want it over. But if we can't reach some understanding, if you don't have anything to put on the table, well, I can't be responsible for what my big friend here might do. Give us something to work with. Anything."

While Hurley seemed to fold up inside himself and weigh his options, which were pretty much none and zero, Lyons heard Schwarz call him over. Blancanales was busy putting on some more gentle persuasion when Lyons read the dark look on Schwarz's face.

"What is it?"

"While Pol was gone, I did some digging on this prick at the State Department."

"Yeah? And?"

"This guy Carlington, before he somehow landed himself the job at State as chief liaison officer to Moscow?"

Schwarz paused again, and Lyons restrained himself from snapping. "Come on, what?"

"He was the CIA's chief station officer in Moscow about the time Mosnivoc was shooting and extorting his way to the top in Russia."

Lyons felt his jaw drop open. Something was beginning to smell real bad over at the State Department. The problem, as Lyons saw it, was the stench had blown his way, putting the lives of Able Team and the other FBI agents guarding on Mosnivoc on the line. He was starting to wonder if maybe the good guys were nothing more than sacrificial lambs in some bigger scheme.

"Guys."

Lyons looked at Blancanales. "He says he can help us. He knows two locations where we can find a few of the Russian shooters."

Lyons bared his teeth in a grim smile. "A preemptive strike. Sounds like a plan I can work with."

Hawaii

HOTEL STREET was Honolulu's version of Bourbon Street at Mardi Gras crossed with the seedier days of Times Square-Broadway. It was all noise, whores, drunken sailors and Marines. The city council and the cops had tried to clean it up over the past few years, but money talked and it was still business as usual. Everywhere Bolan saw the hookers, the pimps and the staggering sailors and Marines marching their way in and out of hotels, peep shows and strip clubs. The Golden Dragon stood out like a king's palace among the squalor of the peasants at the far end of Hotel Street.

"I have helped you, yes?"

Bolan slowly drove for Chengdu's restaurant, found an alley, rolled in and parked. He looked at his Chinese tour guide. His name was Yuhan, stated he was merely a dock worker, but knew, yes, that the eighteen-wheeler the big American had blown up had been loaded up with heroin for distribution on some other island, along with cash that was to be shipped back to mainland China, he supposed. Yuhan told Bolan he was a simple man, with family he'd brought from Beijing on a boat owned by Mr. Chengdu. Chengdu brought Chinese here to work for him at the warehouse, his restaurant. Bolan had the whole sordid picture nailed. Chengdu was importing slaves who would never be free no matter how much they dreamed of a better life.

Bolan reached over and uncuffed Yuhan. He would get little more from the man, who, if nothing else, confirmed Bolan's suspicions that he'd blown up the mother lode back at the warehouse. Maybe this stop, he decided, would be his next-to-last crushing blow against Chengdu's Triad. There was still plenty of work to do, but Bolan figured he at least had the rats running scared. With any luck he'd find himself staring down into that barrel of rats soon enough. A turkey shoot maybe.

"I free to leave?"

"Yes."

Yuhan looked at Bolan, suspicious. "Just like that?"

"Just like that. Some free advice. Chengdu's finished in Oahu. I suggest you find another employer."

Yuhan bobbed his head. "Yes, yes, good advice. Chengdu is bad man. Thank you."

When Yuhan was out the door, Bolan unzipped his war bag and filled his pockets with three thermite grenades.

The Executioner disgorged, locked up the rental, shrugged a shoulder as he felt the weight of the mini-Uzi in its special rigging.

This was another crash-and-burn job, nothing tricky about it.

Half a block later Bolan went through the front door, marched down the foyer of the Golden Dragon. It was a mixed dining crowd of Americans and Asians, decor all glitz and oil prints, with tropical shrubbery spread around. Maybe it was the grim look on the big warrior's face that caught a few wary eyes. But the mini-Uzi that came out definitely grabbed everyone's attention.

"Everyone clear out, there's a fire in the kitchen."

A short burst, sprayed at the ceiling, got the stampede started. He rolled through the dining room, an elbow thrown here and there to clear his way. As he palmed a thermite grenade, two goons brandishing pistols hustled around the far end of the bar. Bolan chopped them off their feet with a lightning double-tap of stuttering mini-Uzi fire, a fresh wave of screams assaulting his senses as more diners packed into the herd.

When he had clearance, he armed the hellbomb and dropped the steel egg behind the now vacant bar.

Another Chinese thug charged through the swing doors to the kitchen, hollering at the top of his lungs, his compact Ingram subgun spraying lead the big American's way. Bolan was bolting across the dining room as hot lead sought him out, when the bar erupted in a ball of blinding white fire. The soldier dropped to cover beneath a vacated table. Plates were blown up and food was flying over Bolan's head as he aimed the mini-Uzi at the knees of the shooter. A 3-round stitching, and the soldier turned those knees to red ruins with protruding shards of bone. Shrieking, the Chinese goon toppled, Bolan rising and pumping a mercy burst into his face.

By now the superheated white phosphorous was racing out beyond the bar, eating up the carpet as if it were nothing more than kindling that had sat out in a blazing sun for too long. Just for good measure, the soldier armed another firebomb, pitching it into the abandoned dining room. There was all manner of racket in the kitchen, a round brown face plastered to the window of the swing door. That face pulled away, the figure running deeper into the kitchen as the second fireball roared through the dining room.

Bolan stowed the mini-Uzi in its special rigging and retraced his steps for the front door. By the time the soldier hit the sidewalk, averting any eyes, his head bent and melting into the running stampede, the Golden Dragon was belching smoke and fire in his wake, well on the way to burning down to smoldering ash, warning Huan Chengdu in the process that he was going out of business.

CHAPTER SEVEN

Adriatic Coast

David McCarter found a feast fit for kings waiting for him in the dining room, saw the men eating up as if there were no tomorrow. In their line of work, there was always the chance the next minute could prove their last on earth. So he could well understand their appetites after spending a long week in Senegal, dodging bullets, killing warlords and snatching the good senator from Maine, along with his UN peace-keeping force, out of the clutches of a tyrant who made Idi Amin seem a prepuberty choirboy.

"I just got off the horn with Barbara, mates. Looks like we have to eat while we fly back to Aviano."

The former SAS commando gazed at the spread Jack Grimaldi had cooked up and laid out for the men of Phoenix Force. Damn shame, he thought, to not be able to sit down and partake of what Stony Man's top gun had gone through so much trouble to prepare. The British leader of Phoenix Force saw enough grilled rack of lamb, veal parm and marsala and bowls of pasta smothered in marinara to anchor the USS *Enterprise*.

Grimaldi, who was twirling linguine around his spoon, drinking red wine, glanced up. "Oh, well. I knew Hal landing us our own little slice of heaven by the Adriatic, not to mention having all the goodies I asked for on the flight back here ready and waiting, was too good to be true."

T. J. Hawkins devoured some lamb, worked on a glass of Jack Daniel's whiskey like he might never eat or drink again. For a Southerner, McCarter decided Hawkins was showing quite the zeal for Italian cuisine. Gary Manning and Rafael Encizo stopped eating long enough to give their leader the grim attention of soldiers who knew duty called.

"We're on standby, mates, as of now," McCarter said. "Let's saddle up."

Hawkins cocked a grin that was somewhere between wry and disappointment, chomped down on some veal parm. "Jack, I can't say how much I appreciate you rediscovering your Italian roots. You showed this Southern boy here what he's been missing all these years."

Encizo grinned at Grimaldi. "We have a pilot 'and' a gourmet chef," the muscular Cuban commented. "Somehow, we have to find a way to install a broiler and a grill on board whatever Jack's flying us around in. Since he's top gun, shouldn't be much of a problem for him to fly and cook at the same time."

"Be just like walking and chewing gum for our number-one flyboy," Hawkins said.

"Where's Cal?" McCarter asked.

Hawkins aimed a thumb over his shoulder, pointing at the balcony, beyond which McCarter heard the surf breaking on the beach. "Took a dip. Said he needed to relieve some tension before working up a suitable appetite."

"Must be the SEAL in him," Gary Manning said, already standing and ready to pack it up. "Never happy unless he's kicking down doors and shooting things up."

"Look who's talking," Hawkins said, grinning at the big Canadian who was also the team's demolitions master. "You must have placed enough C-4 around that warlord's palace, hell, I think you sent pieces of it clear to the other side in Somalia."

"What can I say? I love my job, T.J."

Outside on the balcony, McCarter scanned the choppy surf, peering into the long shadows now falling over the Adriatic. Nearly a hundred yards out to sea, McCarter spotted the human shark that was Calvin James. The ex-SEAL was a slender missile slicing through the water, turning this way and that, back-stroking, front stroking, rolling, dipping down, coming up. James, McCarter knew, had the energy and stamina of five men, and just like Hawkins said, he was most likely working out the kinks, burning off some excess energy after the Senegal foray.

"Cal!" McCarter shouted again, and saw James stop, bob in the choppy surf, wave. "I need you in here, on the double! We're packing it up!"

Another wave to confirm it, and McCarter wheeled, rolled back into the dining room. Plastic bags were being filled with Grimaldi's labor of love, and McCarter couldn't resist consuming a couple pieces of lamb.

"I can't imagine dining on all this in that bucket of bolts Jack flew us here in," Hawkins said.

"Hey, I cut my teeth on Hueys," Grimaldi said, grinning. "Don't sweat it, T.J. It'll be smooth sailing back to Aviano. You won't even spill the first spoon of pasta on your blacksuit. Besides, with the military taking it in the shorts because of budget cuts back home, not to mention the good airborne stuff is still over in Yugoslavia, I couldn't exactly spot an exec-style Bell JetRanger at Aviano."

"So, what's the story, David? Where are we off to?" Manning asked, turning the banter to serious business.

"Saudi's our next home away from home. There's trouble in Syria, and Barbara and Katz want us in their backyard. We're waiting on the green light."

"Sounds like the Man," Manning said, "hasn't given us the thumbs-up yet."

"Hal's working on him. I'll fill everybody in on the way to Aviano. But the way I'm hearing it, sounds like we've just jumped out of the frying pan and into the fire. Syria's hot, mates, and I'm not talking about the desert sun."

Encizo zipped up his portion of the lamb. "Don't keep us in suspense. What's the proposed gig?"

"We're looking at the possibility of taking down a suspected nuclear-waste reprocessing site in Syria," the Phoenix Force leader told them. "And we may end up having to dodge a few Israeli F-16s along the way, so Katz tells me."

"Katz has friends in high places over there," Grimaldi said. "Shouldn't be a problem if some of their flyboys decide to help us out with a few well-placed Sidewinders."

"Right, shouldn't be, if this was shaping up as your

no-fuss, no-muss surgical strike," McCarter said. "The scuttlebutt from the Farm is that those Sidewinders you mention may be armed with nuclear warheads."

To a man they froze, telling David McCarter they'd just lost their appetites.

New York

LYONS AND Blancanales climbed the steps. The Able Team duo peered up into the murky gloom of the second floor of the decrepit apartment complex Lyons decided was a crack motel. They could have looked like just a couple of rough-and-tumble Brooklynite hoods, lugging nylon cases that could have almost been passed off as pool cue wrap-ups. The unwieldy bulk, though, of the SPAS-12 shotgun in Lyons's casing and the M-16/M-203 in Blancanales's nylon toter would never stand up to close inspection in the drug-saturated tenements and crime-infested neighborhoods near the industrial waterfront just west of Brooklyn Heights. Not that Lyons gave a damn. Life was tough all over, and if they had anything to say about it some Russian goons were a few short moments away from never swilling the vodka again back in the motherland.

Lyons stopped as Blancanales tugged on his shoulder. Despite all the racket of someone's stereo cranked up to decibel levels of a jet taking off, the unceasing shrill of New Yorkers laying on the horns out on the street, Blancanales still felt the need to whisper.

"We've already had one false alarm. I'm starting to think Hurley snowed me."

Lyons shook his head, grimacing as he fought to keep every ungodly noise and smell he could ever dread to find in one place from sending him reeling back down the steps. "Gadgets placed that phone number right at the house we found in Brighton Beach. I know, I know, I kicked the door in, and ransacked the place, but there was a method to my madness."

"Yeah, what was that?"

"Urban pest control. We found the place clean, no sign of anyone living there other than a couple of half-finished blinis in the garbage. The roaches skittered off, smart or paranoid enough to figure Hurley's been bagged. They won't be going back to that place. Anyway, Gadgets wouldn't make that kind of mistake."

"So, if a goon squad is here, what's the plan?"

"Being as I only got two slices of pie for which I paid for all the troops, I figure I'll go for the pizza-delivery angle." Lyons tapped the small satchel around his shoulder. "All else fails, I'll try out Cowboy's latest toy."

"Oh, this should be good."

"Look on the bright side."

Blancanales cocked an eyebrow. "Which is what, I'm almost afraid to ask, since I know that pissed-off pit-bull look in your eyes."

"We actually found a parking place in Brooklyn."

"I think it would have been more practical to have Gadgets come along and sit with our wheels. This part of town, we may find ourselves walking back to Flat-bush.''

"We need Gadgets right where he is. Finding out things, watching the store and sitting on Hurley. Come on, I've got a good feeling we're going to score this time out.''

They were topping the stairs when Lyons spotted two black guys hanging around, halfway down the hall. One look, and he could tell they were up to something their mothers would never approve of. A moment later, he was sure of it. They were about to bolt when Lyons unsheathed the massive SPAS-12, warned them another step would end their brilliant futures. Closing quickly on the duo, Lyons put a finger to his mouth.

"Don't even breathe.'' He looked at the bag of rock cocaine, took it and shoved it in his pocket for disposal down the nearest sewer later.

"Hey, man...''

"What did I tell you about even breathing—now you want to talk shit to me.'' He flashed his phony Justice Department credentials, getting another round of respectful silence, then stowed them back in his windbreaker. "Get your hands up.'' When they grabbed air, Lyons patted them down, confiscated two pistols, which he examined then dropped in the pocket of his windbreaker, the weapons also destined for the sewer. "Glocks? You guys really are moving on up.'' He saw the bulge in the coat pocket of the Yankees jacket, delved in and pulled his hand back, displaying a wad of cash to Blancanales, who was watching the hall and covering the crack dealers. "You don't mind if I make a donation to your favorite charity, do you?'' Lyons asked the drug dealers, and shoved the money in his pocket.

Yankees Jacket wanted to get some attitude. "Yeah, make it the United Negro College Fund, cop.''

"No sweat. Like they say, a mind's a terrible thing to waste. Okay, today I don't care about you guys, meaning you've bought yourselves a reprieve. You live here?'' A nod, and Lyons pushed on, told them he was looking for some foreign types in the apartment number Hurley had given him.

"Yeah, they inside now. Come out 'bout every hour, checkin' the hall, like they's nervous or somethin', or maybe geekin' on some rock. Big dudes, talkin' some strange tongue I ain't never heard.''

"How many you figure?''

"Don't know, but I walk by, you know, see the door open long as two seconds, big dude comin' out again, lookin' all around. Say five, maybe six. I seen some guns, too, man, like assault rifles.''

"Beat it,'' Lyons growled, and they jogged off, throwing back sulky looks before they hit the stairs and vanished.

Moving on, Lyons found the targeted apartment at the end of the hallway, tucked up against the fire escape. A brief peek out the window, and he found their way out led through an alley that would take them straight back to where they'd parked near the Brooklyn-Queens Expressway. It was about as sweet a setup for a quick evac as he could hope for.

Blancanales hauled out the M-16, and the Able Team warriors took up positions on either side of the door, flanking the jamb.

Lyons knocked. He made out the sound of a television on somewhere dead ahead, a talk show, someone whining about something or other. The volume went down all the way, giving up only the ominous sound of silence on the other side.

"I got a pizza delivery here."

The continued silence beyond the door rose the hackles on the back of Lyons's neck. He put on his best Brooklyn accent, barking, "Hey, open up, this pie's gettin' cold, fella."

"Nobody order any pizza. Go away."

"Hey, I got the right room, right hellhole of a building. Charlie don't make those kinda mistakes."

"One last time. Mistake. Go away."

"I need fifteen bucks from you'se guys, and since this is such a shit neighborhood, me riskin' my neck and all with all the gangbangers around, I damn well better get a good tip."

"I said, 'go away.'"

"I ain't leavin', pal, until I see a face and a hand out with a twenty spot, you'se hear me."

Silence, then Lyons heard a sound he was familiar with from the old days when he'd been an L.A. cop. Blancanales had to have heard it, too, since Lyons read the look in his eyes that told him he was ready for it to hit the fan. Now Lyons felt the hackles sticking out like antennae. Someone had just jacked a shell into the chamber of a shotgun.

MAYBE IT WAS the vodka he'd been sucking down most of the day to calm nerves tweaked out by crack. Or maybe it was the crack alone he'd been smoking since sunup that pushed him out there in the ozone of paranoia. Or maybe, he reasoned, it was simply the waiting around for further orders while the five of them sat and worried whether, if and when they'd get the green light, wondering all the while if American law enforcement was somewhere out there, circling in for a front-door raid.

Back in Moscow it had sounded so simple. As planned, Alexsandr Dirichky's hit team had flown in behind the other teams, with an address where they were to go and sit tight until they were contacted. The crate with their weapons, flown in by diplomatic pouch, making it untouchable, had been waiting for them at JFK. The plan, as he had been told by a Mosnivoc associate in Moscow, was for the teams to be spread around Brooklyn, then link up when the hit was ready to go.

Of course, what Moscow didn't know was that Dirichky had a drug problem. He had been all too eager to come to America, where drugs were more plentiful and far cheaper.

Something told him the party was over. He threw his men a look, nodding for them to grab their AK-47s while he racked a 12-gauge round into the sawed-off Ithaca pump shotgun. The voice on the other side didn't fool him. It was contrived to sound like some Brooklynite, the pizza-delivery angle nothing but bullshit.

The cops had found them. Two days ago, he had handed over the money to the FBI man under Moscow's orders, the American cop actually knowing the location of their safehouse, apparently before he even did. He had been mildly curious as to why he'd been selected as the bag man, but now it looked as if the

FBI man had some change of heart, or had maybe been found out and forced to talk, pointing fingers this way.

Well, Dirichky's orders were explicit. No one was to be captured by the cops. If they were snatched by American law, they would be somehow brought back to Moscow, make no mistake, and made to disappear forever in one of the Siberian gulags, which still existed, he knew, since he'd done a couple of years of hard labor up north in the freezing frontier.

Death was preferable to the gulag.

The Pizza Voice wasn't about to go away, insisting he open up, and now. Enough. Dirichky squeezed the trigger, rode out the shotgun blast as he blew away half the door.

LYONS WAS BRACED for the storm when it blew, but he wasn't expecting the sort of all-out blitz that put them under siege.

It was only normal—no matter how seasoned a combat vet, or how many front doors a commando charged through—to jump back and hold on when a hurricane of buckshot and bullets was eating up chunks of real estate in your face. Despite that, Lyons and Blancanales got busy, searching for any opening, ready to hurl it back. Blancanales triggered a long sweeping burst from the M-16, his eyelids narrowed against all the debris flying around. He had pulled back on an angle with the doorway, directing what amounted to little more than spray and pray. A curse, a voice screaming something in Russian, and it sounded like Blancanales scored a lucky hit. Lyons unloaded a few peals of thunder from the SPAS-12 on the other side, but the Russian shooters were holding their ground beyond the mangled jaws of the door, firing away, bellowing curses and threats.

They were staring down a suicide squad.

"Screw this!" Lyons roared over the din of autofire and shotgun blasts that were shaving off jagged hunks of the doorjamb in a savage locust storm of unyielding weapons fire. "Blow them straight to hell and back to the motherland in a hundred pieces!"

A nod, and Blancanales tapped the trigger of his M-203 grenade launcher. Lyons wasn't sure where Blancanales had aimed his 40 mm charge, but the explosion was deafening, a cloud of dust and smoke blossoming through the doorway. Lyons couldn't believe it as he made out, a second later, the rattle of still more autofire. Teeth gritted against the painful roaring in his ears, he hauled out Little Bulldozer, judged the weapons fire coming from some distant point deep inside the apartment and chugged off two 40 mm HE rounds. Falling back, he rode out the double blasts, nearly bowled off his feet by the twin explosions.

Time to mop it up.

SPAS-12 leading the way, Lyons bulled into the thick smoke and cordite, fanning the wreckage, Blancanales charging in on his heels. Lyons kicked through a severed arm, glimpsed the twisted barrels of smoking AK-47s, the sprawled corpses among the kindling of what had been furniture. They had the adjoining rooms checked and cleared within seconds.

It looked wrapped up to Lyons, nice and bloody.

Lyons gave the carnage in the living room one last

look. "I see five, if you want to add up the missing body parts lying around this dump."

"Five down, and what did Hurley say?"

"Twenty-five left, give or take."

"Brooklyn's a big place, Carl. I'm not sure we have the time to ride around and look for buzz cut ex-KGB types in dark sedans."

"Your point being?"

"This was the last of the addresses Hurley gave us. He said it was this place where the guy handed him over his money two days ago."

"Maybe we need to jog Hurley's memory some more."

Lyons led Blancanales out into the hallway, angling off for the fire escape. A quick search, and Lyons found no one had ventured from the squalor of their cubicles. But this was New York, he figured, see no evil, like that, which suited him just fine. He had enough problems already without having to explain himself to the local NYPD blue.

Hawaii

THE MODEST ESTATE north of Diamond Head Beach was marked in the Justice Department's files on Fugasami as a suspected cash cow barn. It was one piece of the report on the Yakuza that had been faxed on earlier to Bolan as part of the Farm's intel package. But here Bolan hoped to find enough Yankee dollars on-site to fill up a dump truck. To make life a tab more miserable for Benny Fugasami, the soldier was bringing along a large empty nylon pouch to help himself to some of the Yakuza's dirty money when the smoke cleared and the bodies stopped twitching. The rest of the cash would go up in flames when Bolan dropped off a few thermite grenades before departing the premises. The report stated the cash house was a suspected money-laundering and clearinghouse from the various backroom gaming houses the Yakuza ran in Honolulu and Waikiki. That the place could operate openly and freely told Bolan a few cops were on Benny's payroll.

In due time, the soldier would sweep up all the dirt. First another firestorm in paradise.

When rolling away from Hotel Street, the soldier had figured he could at least drop a double whammy on Fugasami as he'd done to his rival. Two for two, but going for the grand slam now, just to keep the scorecard even on both sides of the enemy's fence. By now, he suspected word was spreading through the ranks on both sides about a big American shooting up the island, blowing up and burning down major gold mines on both sides of the Triad and the Yakuza. He was hoping that, sometime during the night, the strange and bloody events of the day would have both sides clashing to the death.

And Bolan lived in grim hope to see the savages devour each other before he made the grand and final entrance, wherever that was.

Shadows were now stretching over the lush vegetation as Bolan closed on the red-tiled, white-stuccoed building. A sat picture of the hard site marked the distance off as a half mile due west of the prehistoric-looking 760-foot peak of the extinct volcano that looked out over the white sands of Diamond Head Beach, and Bolan used nature's landmark to guide him in. With nightfall fast approaching, Bolan now opted for his combat blacksuit, webbing outfitted with all the grenades and spare clips for his side arms and the mini-Uzi he would need on this smash and grab.

The Executioner took the path of least resistance, coming up on open ground south of the building. There was no gate, no kind of surveillance equipment he could detect, but that didn't mean they weren't there. Just the same, he checked the grounds, the dense vegetation all around. Sure enough, he spotted a mounted camera that slowly swung from left to right. He could have cursed the oversight, but it was too late. With any luck the camera would have been aimed the other way when he'd skirted up the trail. He darted ahead as the camera came within inches of panning his way.

Bolan wasn't banking on luck.

He counted five luxury vehicles in the motor pool. Figure roughly twenty guys inside, maybe up to thirty if the cash cow was that fat, a squad of gunmen at least guarding the bean counters. Whatever, he'd tackle the odds, shoot first. With skill, daring and the advantage of striking first on his side, he should make it out, move on.

Should. Whatever.

The soldier was weaving his way through narrow breaks in the tropical vegetation when he discovered he'd have to make his own luck.

The front doors opened, and a big Yakuza thug in silk threads came barreling outside, barking something in Japanese at two more goons armed with Ingram submachine guns. Since the soldier was once again on a bulldoze-and-burn outing, he decided to start the ram and slam.

The two goons were splitting up when the warrior palmed the Beretta 93-R and drilled two lightning rounds out the sound-suppressed muzzle. The Yakuza lost two more shooters as quiet death cored them between the eyes and kicked them off their feet.

The estate boss was stunned for all of a second, then he swung up his own compact subgun when the big invader in black surged out of the brush. Bolan shot him in the face, charged past his falling body.

The Beretta tucked away, the mini-Uzi was back up and tracking as Bolan sprinted down the foyer and hit the sprawling living room. What he found were fifteen or so guys in aloha or sports shirts grouped around big tables. They were running stacks of cash through money counters, fielding phone calls to take bets or maybe warn the losers to pay up, when the Executioner went to work ruining the Yakuza's day some more.

A few pistols were coming up from the tables when Bolan hosed down any wannabe samurai. Up the steps two hardmen were bounding Bolan's way, their Ingram subguns barking for all of two heartbeats. Slugs snapped around Bolan's head before he adjusted his aim and drilled the shooters in the chest with two 3-round bursts. They were tumbling in a twisted heap when Bolan surged ahead, firing the mini-Uzi at two gunners in aloha shirts backpedaling for the French doors, the bean counters winging wild pistol fire around the room as they scrambled in their evac.

The runners were doomed to hell.

A long burst up their backs, and Bolan sent them sailing through the doors in a crash of glass.

The soldier was cracking home a fresh clip when he saw a money counter thrusting hands up and shouting in a mix of Japanese and broken English. He sought out a defiant face.

Bolan dumped his pouch on top of a dozen or so stacks of hundred-dollar bills. "You. I need some vacation funds. It seems my credit cards have maxed out. Fill it up."

The defiant one cursed, something about the gaijin could go to hell, was reaching for something behind his back when Bolan squeezed the subgun's trigger, marched a line of 9 mm slugs across his chest.

"Anybody else looking to commit seppuku?"

Two of the money counters moved fast to fill Bolan's pouch. He ignored the hate and anger boring his way, plucked a thermite grenade off his webbing. "You have maybe four seconds to clear out before I burn the house down." Bolan selected a volunteer to deliver a message to Fugasami. "You, in the purple shirt. I like the flowers, by the way. Tell Benny his time on the island is now measured in hours. Repeat that." Purple Shirt did, and Bolan barked for them to move out. He watched the stampede carefully as they filed out the front way, doors opening and thudding shut, big engines growling to life a few moments later. Hefting his cut of the action, Bolan figured he was walking off with at least a quarter million. Not much by Fugasami's standards, but it was the brazenness of the rip-off and the goring of his cash cow that would have Benny frothing at the mouth.

Quickly and smoothly, the Executioner strategically lobbed three thermite hellbombs around. One for the living room, one for the kitchen, the third scorcher flung upstairs, and he was breaking for the foyer. Mini-Uzi leading the way and poised to cut down the first glimpse of trouble, Bolan was flying out the front doors when the hellbombs thundered off in rapid succession. Glass shot over the grounds as the concussive force and tongues of white fire blew out the windows on the first floor.

Straight ahead, the way was clear for the soldier to reroute his path back to his vehicle. The Executioner couldn't resist a last look back to admire his work. By the time he hit the trail, the soldier figured the House of Fugasami was burning bright enough for the Yakuza boss to see the flames dancing all the way to the Golden Palace.

As far as the Executioner was concerned, things were only just heating up. He was saving the hottest taste of hell for his enemies for last.

THE HORRIFIC REPORTS coming in from his samurai were not only mind-boggling, but stoked his fury to strike back right away. The problem was whom to take out his rage on, and where, no less, to find the source of all this mystery and misery coming at him from every turn, every hour on the hour it seemed.

Incredible as he found it all, some big gaijin was apparently running amok on the island. First Barzama had been dishonored, the gaijin leaving ominous messages to be delivered that Yakamu Fugasami was finished on the island, his hour of doom fast approaching. If that was true, why didn't this barbarian simply come to him, face him down and do battle, a warrior of honor instead of these ninja sneak attacks? Or was there some angle, some game the gaijin was playing on him? But what? It didn't please him much, either, that Chengdu had also been hit by this same madman. The Triad boss was now staring at the ashes of his warehouse by the harbor, where he kept his contraband, then having to answer a bunch of questions fired at him by local law enforcement about why someone would come in, shoot up his restaurant, then burn it to the ground. And now, the latest blow, a huge slap in the face of Fugasami. This madman had actually stormed the money house where, reportedly, he'd lost nearly ten million in cash that was slated to be flown to a bank in Tokyo where he cleaned up the money, then had it rerouted back to Oahu where he could make legitimate investments. Then he felt his blood turn to fire, recalling the report from one of his money counters how this gaijin had helped himself to close to three hundred thousand dollars, before passing on more threatening words. Naturally any survivors of this latest debacle would be offered a choice. The short sword, or a bullet pumped into their heads from one of his samurai.

Fugasami needed to clean house anyway, get himself back on top, take charge. Restructuring the order of his organization, finding out who was who and what was what was a long time in coming anyway. One good thing about this hurricane, he thought, it showed him who was samurai and who was just riding his coattails.

Control, he told himself, he must regain control of his emotions at the moment. The situation was salvageable. If he marshalled his samurai and hunkered down here at the Golden Palace he could hazard a good guess both Chengdu and this gaijin crazy man would come to him. He was being hunted, after all, and it stood to reason, since his places of business had come under siege by the gaijin, well, he could only hope the wild man would soon enough be coming to the club.

Fugasami stood and walked around his massive teak desk, his mind racing with a slew of unanswered questions. He gritted his teeth against the steady thumping of American rock and roll pounding through the closed door of his back office, noise that seemed to fan the fires of his rage. It may be fun and games out there on the dance floor, but Fugasami knew his empire was crumbling, and he was facing a threat unlike any he had ever known. He fingered the hilt of his long sword, looked around the four samurai who had brought Barzama to him.

"Majiki," Fugasami told the samurai standing by the door. "One hour, you are to close the club send everyone home. I want every warrior we have left contacted and brought here. You will have my men bring every weapon, sword, throwing stars, machine guns, whatever, anything they can lay their hands on here. You will place two men down the street with handheld radios, one out back in the alley. Anyone— I do not care if it looks like a beggar—approaches the club, I am to be contacted immediately. Go."

Majiki bowed, wheeled. When the door closed behind him, Fugasami rested a dark gaze on Barzama, who was kneeling, head bowed, on thick plastic sheeting.

"Barzama, listen to me very carefully. This is a

dark hour for all of us, let us be clear. We have some crazy gaijin who seeks to destroy us. Who he is and what he wants I do not know. As for you, I wish to tell you a short story about my father's death. My father, who created what is now an empire at my command, committed ritual seppuku. I have never told anyone this tale of shame, but I tell you know so you understand what I expect. What happened, he was beaten severely, near to death, by a gang of drunken GI barbarians. As he was lying in his own blood, he was forced to watch them rape my mother, and many times. In the face of such dishonor he cleansed my mother of her shame, then put the short sword in his own belly. For the moment, your life is being spared, but we are both clear, I can tell you, you have been dishonored. Had you dealt like a warrior with this crazy gaijin, I perhaps would not be faced with such trouble. I need you at this time, I cannot spare the first man. War will be coming here, to this club. The war has been created by others, but it is destiny, I can feel it in my heart. We have been on top too long, too soft, I can see now, while there have been jackals everywhere wishing only to eat us alive and attempt to take what we have. So be it. Barzama, should you not die in what I feel in my heart is a coming great and final battle between us, the Triad and this wild man, you will do what you must to reclaim your honor.''

Barzama bowed his head. "Yes, my lord. I understand.''

When the phone on his desk rang, Fugasami couldn't hold back a grim chuckle. "Ah, I hear more bad news already.'' He picked up the phone, right away recognized the voice of his hated rival.

''I would ask if you are somehow responsible for my present predicament,'' Huan Chengdu said, his silk-smooth voice tinged with bitter anger on the other end. ''But I figure you for nothing more than a liar.''

''Perhaps we could meet and discuss our mutual troubles.''

A pause, Chengdu's mind, he figured, reading between the lines. ''As you wish. I believe it necessary for the both of us to conclude some business.''

''You know where to find me. Let us say eleven tonight.''

''Perhaps sooner. I am most eager to meet with you.''

''The club will be emptied out by then. I will even leave the front door open for you.''

Chengdu hung up and Fugasami felt the smile cutting his lips as he listened to the buzzing dial tone of empty air.

Putting the receiver down, he told Barzama to rise. ''This is destiny. I feel a divine wind surrounding all of us. The Russians are coming to deliver five million dollars for what the American will be dropping off in two hours. The Triad will be arriving shortly after for what I know will be battle. And do you know something? After all I have worked so long and so hard for, I do not care about the Russians' money. Our honor will also be reclaimed, because I know we will handle Chengdu and his ninja. However, given all of this, all I want is to meet this crazy gaijin. All I want is the chance to carve him up into a dozen bloody pieces and hear him beg for his life.''

"If it is the destiny you believe, my lord," Barzama said, "then it will come to pass. You have always been right."

"Indeed I have," the Yakuza boss said. "I am samurai. I am shogun."

CHAPTER EIGHT

Stony Man Farm, Virginia

Brognola stared at the computerized-graphic wall map of the world with its bank of clocks marking every time zone and miles in between the zones. He was mentally mapping out the logistical bits and pieces for Phoenix Force himself when Price signed off with McCarter.

"Phoenix is airborne for Saudi Arabia. I've faxed David all pertinent intelligence as we have it so far," Price reported to Brognola. "On the plus side, there was a military jet on hand, and since the base commander at Aviano suspects David and company are something a little more than he cares to know about, the good general was more than happy to see them off. Jack is at the helm of a Gulfstream C-20 as we speak."

Brognola nodded as he studied the wall map. Price had already paved the way for Phoenix Force to land at an American military base near the Saudi-Iraqi border, putting them as close to the Syrian backyard as possible.

"Okay, according to the map, that's roughly a two-thousand-mile flight as the crow flies. Max speed on one of those Gulfstream C-20s is what?''

"Five-sixty-one an hour.''

Brognola nodded. "Call it four hours, then, to touchdown."

"When I first heard about the Syrian situation, I went over an inventory of all the requisite hardware, gear and some techno-goodies with Cowboy that Phoenix will need. I had a crew of blacksuits load up one of our own Gulfstreams. They left the Farm," she said, checking the wall clock, "almost seven hours ago. One stop to refuel in Germany, and with any luck they may touch down right behind Phoenix. I spoke with Jack, and he told me what he would need for air-firepower support for the guys but I was already way ahead of him. He's asking for an AC-130 Spectre."

Brognola whistled. "Our resident top gun doesn't want much, does he? That kind of flying death is just this side of a nuked-up B-52."

"I may have jumped the gun, Hal, but I was anticipating getting Phoenix Force into the game, and hours ago. I didn't mention it to Jack, but I already had a Spectre in mind. I had already found one sitting on the tarmac down at Langley Air Force Base near Norfolk."

"Called initiative. I always appreciate that kind of jumping the gun," Brognola said, mentally calculating distances, refueling layovers, aware it would be several long hours before Phoenix Force was in place, with weapons and gear delivered, everything on-site and ready to go. He paused a moment, unable to keep from marveling at the tireless dedication of his team here. Near the big Fed the computer wizards were hard at work in cyberspace, tapping keyboards like concert pianists, intent stares locked on their monitors.

From the Communications Room Brognola heard Katz going back and forth with Colonel Avi Meissel again. The speaker hookup to Katz's satcom was on, and what Brognola was hearing didn't bode well for inserting Phoenix Force as a solo act, if the President even sanctioned them for a go. He also had an update from Lyons through Kurtzman. Things were likewise turning ugly in Brooklyn, but Able Team had control of the situation. Still no call from the big guy, leaving Brognola chewing on more raw nerves about the mess and the mystery in Oahu. Usually, though, no news from Striker was good news.

"This is a matter of grave national security, I know you understand that, Katzenelenbogen. I know you understand we cannot let this site remain standing. According to Mossad, it is far larger even than the nuclear plant the Iranians were building before we took care of that particular problem, as you know. Unfortunately, we are not even sure how long this site has been in place, or what precisely is under way. Should the Syrians, however, be well on the way to be producing, at worst, a short-range surface-to-surface missile with nuclear-strike capacity, we believe they would not hesitate to use it on Israel to cement, for just one matter, their claim on Lebanon. Perhaps they would even use nuclear blackmail. From there, who knows?"

"Colonel, I well appreciate what you are faced

with. You know my background in military and intelligence service to Israel—"

"Which is the only reason I even stand here and give you all due respect as to some of our intentions."

"That's why I'm a little nervous on this end, Colonel. As of our last communication, you informed me you were outfitting a few F-16s with nukes. Is that plan still on the table?"

Brognola and Price were walking for the open doorway to the Comm Room when a new voice broke over the sat link.

"Mr. Katzenelenbogen, we have been very patient so far in dealing with this situation, what with our politicians haggling and bickering over what to do, and your constant calls here are becoming bothersome. All you need to know, sir, is soon, very soon, I am prepared to give the order to strike this site in Syria. Moreover, I feel we do not need any help from the Americans on this matter."

"Who's talking?" Katz growled.

"I am Major Neissbaum. I am the commanding officer of this operation. I know who you are, I know about your service to Israel. With all due respect to a man who served Israel, Mr. Katzenelenbogen, we will resolve this crisis."

"How? By nuking half of Syria? Maybe starting a war in the Middle East? Do you know what you're saying, Major?"

"You make it sound as if I am mad or perhaps reckless at the least. What was madness was Israel— how would you say in America?—standing on the sidelines during the Gulf War while Iraqi SCUDs blew up apartment buildings and killed innocent Israeli citizens. What is madness is knowing Syrian terrorists just murdered Israeli citizens in the Bekaa and skipped over the border for safe haven in Syria, free to kill again another day."

"Americans were also killed in the Bekaa."

"I know, and I understand American resolve to take action."

"Very well, then, how about both our sides committing to a joint operation?"

"I hear ego on your end. I have no room on this operation for egos."

"I'm not talking about stroking egos here, Major," Katz snarled. "I'm talking about us doing the dirty work, so Israel doesn't get blamed and is forced to shore up the borders with half its military while putting the entire country on high alert against renewed terrorist attacks."

"This will be our last communication. Do not attempt to contact the colonel again. You will hear nothing but silence. Good day."

Brognola watched as Katz slammed his fist on the table so hard the radio console seemed to jump. "I'm running a background check on this Major Neiss-whatever-the-hell. He's talking to me about egos? Politics? He's going to forge ahead and create major disaster. I'm here to tell you if the Israelis start nuking Syria, and with the Russian crisis...I don't have to look into any crystal ball to see how bleak the future looks if Moscow decides to go on the muscle. And all this because I just heard a guy who sees a huge career move in his future if he pulls off this stunt."

"I heard the same thing," Brognola said. "I'm bringing the Man up-to-speed. With any luck, he can finagle the prime minister into reining in his people before this gets ugly to the point there is no point of return. In fact, I'll have Phoenix ready to go the next time you see me.'' Brognola chomped on his cigar, his eyes fired up with renewed grim resolve. "First you and Barbara give me your proposed plan of attack. That way I have some live ammo to fire off while I'm bending the Man's arm."

New York

LYONS WENT with his gut, trusting Masterson, filling him in on his hunt and subsequent takedown of the five Russian shooters, but skipped the part where he and Blancanales blew up the apartment in a show of force that was more acceptable in, say, Sri Lanka. The FBI SAC also knew Agent Lemon had backup, but didn't know where, or that they were actually three commandos working for the country's most covert operations force ever assembled.

They were standing in the bedroom, alone, with Masterson spreading a map of Brooklyn on the bed.

"Easiest way to transport Mosnivoc, the way I see it, is straight up Flatbush Avenue, all the way to the courthouse in downtown Brooklyn."

"I already have it covered," Lyons said, and watched Masterson peering at him. "Only the two of us are going to know this until we head out of here in the morning. I have two Justice Department choppers on standby at LaGuardia. They'll be landing in an open field near the Picnic House in Prospect Park to pick up the boss. Where we are now from the park, it's a hop, skip and a jump to get there by car."

"And then?"

"Then what? He'll be choppered to the courthouse, where you'll already have a team waiting on the front steps to hold his hand and walk him inside. Driving him in is simply too risky. Say our Russian friends are right now riding around all over Brooklyn. Say they accidentally spot our street surveillance. I mean, it doesn't take any rocket scientist to figure out what they are. If we get caught driving Mosnivoc, we become too easy a target for a bunch of shooters to cut us off in traffic and go for broke."

"After what you told me happened when you hit that door, maybe you're right."

"No 'maybe' about it, my friend."

"It's your show."

"It's our show."

Masterson turned grim. "You know, I've been on this job for fifteen years. And I have never seen even the first inkling of one of ours going bad. I can't tell you how much it galls me to know about Hurley and Peters. If it was up to me, I'd have them squirming on death row up at Attica tomorrow."

Being a former cop, and knowing that a rare few with the law on their side did go bad, Lyons could well understand Masterson's bitter anger and disappointment. The law was the law, bottom line. When a man pledged his honor and devotion before man and God to uphold that law, he was only as good as how far he was willing to go to do the job and do it right. No shades of gray, no wilting, no waffling in the face of whatever temptation was flung his direction that wanted to try to snap the required backbone to be out there and walk the walk of a stand-up cop.

"Speaking of Peters, how's he holding up?"

"The agent I assigned to him took a stroll away from the car an hour ago to give me a report. Told me he's shaky, plain to see he's feeling his nerves."

"I've got an idea, regarding Hurley, that might soothe any of our own nerves on this side."

"And what's that?"

"A little diversion tactic. If it works, we'll see Mosnivoc safely inside that courtroom and be able to drop the net over his shooters before those choppers lift off from Prospect."

"Not that I doubt you, but if it doesn't go down according to plan?"

"Then we'll just bring running all Mosnivoc's merry marauding shooters to us that much sooner."

And Lyons went ahead, laying out his next move to Masterson.

LYONS DROVE Hurley back to the same pay phone where Blancanales had ruined his day and ended his career with a future that would dead-end in a cell block at Riker's. He could have made Hurley put the call in from the room, Gadgets hooking up his tracer monitor to nail down the location of the FBI man's Muscovite cash cow. But given the prior experience when Hurley was abruptly shut off, Lyons figured it was a waste of time. Unless Lyons missed his guess, the Russians smelled something on Hurley's end. So the message to be delivered to Hurley's Russian sponsor was going to be short and point-blank. Hopefully, a few choice words would shake up the hitters on the other end, with a meeting arranged for the dirty Fed to hand over the address of the safehouse where the

FBI was sitting on Mosnivoc. Of course, it was a smoke job, but Lyons was tired of sitting on his hands, knowing a small army of imported hit men was still on the prowl. When the Russian hitters moved in on the abandoned tenement building, which Lyons had previously scoped out during the earlier "bombing run" on the crack motel near the industrial waterfront, Able Team would cut them down from behind. In fact, Lyons intended to unload Little Bulldozer again, save the three of them and the FBI from jumping around any longer on their own nerves.

Hurley started talking to the mystery Russian. Lyons listened to the guy fumble along with his song and dance about his money, his paranoia, his need to be cautious. While Lyons checked the street for anything out of the ordinary, the teeming rush-hour crowd petering out into the early-dinner force as the sun began dropping west of the city, a warning bell sounded in his head. Hurley gave the address, complete with directions to the vacant hellhole, but was forced to repeat them, spelling it out as if he were talking to someone who could barely understand English. Lyons couldn't hear the other end of the conversation, of course, but it sounded as if Hurley was being kept on the line a little longer than necessary.

"Yeah, yeah, I heard something about that problem. Now you see why I have to move like I've got the SAC breathing down my neck. Hey, I can't say what that was all about, I didn't have a damn thing to do with it.... What are you saying...? Okay, okay, but we'll meet there, right? Good. I don't feel safe giving up the place over the phone."

Lyons caught Hurley's eye, mouthed, "Hang up." Bared his teeth, and whispered, "Now!"

"Look, I've gotta go. An hour. Sounds good.... No, there's nothing to worry about, how many times I have to tell you that? I'll see you, sixty minutes. Don't keep me waiting."

Lyons snatched the phone from Hurley and hung it up. Something right then felt all out of tilt to Lyons, warning him his big plans for another preemptive strike were about to blow up in his face.

BYLOKIV SAW Chechkin smile, nod, heard him say, "We have them. A pay phone in Flatbush. It is outside a pizzeria." He went on, naming the place, complete with street and address.

Outstanding. They were so close, he thought, it was just like Ma Bell said in America—they could almost reach out from their own brownstone on Bedford Avenue and touch them. Chechkin went over the directions and address where Bylokiv was supposed to meet their FBI man, but the conversation had also been played over an attached speakerphone. It was an unneccesary relaying of information Bylokiv already knew, but he read the unease behind Chechkin's dark eyes. The FBI man had turned double rat. Why, Bylokiv didn't know or care. He had what he needed.

Chechkin was unhooking the wires from the phone, double-checking the triangulation on the monitor of his computer for the location of the pay phone, when Bylokiv decided vodka all around was in order. He was feeling so pleased that he uncapped the chilled bottle and poured the shots himself.

"These Americans," he said, then chuckled, indicating ten of the best men he'd brought with him from Moscow should step up to the wet bar and help themselves. "They must think we are stupid peasants. They must either not know or care that many of us are either former KGB or Spetsnaz. We have access to the best in high-tech equipment. We have intelligence resources that can put their CIA to shame. We have a man on the inside they would never even suspect. Drink up, comrades, before I hand out the new orders. Success, victory is within our grasp."

"I do not like it, Comrade Bylokiv. It is too easy."

Bylokiv drank, then looked at Ivan Mykov. "But, of course, it looks too easy, that is the whole problem. I know what they are attempting to do. Earlier, when I could not raise him, I drove near the waterfront and saw where Dirichky and the others were staying. I drove straight through a police barricade, and with a flash of my phony passport and ID, the stupid American cops let me go on my way. More cops, ambulances, fire trucks up and down the block than you could imagine. Dirichky and his men were hit. I even saw the body bag some incompetent left unzipped. I saw what was left of his face, but I clearly saw the diamond ring that only Dirichky wears on the left pinky finger of his hand. This Hurley has been found out. He gave up Dirichky, who was my money man to the FBI. This call, it was a trap. The arrogant Americans think we will blindly go to their new trap, not even two blocks away from where they hit Dirichky. It is unbelievable, their stupidity. I would love to meet the genius running this FBI operation."

"What next?" Boris Kyricik wanted to know.

"For the moment, we do nothing. We let the stupid

American FBI go to this abandoned building and sit and wait for someone who will never show up. They will sweat, wonder what's wrong. They will lean on Hurley. They will hear lies and half truths and bullshit, wondering what is what and who is who. In the meantime, Boris, you take two others and reconnoiter this area. Make sure you have your legitimate credentials and paperwork. No guns. Drive around, you will know an FBI man when you see one. All we need to know is the general area, just narrow it down to one block even. Comrade Yuri, I am informed, is to be taken to the courthouse in downtown Brooklyn first thing in the morning."

Bylokiv smiled as he poured another shot of vodka. "When that happens, we will be there. And, if necessary, we will blow up half of this borough if that's what it takes to free, or kill, whatever the case may be, our once fearless leader. Let us be clear. No matter what happens, New York will never be the same after tomorrow. And you will never hear again someone in this city say, 'I love New York.'"

Bylokiv drank up, laughed. So much for their vaunted FBI. This was shaping up to be so easy, it struck Bylokiv as damn near comic. Another round of vodka for the troops to celebrate, glasses clinking, cheers all around.

Bylokiv chuckled. There were clown suits in the near future, donning FBI insignia, to be sure, only he would be the one laughing all the way back to Moscow.

"THEY KNOW. Don't ask me how, Carl, but they know."

Lyons had to agree with what Blancanales read on the situation. By the time they made the crumbling ruins of the abandoned tenement building, darkness had blanketed the industrial waterfront. The Manhattan skyline was lit up across the East River in the rearview glass of their rental.

Lyons reevaluated his ploy. Both Hurley and Peters had been handed over to Masterson after Hurley arranged a rendezvous with the Russian shooters that, Lyons suspected, was never going to happen. Hurley had squawked when Masterson cuffed him a block away on the street from the pizzeria, whining that Blancanales had promised to help him out. Lyons had taken the man's temper tantrum in stride, resisting the urge to wave goodbye to Hurley as he was driven off by a couple of FBI agents to the field office in Manhattan where he'd find his buddy, Peters, waiting for the short trip to Riker's Island. The destiny of two dirty Feds was no longer his problem.

From the back seat Schwarz spoke up. "The Russian Mafia is made up of a large percentage of KGB agents and officers and Spetsnaz commandos who suddenly found themselves out of work when the Wall came down and the West started celebrating so-called democracy in Russia."

"I know you're going somewhere with this, Gadgets," Lyons said gruffly, not meaning to sound so brusque, but he was annoyed with himself for getting duped, with Schwarz about to point it all out.

"High-tech toys. If I had a trace monitor on their phone, what's to say they didn't bring along something other than their AKs and good looks from Moscow."

Lyons searched the building from the weed-choked, vacant lot across the way. Silently, he urged some big goons with big guns to show up, but knew this game was dead.

Blancanales, looking wound up tight and itching for action as he sat behind the wheel, said, "You're telling us they had a trace put on that pay phone where Hurley put in the call."

"You got it."

"Damn," Lyons rasped. "Let's move it out, Pol. If that's even close to true, we're looking at a real long and nervous night ahead of us."

Blancanales fired up the engine and had them rolling a moment later. Lyons cursed. He was nobody's fool, but life was definitely showing him something lately about himself. It was time to tighten up. If it was anatomically possible, Carl Lyons would have kicked himself in the ass, but decided to save that little piece of joy for the bad guys. Soon enough, maybe even before the night was over, he suspected there would be enough Russian butt to kick to go around for a lifetime to come.

Or so he lived in hope.

CHAPTER NINE

"Phoenix has the green light, folks."

Brognola nearly raced into the Computer Room to make the announcement. Everyone stopped whatever they were doing, turned, and for the first time since they had gathered in the War Room he saw something close to relief on their faces. Good news for a change, only Brognola was chafing at the bit, hoping against hope it didn't prove too little too late.

"When the President heard the Israelis are intent on going nuclear, he informed me he wants this wrapped up, and like ten minutes ago."

A thumbs-up from Kurtzman.

"Outstanding," Katz said, already perusing the situation board. "Now, all we have to do is get Phoenix Force inserted, have them fall from the sky, say, at around thirty thousand feet for a HALO, have them land in this remote area," he said, tapping a piece of Syrian turf he'd already circled in red with his prosthesis, "about four miles east of the compound, leg it in through this wadi, break in, set the charges, wax about a hundred Syrian soldiers and maybe half that many terrorists if they are on-site as my Israel contact believes they are. Blow the place down, run like hell without getting irradiated by any fissionable matériel that may or may not be buried when the place goes up and U-238 or P-239 is raining down all over the desert. In the meantime, Jack will lend any air fire support with the Spectre's blazing guns, taking out the Russian Hinds and the four MiGs here, then touch down here," he said, tapping again, "and fly them back to the Saudi border while hoping the Israelis don't show up and start lobbing nukes around. Piece of cake."

"We all know you're not being a smartass, Katz," Kurtzman said, angling his wheelchair toward Katz and Price.

"Never. The fact is I pretty much just laid out the whole program. Keep it simple."

"Five men against a hundred?" Hunt Wethers said. "Even for Phoenix, Katz, that's stretching it."

"Our satellite recon shows that half of that contingent rolls out just before dawn to patrol the border near Lebanon," Katz said.

"Shaves the odds by half if it plays that way," Price said. "Now, David didn't care too much for the idea of lumbering around in nuclear-biological-chemical spacesuits I had shipped to them, but their Geiger counters will indicate whether they'll need to put them on."

"I already have the buildings marked off," Katz said. "Barracks, what I think is the armory, HQ and, of course, the entrance to the hot zone. They'll know what to blow, what not to. It's straight-ahead bulldoze and burn. Nothing cute, nothing fancy. A few well-placed charges on the critical matériel belowground, run like hell to the surface and you have useless scrap and an area that will be uninhabitable for a long, long time.''

"And if the Israelis show up and do just what we're afraid of?" Carmen Delahunt asked.

"Then we've got major problems, Carmen," Katz said. "And if you're the praying sort, you might want to say one. Silence on the Israeli end in this case is not golden.''

"How soon can we get Phoenix on the way into Syria?" Brognola asked.

Wethers announced Saudi time, factored in the flight from Italy to touchdown. "I don't think we'll beat the dawn time frame for getting them airborne as soon as they land. You'll be looking at full-blown daylight, by several hours.''

"We may have to hold off getting them in the air until the sun starts going down and they have night cover," Price said.

Brognola clenched his teeth. "Damn, but I hate it whenever it feels as if we're doing a major covert operation by the seat of the pants.''

"No choice, Hal, the clock is ticking. If it has to be a daylight hit...I'd feel the odds would be a little better if Striker was on board for the party," Kurtzman said. "By the way, Hal, I heard from Mack. Seems like he has his own party under way on the island.''

Brognola listened as Kurtzman filled him in.

"I briefed him on the Russian situation," Kurtzman finished. "Able Team is shipping the don out in the morning. Hurley and Peters are under arrest, but the situation, Lyons tells me, is far from being under control.''

"Meaning?"

"They took out a team of five Russian hit men," Kurtzman said. "But according to Hurley, who spilled his guts, there's at least another twenty-five or so shooters on the loose in Brooklyn."

It was all reaching critical mass, Brognola knew. He had three separate firestorms raging, and the flames were a long way from being doused.

"We were running down those names you gave us, Hal," Delahunt suddenly said.

"You mean the ones my contact over at the Pentagon laid on me about Centurion X?"

"They all worked for NASA," Delahunt said, "and the project was so classified whatever documents I was able to steal through cyberspace were full of blacked-out deletions."

"But the mystery marches on," Wethers added. "Using the Social Security numbers of Feinstein and the others on your file, we traced their movements all the way to Hawaii. Specifically a bank in Molokai."

Akira Tokaido chipped in. "Three- to four-year stints for each of the aerospace engineers who were shipped out there."

"The light show Striker mentioned," Brognola said. "He's on to something out there. When he calls back, fill him in on that piece of news. We're a long way from seeing daylight, people, but I'm starting to see a little light at the end of the tunnel." He stepped toward Katz and Price. "Okay, fill me in on the plan from *A* to *Z*. I didn't give the Man many more details other than what you've already laid on me. But it's our show from here on, and I don't think he'll sleep until this is a wrap."

"First," Price said, "I've wheeled in a television monitor," she said, indicating a giant-screen TV in the far corner of the room. "Each commando will have a minicam fixed to the shoulder of his combat harness. It'll monitor the action, front and back. We'll be in constant satcom."

"I like it," Brognola said. "I just hope I don't see that guy from CNN on the premises when the bullets start flying."

Hawaii

THE GOLDEN PALACE occupied its own stretch of real estate between King and Young Streets. Situated away from the chains of restaurants, hotels and other businesses, it was easy enough for Bolan to maintain surveillance from where he sat in his rental, a block down in an alley.

The nightlife was in high gear, with sidewalks jammed with couples, soldiers on the prowl for a good time, the obligatory cop here and there. The Executioner didn't want to sit there on his hands all night, a plan of attack already shaping up in his mind. Why stray from the program now? Why not just roll in, kick ass and take names?

For one thing, it looked as if the gentlemen's club had been shut down, cleared of all noncombatants, Bolan having seen the Golden Palace disgorging all the fancy suits and gaudily decked out dancing girls maybe twenty minutes ago. Benny was braced for a blitz. Was Chengdu on the way with his army of ninja? Or was the Yakuza boss expecting a lone gaijin to come strolling in and start shooting the place up?

Second, Bolan had just seen four very large, grim-faced Westerners allowed in by the two Japanese thugs guarding the front doors. After the Farm dropping the Russian bomb on him, he made an educated guess that some of Moscow's worst had just entered the club. But to conduct or conclude what business? Kurtzman had informed him that Rivers's report stated the Russians had been on Oahu for nearly two months. Had Rivers conveniently neglected mentioning that tidbit, or had the man been so ashamed and afraid for himself his mouth simply couldn't work out all the facts? Whatever, a journey through cyberspace, and Kurtzman had matched up the faces with the names of the Russian gangsters in question, and Bolan had them mentally pegged.

And another mystery guest had entered the club less than five minutes ago. He was another Westerner, tall with gray hair, lugging a briefcase, decked out in a Brooks Brothers suit. Tall One had moved with the sort of military bearing Bolan knew all too well, but there was obvious paranoia in the way Tall One searched the street, as if his worst fears would become reality any second. With any luck, Bolan would have a chat with him soon enough.

The Executioner decided to give it a little more time, sensing he was about to hit the jackpot, that Chengdu would make some attempt to hit Fugasami here. There was a definite charge of jumpy nerves in the air, if Bolan read their faces and movements right. The soldier watched as the goons were forced to turn away some suits then a few drunken Marines who wanted an eyeful of Golden Palace delight.

Checking his surroundings, finding he was still unnoticed by the marching throngs, the soldier fed the mini-Uzi a fresh clip.

"IS THIS necessary? It's real, it's what you wanted."

Sitting behind his desk, Fugasami kept the smile off his face as the Navy admiral fidgeted in his seat and glowered at the Russians. The Russian made a big production of bringing up the disk on the laptop. Fugasami saw "Access Denied" flash onto the monitor.

The Russian computer wizard returned Admiral Ralph Howard's glare. "The code?"

Howard seemed on the verge of reconsidering something, but Fugasami met his stare. "Admiral, you have been paid. I have been paid. What little honor you cling to, do not cause me any delays. I have other urgent business."

"Forbidden Isle," Howard growled.

The Russian tapped it in, and Fugasami saw what looked like blueprint specs for some sort of aircraft flash onto the screen.

The Russian with the black mustache and bald head Fugasami knew as Drylov said, "And our other arrangement, Admiral?"

"Goddammit, you're asking me to hijack a freaking C-130."

"You have already committed high treason, need I remind you," Drylov said.

"You just expect me to have that sort of classified matériel loaded up and flown to Russia? Do you know what is being crated up as we speak?"

"Precisely. The shell to a flying saucer. You are in charge of that compound. Your word, your orders

If offer card is missing write to: Gold Eagle Reader Service, 3010 Walden Ave., P.O. Box 1867, Buffalo NY 14240-1867

NO POSTAGE
NECESSARY
IF MAILED
IN THE
UNITED STATES

BUSINESS REPLY MAIL

FIRST-CLASS MAIL   PERMIT NO. 717   BUFFALO, NY

POSTAGE WILL BE PAID BY ADDRESSEE

GOLD EAGLE READER SERVICE
3010 WALDEN AVE
PO BOX 1867
BUFFALO NY 14240-9952

GET FREE BOOKS
and a
FREE GIFT WHEN YOU PLAY THE...

LAS VEGAS
GAME

*Just scratch off the gold box
with a coin. Then check
below to see the gifts you get!*

YES!
I have scratched off the gold Box. Please send me my
2 FREE BOOKS and **gift for which I qualify**. I understand
that I am under no obligation to purchase any books
as explained on the back of this card.

▲ DETACH AND MAIL CARD TODAY! ▲

© 2001 GOLD EAGLE

366 ADL C6RD

166 ADL C6RC
(MB-OS-03/01)

NAME   (PLEASE PRINT CLEARLY)

ADDRESS

APT.#   CITY

STATE/PROV.   ZIP/POSTAL CODE

7	7	7	Worth TWO FREE BOOKS plus a BONUS Mystery Gift!
🍒	🍒	🍒	Worth TWO FREE BOOKS!
🔔	🔔	♣	TRY AGAIN!

are—how would I say?—written in stone. Besides, once your people discover that plane will not be flying to your Area 51 in Nevada, they will come looking to question you."

"And I'm supposed to just go skipping off on board to finish out my days in a dacha in Moscow."

"Sergei here, he is expert pilot."

"How the hell do you expect me to get him cleared through the front gate?"

"You can make it happen. We can duplicate the necessary credentials right here," Drylov said, patting his briefcase. "Much planning has gone into this. It is all covered on both our ends. It only takes some daring on your part, some bluster, some balls."

"Daring, some balls, you say. We could get shot down as soon as we're three miles out to sea."

"No, I think not. Our SVR was aware of your Centurion X program long ago. However, we could not very well have SVR agents traipsing all over the islands."

"So they made a deal with your don instead," Howard rasped.

Drylov lowered his tone, put a menacing edge to his voice. "You Americans think we cannot move mountains when we wish. Well, the mountain, Admiral, has been moved. It will come crashing down on you if you do not cooperate. I have a special black box that can hooked up to the transponder. Very clever thing, it is. It will show your radar the C-130 is on its scheduled flight, but it can also jam the most sophisticated radar."

"What about satellites?"

"All I can say is 'trust us.'"

Fugasami saw the Russian grinning around his mustache.

"Trust you. And how about those negatives?" he asked Fugasami.

"I will keep them for the time being." Fugasami next played a dangerous hand, withdrawing the disk from his jacket pocket.

"What is that?" Drylov wanted to know.

"Insurance. Until you are safely on your way. Until the admiral has fully cooperated. I do not like surprises."

"Meaning he doesn't trust you," Howard said.

"It looks to be real," the computer expert told Drylov.

In the other corner of the office, Fugasami saw his samurai finish running the American cash through a money counter.

"Five million, my lord," Tayaki said.

"So, there we are. Everyone is happy," Fugasami said.

"Then I'm out of here."

"Not so fast." Drylov handed the short, stocky Russian the briefcase, said something at length in his native tongue. "Sergei will go with you. He will know what to do."

He addressed Fugasami. "Your keeping a copy of the blueprints was not part of any agreement I was aware of."

"Why should you fear if I hold on to it? I have no experience in matters such as this. I would not know a blueprint of an aircraft from an oil print."

"So you say."

"So I mean. I keep it for now."

Drylov looked set to pursue his argument but grumbled something in Russian and waved the matter off.

Howard rubbed his face, the expression of despair striking Fugasami that the man was about to crack under the strain.

"You have no choice, Admiral," Fugasami warned. "You go with them."

"A few dirty pictures, I can't believe it."

"And no one but those of us here will ever know of it," Fugasami said. "I hope you enjoy your golden years in Russia, Admiral."

"You—"

Fugasami draped a hand over the hilt of his sword, the motion alone stifling any insult the admiral was about to issue. The traitor shook his head, looking away, the Yakuza boss figuring he was thinking any life, even a bad one on the run, was better than none at all.

"I wish to examine this," the Russian computer expert said, "for a few minutes more."

"Be quick about it," Fugasami snapped.

"Let's go," Howard growled at his Russian escort. "I tell you what, you'd better be up for this when I'm ready to fly."

"No, Admiral," Drylov pointed out, "success or failure is all in your hands. Be grateful, at least, your children are all grown, that your wife is not alive to see you like this."

Fugasami was sure Howard would blow up, but the admiral simply accepted the insult, then was marched out of the office to meet whatever fate awaited him.

The Yakuza boss heard his handheld radio crackle. He picked up, punched On and heard his samurai out back tell him in Japanese that a suspicious black sedan with four Chinese-looking types had just pulled into the alley. Fugasami felt the adrenaline rush.

Chengdu was coming for him. It was a little early, according to his watch, but it would be good to get it done. With the Triad out of the way, he could concentrate all of his energy and focus on hunting down the crazy gaijin.

Fugasami envisioned a clean sweep that night.

BOLAN SAW Tall One ushered out the front door by his grim escort the soldier knew from his intel package as Sergei Kuschik. Something felt all out of whack to Bolan, as if the immediate world around him were about to blow up in his face. No sooner were the two men on the sidewalk, allowed to skip right past the hardmen, than a black Lexus rolled up curbside. Tall One was shoved into the back, his gangster escort sliding in beside him, and the Lexus rolled away.

Something had gone down inside, a deal of some type, but the only way Bolan would get some answers was a trip into the Golden Palace.

A long blood ride, he knew, was just ahead, if he had anything to say about it. And he would let his weapons speak volumes for him soon enough.

He was reaching for the door handle when it happened. The Executioner watched as two teams of four small men in black garb converged on Benny's guards from both sides. By now the Yakuza samurai had the area in front of the Golden Palace free of human traffic, following a few brief encounters with passersby. They had been so intent on watching Tall One and escort leave the premises that they didn't see the eight shadows until they were nearly on top of them. It happened so fast even Bolan nearly couldn't believe what he saw. It was such a brazen display, the Executioner knew a final whopping round of bloodletting was about to descend on the Golden Palace.

Benny's samurai were wheeling toward one group of black-clad hitters, engaging in a brief exchange Bolan couldn't hear, when the second foursome hit them from the blind side. A flash of steel in the lights of the Golden Palace, the knives buried deep into the lower backs of the samurai, telling Bolan they were going for the kidneys, and it was over. Before they even found themselves dead on their feet, the front doors were open and the limp forms were whisked off the sidewalk and inside the murky shadows of the club. One of the killers took up the vacated sentry duty.

Not even five seconds later, a black Cadillac slid up curbside, and a slight figure in a suit jacket stepped out. Bolan recognized Huan Chengdu from the Farm's intel package as he hit the sidewalk, the door held open for him by the Triad sentry. The Triad boss entered the club. Two more luxury vehicles showed up, Bolan counting ten more Triad hardmen moving in to do battle. Before they hit the doors, they hauled out compact Ingram submachine guns.

The Executioner decided to stay put for a couple of minutes. There was no doubt in his mind the savages were about to go for each other's throats. Why not let the shooting and swordplay at least begin without him? It would help, and soon enough, when he marched in to lend a helping hand.

No mistake, the Executioner considered everyone inside the Golden Palace fair game. Give it another minute or so, and it was show time.

CHAPTER TEN

Juiced up to high voltage on a full pot of coffee and at least a half pound of sugar, Carl Lyons figured he could now make it through the night without caving to some serious wear and tear on his system, which meant he wouldn't nod off to dream about kicking ass instead of doing it in real time. Miami was still clinging to him like some filthy shroud in every way, but the day's action had revived Lyons back to Ironman stature. Now, if they could just ride out the night, he thought, load up the Russian whale and dump his carcass at the courthouse to Your Honor without having the OK Corral drop over Brooklyn, no fuss, no muss.

Fat chance.

It was going to happen, he knew; it was simply a question of when and where.

So far the Farm hadn't said how long this stint would go on. He made a mental note to ask Brognola if Able Team was supposed to hold the fort until the don was sentenced to a 1001 years in Attica, or if the job would end once the remaining goons were found, bagged, tagged and sent back to Moscow.

Right then nothing much mattered to Lyons other

than watching the front door. He was sitting straight up and tense in a leather recliner, the SPAS-12 resting across his lap, a 12-gauge maneater up the snout, with seven in reserve, the .357 Magnum Colt Python in shoulder holster and full view to the troops. He even had Little Bulldozer settled by his feet, just in case the Russians made some mad charge through the door. If that happened, Lyons would send them flying in a hundred mangled body parts over the streets of Flatbush and clear to the East River. His com link was in place, and Schwarz and Blancanales were the only eyes and ears now watching the brownstone. Having clean-cut guys in dark jackets, shades and earplugs standing around on the front stoop was a little too obvious for Lyons's liking.

By now, Masterson and the other FBI men knew he was something a little different from the average G-man. Of course, they didn't know what, didn't even seem to care, appearing only grateful Special Agent Lemon was there and at the helm. Since his veal-chop whacking of the don, Agent Lemon was treated with the utmost respect, which, at times, seemed to straddle some fine line between a sports icon and a matinee idol, if he was any judge of the looks they threw him on occasion. In turn, Lyons showed the FBI troops the respect they deserved. They were all laying it on the line, prepared to go the distance for each other. That was more than good enough for the former L.A. cop. Supposedly, after some manhandling and dire threats issued by their superiors, Hurley and Peters claimed they were only the snakes among the team. Just the same, Lyons was measuring every man there, but his gut told him all rats had been flushed out of the hole and accounted for.

Lyons glared at the mass of flesh stretched out on the couch, snoring away with all the sound and fury of a runaway freight train but sleeping like a newborn.

Masterson was sipping coffee at the kitchen table, the TV turned down low on an *X-Files* episode. Aware of the UFO situation over in Siberia, Lyons wasn't sure how much he cared for the SAC's taste in TV viewing. Lyons could well enough see ghosts, goblins and little gray men without any gasoline to fuel the fire of his own paranoia and raw nerves. The other agents were grouped in various sitting positions around the room, M-16s canted here and there. Four of them were playing a quiet game of Spades to kill some time.

"How can he sleep like that?" Masterson suddenly asked, scowling at Mosnivoc. "The rest of us are ready to jump out of our skin, and there it lies, freaking buzz-sawing our brains out like all that's gonna happen tomorrow is maybe a plane ticket for the Bahamas will be waiting for him at the courthouse."

"Maybe it's because he knows someone does have that ticket for him to ride."

"Not if we have something to say about it."

"You got that right, my friend."

The knock on the door had Lyons up and charging, SPAS-12 leading the way. The FBI men moved, swift and sure, like a well-oiled machine, grabbing up weapons, fanning out in twin lines beside the door, hitting combat crouches, ready to let the lead fly. Lyons briefly considered asking who the hell it was, then gave a hand signal that he would open the door and personally greet whoever was out there. A prearranged hand signal, and the FBI men knew to open fire if it hit the fan when Lyons opened the door.

He did. Unfortunately, he had to unlatch about three locks, dead bolts and chains, giving his play away, but there was nothing he could do. Briefly, he wondered again who was out there, figured if it was some Russian shooters they would have already come through the door, but he wasn't taking any chances. He flung the door wide, glimpsed some scrubby-clean pink face in a fancy suit jacket with eyes popping out of their sockets at the sight of the massive assault shotgun as Lyons snatched some lapel and hauled him in. While two FBI men surged past, hitting the doorway and fanning the street with their M-16s, Lyons threw Fancy Suit to the floor, pinned a knee to his chest and thrust the muzzle of the SPAS-12 under the guy's chin.

"Who the hell are you?"

"That's Carlington."

"What?" Lyons growled, staring up at Masterson.

"That's Mr. Carlington to you people, top liaison officer for U.S.-Russian relations for the State Department. You must be this Agent Lemon."

What the hell were Blancanales and Schwarz doing? he wondered, and tapped his com link. "Able Eyes, wake up."

"We just now spotted him, Ironman. Able G," Blancanales said over the com link, referring to Schwarz, "and myself were watching a suspicious vehicle with some very ugly and wary faces rolling by. They're gone now. By the time—"

"Save it. I have the picture. Anybody else out there with this asshole?"

"Why, you—"

"Shut up!"

"That's a negative. Looks like he came alone."

Lyons told them to tighten up, signed off, but kept the SPAS wedged up under Carlington's chin. "You better have a real good reason for being here."

"And you," Carlington said, fighting to work his jaw around the SPAS muzzle, "are so fired I will personally see to it you spend the rest of your life pushing a mop and a broom in some public high school where there will be nothing but gangbangers and grief for you."

Lyons stood, nodding, a wry smile on his lips. "Well, in that case I guess I don't need to worry about skinning you alive."

Hawaii

THE EXECUTIONER followed the Triad knife men's example, but with a slight variation. The sidewalk on both sides of the front door to the Golden Palace was still free of pedestrian traffic, and it made Bolan's ploy that much easier to pull off. Just the one Triad goon, peering with wary eyes at some drunken Westerner staggering his way.

"Closed! Go away!"

Bolan weaved ahead, cutting the gap to less than six feet. "Hey, come on, Charlie Chan...naked girls...I want to see some naked girls...." Bolan unzipped his jacket halfway for easy access to the Beretta. "Hey...how 'bout some whiskey, Charlie?"

The hardman glared around the street, tensing, obviously poised to get rough on some drunken fool. Bolan also found no watching eyes right then. He was making his move when rock and roll began thundering from beyond the front doors. An eye blink later, the shooting inside the Golden Palace started to announce to Bolan he was right on time.

"One last time, stupid GI. Go!"

"You first," Bolan said, whipping out the sound-suppressed Beretta and blowing the shock right off the hardman's face. Before the blood was even spraying out the back of his skull, Bolan scooped the guy up in his arms and opened the door. The shrieking guitar riffs of some heavy-metal thunder muted the racket of weapons fire. Something about a psycho circus assaulted Bolan's eardrums as he dumped the limp baggage in the foyer, closed the door and hauled out the mini-Uzi.

At first glance, it was nearly impossible to take in the action. Out on the floor guys were shooting each other up in a frenzy. Bodies were sailing over tables, crashing into mirrored columns, bringing down the glass on their bloodied carcasses. The decor was all gold, glass and tropical shrubbery, with a circular bar about the size of a small parking lot taking up real estate in the middle of Benny's club. There was plenty of combat zone—with clustered tables and thick tropical vegetation for shooters to find cover—for all involved to keep on blasting for a long time to come.

And the show had only just begun.

On both sides, hardmen were dying hard and fast. Maybe Benny had put out the word to the local PD that no cops need worry if some shooting was heard from inside his club. The rock and roll would work wonders up to a point, masking the din of subgun fire and the screams of men dying in great pain, but this was going to be a protracted engagement.

Bolan triggered the mini-Uzi on the fly down the short flight of steps, zipping a burst of 9 mm Parabellum manglers into a pack of Triad shooters with their backs turned to him, dropping them in a tattered heap. Somewhere near the bar, a figure in black launched himself over a table, sailing along in a somersault that would have been the envy of an Olympic gymnast. The flyer came down on his feet with the grace of a cheetah, landing right behind two Triad shooters blazing away with Ingram subguns at the empty air above. Before they got their act together, a samurai sword flashed in the winking overhead light, and the lean figure with the gold-braided ponytail had their heads lopped and rolling across the floor in great swathes of crimson. Bolan couldn't be positive, as he swiftly moved off to cut down anything that moved, but he was near sure Fugasami was hard at work, showing his Triad rivals the rewards of all his years of sweat and toil in the dojo.

Four Triad goons wheeled on his right as the Executioner charged up their blind side. Mini-Uzi flaming, the big American hosed them down with head shots, then dashed for the deeper shadows, away from the banks of hanging revolving lights.

Bolan knew it wouldn't be long before they spotted the latest arrival and started returning fire. Even then a few Eastern faces were turning his way, subguns up and barking.

The soldier just made cover behind a booth when the bullets sought him and started snapping over his head. It was time to get serious, crank up the heat and show them just what a slaughter circus was all about.

The Executioner plucked a frag grenade off his webbing.

New York

LYONS INTENSIFIED his take-no-crap stance. He shoved Carlington on the bed, Masterson shutting the door so that the three of them had privacy.

"Do you know who I am?" Carlington bleated.

For a moment Lyons found it incredible this guy was a former Company spook. Then again, it took all types, he figured, to make the spook world go around. Maybe it was his nondescript, baby-pink, nonthreatening look that allowed the guy to fill up space wherever he went and no one would peg him for a spy. The kind of guy who always went through the front door, looking to shoot bad guys first and save the questions for much later, Lyons had never been one for all that sneak-and-peek nonsense, all the double talk and deceit that a spy wore like a second skin. If Carlington was up to bullshit, then Lyons would listen to all of two seconds of it before he went to work extracting the truth.

No mistake, pain always set a man free.

"I know you used to work for the CIA as a station chief in Moscow when Mosnivoc was making his rise to gangster stardom," Lyons said.

The State guy blinked, and Lyons saw the wheels spinning.

"How did you know where to find us?" Lyons growled.

"One phone call to the FBI field office and a word or two with Agent Masterson's superior."

"I can't believe it's that easy."

"Believe me," Carlington said, sitting up and smoothing out the ruffles in his coat sleeves. "That is one man who understands the meaning of career advancement and teamwork and going with the program and living long enough to see his pension intact."

"You mean he kisses ass about as good as you do," Lyons said.

"I don't think your Neanderthal mentality could even begin to grasp the reality of the situation here."

"Try me."

"The CIA is working behind the scenes to see Mosnivoc returned to Moscow."

"Don't make me start having to ask a bunch of 'why' and 'who' questions. I'm having a bad day, Carlington—fact is, I've had a bad few weeks and I'm itching to relieve some major tension. Something here smells, and it's not your bad aftershave."

Carlington worked his peeved look over Lyons, then said, "The Russian Mafia is comprised largely of former KGB agents, Spetsnaz and GRU types who—"

"Found themselves out of a job when the winds of democracy blew over the motherland. I already know all that," Lyons said.

"Then you know the KGB had access to all nuclear facilities and missile silos. They had access codes to every ICBM, IRBM, intermediate, long-range, short-range nuke at their disposal.'' Carlington smoothed back his coiffed black hair with the ivory-sheened tips of fingers that struck Lyons as maybe seeing the scrutiny and concern of Pierre the manicurist twice a week.

"So, you may be able to guess current Russian Mafia types, such as Mosnivoc, have been key players in the dismantling of warheads, and the shipment of uranium and plutonium from said warheads to foreign countries that do not exactly endear themselves to the United States. Mosnivoc, we know, shipped large quantities of nuclear waste, component parts of light water reactors, fuel rods and other requisite matériel out of Russia. Specifically to Syria. The CIA now wants to pick his brain, find out just how much matériel he managed to ship out to who, and when. They want to shut down the entire pipeline of the Russian Mafia's exporting of nuclear technology to various countries that sponsor terrorism. World War III will not begin with Russia and the United States hurling ICBMs at each other. It's one of several scenarios the CIA and the Pentagon have worked out, with China now clearly factored in, but the think tanks believe it will all start to come unraveled when two smaller 'terrorist' nations seek to gain an edge by wiping another country out of next year's edition of the world atlas.''

"And you're looking to cut a deal with Mosnivoc?'' Masterson said.

"Something like that, yes, but the particulars have not been ironed out.''

Lyons put an edge to his voice as he told Carlington, "And they won't be.''

"Says who? You?''

Lyons patted his SPAS-12. "And my autoshotgun friend here."

"When I leave here, I'll carry out the wishes of my former CIA counterparts to lean on the right people to see Mosnivoc gets his deal. Total immunity for full cooperation in tracking down the tens of millions of dollars' worth of nuclear technology and uranium and plutonium he smuggled out of Russia."

"The way you make it sound, it wasn't much of an effort to get all the good stuff into the hands of the Syrians," Lyons said.

"Meaning what?"

Lyons knew he had to touch base with the Farm, have them run down every minute of every day of Carlington's life for the past fifteen years or so. "Meaning I think the CIA is playing some other angle."

"Such as?"

"Such as I don't know. Now, I want you to understand where myself and Agent Masterson and the other dedicated, stand-up FBI men are coming from. You sashaying your little weasel butt right up to our front door may or may not have been spotted by some very mean and nasty Russian hit men who, I'm told, may or may not have just driven past here."

Carlington sputtered, "You're saying...there may be another attack."

"And you know what?" Lyons grinned, as cold as Siberian ice. "If that happens, you'll be right there with us on the front lines."

"What are you saying?"

"I'm saying, you're under house arrest."

"You can't do that!"

"Watch me."

"I'll have your job!"

"I thought you told me I was already fired, something about pushing a broom the rest of my days."

"Masterson?"

The FBI SAC shrugged. "I have my orders from the Justice Department. It's Agent Lemon's call."

"Then I'll have your job, too."

Lyons saw Masterson glance his way, a crooked grin on his mouth.

"If that's the way you feel, then, like the song says, you can take this job and shove it. After, of course, I see your palski sentenced to life without parole."

It was all Lyons could do to keep from chuckling, but, by God, he was really starting to like the guy.

Right then, though, Lyons knew the future for everyone under the roof of the brownstone and across the street was up for grabs.

Fair enough.

At least, he thought, there was still something to be said about guys going the distance. Better yet it recharged the battery to find good old-fashioned guts shining through in a PC, money-grubbing, status-seeking world that wanted the few, the proud and the brave to crawl.

Hawaii

THE WAR BETWEEN the Yakuza and the Triad would have happened with or without him, Bolan knew. The soldier had simply been on the scene when things were heating up, merely lighting the fuse, sowing the seeds of confusion and long-simmering distrust and hatred on both sides.

Call it fate, good timing, luck or whatever, but Bolan was now part of something engineered long before he hit the island. Chalk it up, he figured, to cosmic justice working in mysterious ways. Going in, he had carried some remote hope he would find the truth behind the extortion angle in the Golden Palace, and maybe whatever reached beyond Benny to the Forbidden Isle and the light show over the channel. Now Bolan found it all a long shot if he was lucky enough to stumble across the first bloodied survivor who might feel so inclined to answer a few questions.

All provided, of course, he even walked on out the other side in one piece.

Time to get busy helping the savages do what had to be done.

The stuffing was being blown out of the booth in shredded white clouds when Bolan let the armed steel egg fly. It wouldn't take much accuracy, since half the Golden Palace at least was packed with shooters and swordsmen going at it in a demonic frenzy. No sooner did the first hellbomb blow than Bolan pulled the pin on his next frag grenade, counted off two doomsday numbers and pitched it at a group of Triad shooters charging his way, subguns blazing up to the final heartbeat.

Bolan dropped beneath the table as lead hammered his position, riding it out.

It felt as if the building would come down on his head, as the floor shook, rattled and rolled and Bolan glimpsed mangled bodies sailing away from blast number two. He had to have hit another homer, he believed, since the shooting abruptly stopped eating up his cover from dead ahead.

The Executioner threw himself around the corner of the booth and waxed a Triad gunman who clambered from the smoke. The hardman was missing an arm, severed at the elbow, no doubt from getting amputated by flying shrapnel. The guy would never have to worry about a prosthesis, as Bolan sent him on his way. The amputee's scream lasted all of one eye blink before Bolan triggered the mini-Uzi and punched him off his feet.

The Executioner found them still going at it on roughly half the points of the compass. The battle looked confined to the far side of the club, but he next found the thug he knew as Barzama hosing down a few Triad goons at twelve o'clock, an Ingram subgun blazing away in one hand, while the shaved-head Yakuza man gored, slashed and decapitated another three Chinese gangsters with the sweeping razor's edge of a samurai sword.

Short work, and Barzama was already sniffing for fresh blood.

Heavy-metal thunder and the roar of unceasing subgun and pistol fire in his ears, the Executioner aimed his own compact SMG toward the ceiling. Holding back on the trigger, Bolan blasted out maybe three-quarters of the lights to rain still more chaos and confusion, lend him a few critical seconds to seek out and nail the enemy without immediate concern over catching a bullet. Glass shrapnel, large and small, began showering the combatants around the bar, and dead ahead of Bolan. There were some shriekers, a couple of runners headed his way as they made a vain attempt to flee the glass avalanche.

Blind runners with flapping arms made easy targets for the Executioner's death sights.

Cracking a fresh clip home, Bolan rose and nailed them with a long burst of 9 mm rock and roll. One clip left for the mini-Uzi, two spares for his side arms and he had to wonder how far he could go.

No matter.

It shouldn't be any problem at all if he burned up every last clip, since he spotted plenty of firepower scattered all over the floor like some backgammon board flipped up in the air by a sore loser to send the chips flying.

On the run, streaking for the cover of several long tables at nine o'clock, Bolan armed his last grenade as wild eyes searched him out from behind the bar and flaming SMG fire tracked on. He pulled the pin, aimed his toss for a group of shooters hunkered down that way and hit the club with spray-and-pray subgun fire. Wheeling, the Executioner tapped the subgun's trigger as bullets whizzed past his ear. Two more thugs—Triad or Yakuza, it didn't much matter—were sent flying back, tasting their own blood on lips slit to scream as they skidded off tables and twitched all the way down into a bed of glass.

Bolan nose-dived as still more shooters surged from beside the bar. Blast three scored screams and flying body parts, a gaping hole punched into the bar front, rows of liquor obliterated in glass minefields, all the way to the top shelf.

A wave of sizzling lead scorching the air behind

him, Bolan flung himself to cover behind an upturned table.

Barzama.

Unleathering both the Beretta and .44 Magnum Desert Eagle, Bolan poked up his head and saw Barzama rolling his way. The shaved-head Yakuza thug's snarls and curses audible above the pounding rock and roll and hellish racket of weapons fire.

Barzama burned out the clip of his Ingram, chucked the weapon away and made a straight-on charge for Bolan, with clearly nothing more than a heart full of rage and a sword in hand.

Bad move.

The fat lady started singing for Barzama.

The Beretta chugged and the Desert Eagle thundered. Barzama's chest opened up, ruined by the 9 mm .44 Magnum combo. Spewing gore, Barzama, incredibly, staggered on, his sword raised high over his mask of fury and pain. A hornet's nest of lead from ten o'clock forced Bolan to cover, Barzama forging on through his own blood, some sort of primal banzai scream flaying the Executioner's senses. It was a waste of precious ammo, but the big American was forced to empty out both clips—his aiming for the bald dome thrown off as he twisted, rolled and dodged bullets—before Barzama toppled.

There was action on the other side of the bar, a wink of light off steel, Bolan pinpointing the source of slaughter. Fugasami was alternately triggering what looked and sounded to Bolan like a stainless-steel .45 Colt while skewering Triad goons into tomorrow's take-out garbage.

Bodies dropped, piling up by the threes and fours,

handing out a scorecard that would give the city morgue capacity status in a few short hours. And it was still a long way, Bolan saw, taking a rapid head count, from wrapped up.

At least one full squad of Triad shooters was leapfrogging its way through a cluster of tables and booths. Benny had his hands full, but Bolan could plainly see the guy would commit seppuku before yielding the first foot of turf.

Bolan nailed four problems for Fugasami, head shots that dropped Triad thugs as if they'd been hammered down by a major-league slugger's bat.

The Executioner's ammo gone, he stowed the pieces, was charging for a discarded Ingram subgun when a flying samurai appeared out of nowhere.

Bolan would never reach the subgun in time, knew he had to come up with an answer to what next.

The attacker rushed him, all swishing steel and bellowing in a banzai charge.

The Executioner rose, searching for any opening to take out the swordsman, but found his next set of problems had only just begun.

CHAPTER ELEVEN

Hawaii

One glance toward the street side of the bar, and Fugasami knew it was the crazy gaijin on the rampage. The big American had waded right into the killing, mere moments after Fugasami's samurai and Chengdu's thugs opened up with weapons on each other. The first dozen or so casualties on both sides went down in a matter of seconds under the first salvo. No hesitation, no flinching by the gaijin, killing Fugasami's samurai while at the same time cutting down Triad shooters as if it were second nature. The wild man had helped shoot the place to hell, even pitched around a few grenades, which made Fugasami wonder if he was military, perhaps some kind of Navy SEAL commando or Special Forces lone wolf who did his own thing, some crusader who believed he was battling the forces of evil here on Oahu. Whoever he was, whatever the intent in his heart, Fugasami knew a warrior when he saw one. At the moment the gaijin had his hands full with Hataki, a samurai Fugasami rated as one of his best swordsmen.

No problem that way.

It was a good night, he decided, tasting the blood of the dead on his lips, to test his own skills to the ultimate limits.

He was samurai.

Fugasami indulged a brief but dangerous time-out to see that his enemies were stacking up around him like so much cordwood, a lopped-off head here, a severed arm there. If Hataki didn't finish the gaijin, if Fugasami could only keep track of the big American, somehow make a path toward him...

First the Triad. Fugasami heard the autofire snapping his way, telling him there was still plenty of killing left to do.

There were so many bodies strewed around Fugasami he had to watch his step or risk stumbling into a nosedive at a critical moment. Just as treacherous— with all the running blood and teeming quagmires of guts and other and all manner of reeking body fluids—there were thick pools of slick gore that could send a man falling for his back on one careless step. A head count of his remaining samurai, and he couldn't believe he was down to six warriors. Drenched in the blood of his slain enemies, Fugasami hit a crouch at the edge of the bar as autofire kept roaring on, slugs blasting beer bottles and spraying glass over his head. He'd already glimpsed Chengdu firing from inside a ring of tables with an Ingram MAC-10. If he was right, Fugasami guessed his hated enemy was down to perhaps five men himself. Mentally, he marked off the distance to the Triad shooters. Say a thirty-foot charge, he figured, then his planning was interrupted by a sudden outburst from the Russian.

"This is not my fight! I am leaving now!"

Fugasami whipped a ferocious look toward Drylov. When the shooting started, two of the Russians had gone down, caught in the cross fire. Drylov had a Makarov pistol that he'd brought to the meeting, but the Russian didn't seem inclined to use it. Instead of fighting, the Russian had kept himself hidden in a booth, riding it out, watching as others did the killing and the dying.

Despicable.

The Russian had what he wanted, didn't give a damn if anyone else's world came crashing down as long as he left in one piece with his precious disc.

"You stay!" Fugasami shouted over the chatter of subgun fire.

The Russian cursed, stood, was making a beeline for the back exit when Fugasami laid down his sword, rammed a fresh clip into his .45 Colt and shot the man through the ribs. Drylov spun, confused eyes seeking out Fugasami, then he dropped.

His Russian problem out of the way, and with his remaining samurai gathered around him, Fugasami told his warriors, "Fire and drive them to cover, then follow my lead. We charge them. Banzai!"

Two samurai with Uzi submachine guns and four others wielding Ingram MAC-10 SMGs caught a lull in the Triad shooting, rose up and poured on the lead. With a war cry, Fugasami, snapping up his sword, broke cover. He saw the Triad shooters ducking under the wave of sizzling lead, but not before his enemies' eyes betrayed their shock and worry over this new display of insanity.

Sword thrust out before him in one hand, Fugasami

triggered the .45 Colt on the run. A head popped up over the table, and Fugasami cannoned off a round that all but blew the look of terror off his target's face. The lead hurricane went on savaging the tables, wild shots ricocheting off the floor, Triad hardmen screaming and lurching up, the enemy firing one-handed, while grabbing at bloodied arms and legs. Fugasami didn't spot Chengdu, wondered if the Triad boss was dead, then put the man out of mind as he bored ahead, the Colt thundering, drilling another Chinese goon in the chest and hurling him back over the stage where he jerked into some bizarre dance step of his own, bounced off a mirrored section where the girls watched themselves perform and brought whole sheets of jagged glass down on his head.

Blood and wet cloth hitting him in the face, Fugasami cranked out the rest of the clip, a wall of lead from his samurai bowling down the remaining Triad enemy, flinging their blood and screams back in their faces. Tucking the Colt .45 inside his sash, Fugasami held the sword out in a double-fisted grip.

Where was Chengdu?

He was searching the sprawled corpses, felt his feet wanting to stick to all the blood like glue, when he found a small figure crawling on hands and knees for deeper cover behind a table already overturned by flying bodies. A flicker from what remained of the overhead lights, and Fugasami saw Chengdu glance his way.

"It is over, dog. Stand up and die with honor."

Chengdu snorted, cursed, bared his teeth in feral rage, but stood. Fugasami was unwilling to give the Triad boss any show of respect in his moment of truth. The man had stolen, lied, cheated his way into the Yakuza's backyard. Should the other side of the coin now flip over, Fugasami knew the little man would have shown him no mercy.

"Then do it," the Triad boss rasped, his voice bitter but coming to Fugasami clear enough even through the ringing echo in his ears from weapons fire and the thunder of the rock music. "Quickly."

"Not tonight."

One sweep of the sword took off Chengdu's left arm just below the shoulder. The Triad boss looked ready to vomit and topple at the sight of his arm dropping by his feet. Fugasami drank in the expression of horror for a long moment, then took the other arm off with another driving blow of tempered steel. He considered leaving Chengdu like that, a walking message to any other rivals in Oahu who might want to try to take what Yakamu Fugasami had spent a lifetime working to attain.

No. When this was finished and the gaijin was also dead by his hand, there would be warning enough, and tales of glory about what happened here tonight, sounding so loud and fearsome they would hear it all the way back to Beijing that Fugasami was shogun for life.

Fugasami stepped up, brought the sword back and drove it with all the strength and rage of his vengeance through Chengdu's neck.

Done.

The head thudded on the floor, Chengdu's body seeming to fold at the knees, pitch forward. Fugasami kicked the head away, then heard one of his samurai calling to him. The Yakuza boss looked to where Hataki had been poised to disembowel the big American. The gaijin was nowhere to be found, but Fugasami picked out the wide lifeless eyes of Hataki seeking him out from a litter of Triad corpses.

A BEER BOTTLE turned it around for Bolan.

The sword was swishing back and forth, a flashing blur in the hands of the samurai who came at him, hell-bent on gutting him like some slab of tuna. The soldier lunged back, glimpsing the beer bottle as the blade came within inches of disemboweling him. Bolan rolled over the table, snatching the bottle as he dropped to the other side. The samurai vaulted on top of the table, only to catch a face full of the Executioner's glass missile. Unlike celluloid lore, the bottle didn't shatter when it smashed into the samurai's nose but it was enough to stagger the swordsman, a heartbeat long enough for Bolan to slam his arm through the man's legs, chopping him off his feet.

Even as he hammered off the tabletop, the samurai made one last attempt to strike back, going for a backhand slash, but Bolan was all over him, wrapping a fist around the sword hands, then whiplashing his elbow across jawbone like a steel spike marking off the turf. The lights started to fade in the samurai's eyes, but before his mind could register he was facing down no ordinary warrior, Bolan ripped the sword free, stepped back and thrust the blade deep into the enemy's belly.

Human sushi.

At the other end of the bar, out of the corner of his eye, the soldier glimpsed Fugasami as the Yakuza boss bellowed and made for a banzai charge at what

Bolan had to believe were the last surviving Triad shooters. He left them to it, as his own samurai problem rolled off the table, wrenching himself free of Bolan's confiscated sword.

The Executioner made swift work of the dying swordsman, shuffling ahead a step while slicing the edge of the sword across the samurai's throat.

Crouching, releasing the sword, Bolan moved off, keeping himself hidden from sight of Fugasami and his samurai as they went about their own grisly business of mopping up Chengdu and company. Searching the carnage, Bolan found two discarded Ingram MAC-10 subguns. He checked the clips and saw they were near empty of 9 mm rounds. A rough frisk of a dead man, and he scored two full magazines, plus one spare clip. Locked and loaded, as he listened to the dying and the damned wailing up a storm, the Executioner sprinted down and around the blind side of the bar to the last combatants.

Careful to avoid stumbling over bodies and body parts, working his way around pooling blood, the soldier was in position a half minute later. Fugasami was looking at the spot Bolan had vacated, barking out orders in Japanese for his samurai to fan out, when the Executioner went for broke, squeezing the triggers of the SMGs, raking them left to right. Fugasami was already racing away from the twin flaming lines of Bolan's double-fisted Ingram doom, gone from the soldier's gun sights, but a few of the Yakuza hardmen froze like deer framed in headlights. The Ingram MAC-10 capable of spitting out 1090 rounds per minute, the Executioner had them dancing and dropping under the double stuttering death knell.

That left Benny.

Checking his clips, finding them half-empty, Bolan was slapping them back home when Fugasami lunged up on the far side of the bar and began capping off .45ACP rounds. Hunched and running, Bolan secured cover beneath the bar as bullets gouged up chunks of the bar top.

"Come on, gaijin! Show yourself! It is only the two of us!"

Pinpointing Fugasami's voice, the soldier popped up, tapping both subgun triggers. Fugasami was there; then he was gone in the next eye blink as hot lead found nothing but empty air.

Then the music died. In the silence Bolan made out the sound of glass crunching as Fugasami moved down the bar, the Yakuza boss going for an outflanking maneuver from the sound of it. The soldier filled one Ingram with his last clip, stood and rolled on his haunches over the bar.

The music started up again. Bolan recognized the oldie but goodie he remembered as a soldier's favorite tune from his Vietnam days.

Wild horses, indeed.

The soldier cut the gap to where he could nearly feel his enemy on the other side of the bar. Ingram aimed up, he glanced down at a fallen liquor bottle. Scooping up the bottle, he chucked it about a dozen feet down the bar aisle. Figure nerves and rage combined, and he held on, hoping Fugasami would bite.

Benny did.

The Yakuza boss seemed to spring up into the air, dropping on the bartop, his .45 Colt blasting away before he realized he was shooting at nothing, then wheeled, the look on his face telling Bolan the guy knew he was plunged into a world of hurt.

Wrap it up.

The Executioner held back on both triggers, riding it out, stitching the Yakuza boss from buttocks on up the spine. One SMG ran dry of 9 mm rounds, Fugasami roaring and turning Bolan's way as the other Ingram finished it for the soldier. A final chattering burst of subgun fire, and the Executioner sent Fugasami flailing out of sight to drop on the customer side of business. One look over the bar, and Bolan knew Fugasami was a done deal.

"AMERICAN? Who...are you?"

"You're not going to make it, Drylov."

"How do you know?... Oh, I hurt...bad..."

"I can make it quick and painless. A few questions, then I'll be on my way."

Bolan had found the Russian crabbing across the floor, clutching a computer disk, trailing blood and croaking in pain. The soldier had relieved the dying man of the disk.

The Executioner stood over the Russian in the middle of a lake of bodies, his nose full of the stink of death. He checked the clip on his Ingram, found he still had a few bullets left. "What's on the disk?"

The Russian chuckled, rolled over on his back. "Does not matter...blueprints for American flying saucer...too late...my man...gone to Molokai...no catch him..."

"With the tall man, white hair?"

"The admiral...fly out in transport plane...soon... pieces of particle reactor...antigravity...shell of UFO...

Mosnivoc…it was to be his big gamble…hand it over to military…SVR…knew about American UFO for… long time…you have disk…have fun…code…Forbidden Isle…."

Bolan knew he had just stumbled over some of the truth here. A Navy man had been snagged by Benny's extortion net, forced to hand over through Fugasami to the Russian Mafia specs for a prototype aircraft. How the Russians knew the base existed on Molokai, how it had all come to this, Bolan could only guess.

But still more truth awaited him on the Forbidden Isle, and the soldier reckoned it would all reveal itself in due time if he stayed the course of kicking ass and taking names.

"Long live…the shogun…that piece of…shot me…."

Bolan listened to a fit of choking laughter, knew the Russian was lapsing into shock, delirious now from pain. He'd heard enough, aware he was long overdue to quit that place anyway. A quick exit out the back door, just in case local authorities came barreling inside the front way, and he'd leg it back to his vehicle. It looked like a tour of the former leper colony was up next. There was no way the soldier would stand by and see a one-of-a-kind classified U.S. aircraft fall into the hands of the Russian Mafia, whether as a trophy for Mosnivoc or for someone in his organization to put it up on the auction block for the highest bidder.

The game here was dead.

"If it makes you feel any better," Bolan told the dying Russian gangster, lifting the Ingram subgun, "I took care of Benny."

"Then...I shall see him...in hell...."

True to his pledge, the Executioner put the Russian out of his misery, then marched a path for the back exit.

Hawaii

THE SNAFUS WERE stacking up across the board to make life a living hell for Brognola.

Unwrapping a fresh stogie and sticking it in his mouth, jacked up on a full pot of Kurtzman's coffee, one ear tuned to Katz and Price, the big Fed stood in the middle of the Computer Room and wished to God he could do something to reverse course and get Phoenix Force on the way. He heard how the Spectre was grounded at an American air base in Turkey. Something about hydraulic leaks and problems with the reverse thruster, plus the Litton AN-ALR-69 radar-warning receiver was on the fritz, meaning Grimaldi could find a few MiGs up his rear before he knew what hit them unless the problem was solved.

Brognola heard a doomsday clock ticking in his head.

"It seems," Brognola heard Price tell him, "I put my hands on the same Spectre that took a few hits from the Iraqis and dropped into the waters off the Kuwaiti coast during the Gulf War. It was going to be scrapped, but the Air Force put it back together right after the war, for whatever reason, I can't say. I only learned of this when it hit the fan and the AC-130 landed in Turkey on fumes. A crew of engineers is hard at work patching up the problems. I'm hearing one, two hours tops before it's in the air and on the way to Saudi.''

Time travel and top speed for the AC-130 factored, and with any luck Brognola hoped it would land in Saudi before the sun went down.

Good luck and godspeed, he thought.

"Speaking of crews," Katz said, "it takes fourteen good men to normally fly an AC-130."

Numbers crunch. Two pilots, one navigator, three sensor operators not to mention flight engineer, a radioman and gun crews. The good news was Price had that covered, Katz stated, the mission controller having already handpicked and shipped out long ago a six-man crew that could handle the aircraft. A squadron of Thunderbolts, F-16s and Fighting Falcons was on the ground in Saudi, ready to escort the Spectre to its destination.

Whenever that happened.

"It was a long shot," the big Fed heard Price tell him, "to get Phoenix launched before sunup. As soon as the Spectre touches down, they'll be wheels up and on the way."

"And no news from my Israeli contact in Mossad is good news," Katz said. "We're monitoring that part of the world, courtesy of our NRO friends."

That was true enough. Constant sat imagery watched for any air traffic leaving Israel and heading northeast. So far a shaky situation was holding.

Brognola had just touched base with the Man. Nerves were fraying all over in the power structure of Israel. But it appeared as if someone with good sense had reined in whoever was in charge of the elite

Israeli commando team and the nuke-armed F-16s. But how long would the Israelis sit on their hands?

Brognola had situations boiling to critical mass over three time zones, and it gave him a headache to even keep the hours straight, since he'd already been on his feet for more than twenty-four hours or so, and he didn't even remember the last time he'd slept. Midnight in Oahu. Near dawn in Brooklyn. Somewhere after midday in Saudi. Endless hours passing, dragging on for all of them. Juggling time zones wasn't exactly his favorite pastime.

Tomorrow was here, and existence was winding down to sheer survival for a whole bunch of folks, Brognola thought.

"I want Phoenix airborne and in Syria before the sun sets," Brognola told Price. "Work it out, whatever you have to do. The Israelis won't wait much longer before they cut their people loose, and God help us if they do that."

Kurtzman updated Brognola on Able Team's situation. Lyons was pulling out of the safehouse, had the pieces in place for delivery of the don, with the FBI already fielding a team around the U.S. Criminal Courthouse in downtown Brooklyn. All hands were braced for urban warfare in the event another small army of Russian hitters wanted to free their boss.

And that was yet another mess. It turned out Kurtzman had tracked down some rather dubious bank accounts under the Social Security number of Henry Carlington. Moscow. Switzerland. Cayman Islands. Carlington had more money than God. Knowing all wasn't what it appeared to be over at State, Lyons had Carlington turned over to the FBI field office for some Q and A. On the surface it looked as if Carlington and maybe a few others over at the State Department had taken money from the Russian Mafia to help Mosnivoc on his ride to the top.

Damn it all. Brognola was seeing Armageddon headed their way.

If little else, Striker at least had his situation under control for the time being. The Yakuza and the Triad had been kicked out of paradise, sent thrashing all the way to hell from the sounds of what Striker had pulled off at the Golden Palace.

The mystery, though, about UFOs and classified military black projects out that way was far from being revealed. In fact, the truth left a slew of questions hanging.

The big guy had transferred the contents of a disk for the craft in question over the fax on his sat link. Whatever Wethers, Kurtzman, Delahunt and Tokaido were now scrolling through had them about as baffled and fascinated as Brognola had ever seen.

Delahunt said, "There are no mathematical or scientific symbols, lettering, alphabet, whatever you want to call it, like this on earth."

"Only the originator of these symbols know what they really mean," Tokaido added.

Brognola stepped up to their workstations, gnawing on his cigar as the fantastic stared him right in the face. What the hell were they looking at? Sure enough, he couldn't make out the squiggly, jagged or rounded symbols on the monitors, either. It struck him as something an archaeologist would have found on the walls of one of the Egyptian pyramids, or maybe some offshoot of Chinese or Mandarin unknown to the Western world. Or whatever the hell it was.

"These are definitely the specs for our UFO," Wethers announced, and scrolled up the dimensions for the blueprint of a disk. "You have some sort of chamber here where the pilot navigates the craft. The specs are telling me these oblong shapes hanging in the chamber are amplifier heads, or consoles that state that when the particle reactor is running at full power, an antigravity wave is created...." Wethers turned toward Brognola, a stunned look on his face. "It actually makes the craft invisible."

"How is it fueled?" Brognola asked.

"That, we're not sure of," Wethers said.

"Meaning it could be powered by a nuclear reactor."

"Or even laser propulsion, or a combination of both," Delahunt said. "If and when we ever get it back from the Russians, I wouldn't risk getting anywhere near it without an NBC spacesuit."

And still another problem—denial on both sides the craft even existed. The Russians claimed they had no such craft in their possession. Some cyberspace burglary by Kurtzman and company through the backdoor mainframes over at the Pentagon and Langley, and even their own people were doing a tap dance about the existence of the UFO.

Delahunt stayed glued to her monitor. "This element that Feinstein repeatedly mentions in some of his writings is apparently heavier than anything we know exists on Earth. What he says is that when an element becomes heavier it exerts its own gravity A waves, so incredibly intense that atoms create and possess their own force fields.''

"Meaning what exactly?'' Brognola asked.

"Meaning it can hover,'' Wethers answered. "Meaning it can create its own energy to expand mass. Meaning the theory of relativity is, in a phrase, out the window.''

"There are no edges on these specs,'' Kurtzman said. "It's as if the damn thing is made of…hell, I don't know, wax? This…unknown element…melted down to form a smooth, rounded spherical…whatever it is.''

Brognola knew he couldn't even begin to fathom whatever it was that someone had created. It was beyond him. Right then he needed everyone to focus on what was real, and in their face.

"Hal,'' Kurtzman said, rolling his wheelchair around to face the big Fed. "What do we do with these? Give them back, to maybe say your shadow friend over at the Pentagon?''

"For the moment, let's put all this…whatever you're looking at on the back burner. We'll deal with UFOs later. Barbara, I want you to raise David. I want Phoenix saddled up and off the ground the second the Spectre hits Saudi.''

Price was on it, working the sat link to Phoenix Force, while Brognola stood, feeling as if all of them had just landed on another planet.

Or were about to be blown off, he feared, from the face of the earth if the Israelis went for broke in Syria.

CHAPTER TWELVE

New York

As soon as the FBI men emerged from the safehouse with Mosnivoc cuffed and in tow, the battle to free or kill the Russian Mafia boss would begin.

There was no other way but to just do it, he knew, take their chances and hope that brazen slaughter cleared the way and won the night.

Bylokiv sat in the shotgun seat of the black Cadillac, the AK-47 canted against the door, Kyricik at the wheel, the big man having caught a stroke of luck when he'd spotted the State Department liaison going into the brownstone a little over three hours ago.

Looking down the quiet, darkened street of brownstones and shops, Bylokiv had seen his RPG team climbing the fire escape for the apartment's rooftop minutes earlier. He knew they were up there, in position, with the other teams set to unload from the Flatbush Avenue end. A classic pincer assault, twenty-six former KGB agents and Spetsnaz commandos against perhaps all of twelve FBI agents.

No problem.

"And when this is over?"

It was a question Bylokiv hadn't given much thought to, but now he was being asked for their escape plans.

"Several safehouses have been set up in Brighton Beach," he told Kyricik. "If we are forced to split up, we go there on foot. Wait until we receive a call from a contact there who will arrange flight back to Moscow."

"The address you gave me earlier."

"Yes, that one."

"And Comrade Mosnivoc?"

"He has become a liability to some very important men in Moscow. If he gets killed, no one will miss him. Truth is, that is precisely what Moscow is hoping for."

"And if we do take him from the FBI? If we attempt to leave the country with him, it would be very risky for us."

"I understand, but Moscow is apparently prepared to take care of that. How, I am not sure."

Two blocks down, Bylokiv saw two more black four-door sedans rolling to a stop in front of the brownstone, joining the miniconvoy of escort vehicles already parked curbside. M-16-toting shadows, with FBI stenciled on the backs of their jackets, disgorged from the latest arriving vehicles, grim faces checking the street.

And the front door to the brownstone opened up.

"Show time," Bylokiv said, and snapped up his AK-47.

THEY HAD THE POSITION of the shooters nailed down, thanks to Schwarz's eavesdropping toy. Even though they didn't understand Russian, Blancanales and Schwarz caught the entire conversation, just down the street where the black Cadillac was parked, lights and engine off. And they'd also seen three very big men in black trench coats, lugging large satchels, roll around the far corner of the apartment building. The trap was set. It wasn't so much the words that came over the receiver fixed to the parabolic mike as it was the tone of men speaking in grim wariness, a subtle edge that told the two Able Team commandos they were jacked up on adrenaline, itching to kick some FBI butt.

Blancanales patched through to Lyons. "It's happening. Look alive. We've got shooters at the both ends of the street, maybe a team up on the roof."

Schwarz opened the window, chambering a 5.56 mm round into his M-16. With his own M-16/M203 combo, Blancanales joined Schwarz in the window, his heart racing as he saw Lyons and a phalanx of FBI men moving down the sidewalk for the waiting vehicles that would take the Russian mobster to Prospect Park for the chopper ride.

Only Blancanales knew the Russian hitters were hell-bent on making sure no one on the home team made it off the street.

Out of nowhere, Blancanales saw three, then four large luxury vehicles flying off Flatbush Avenue, yet another vehicle racing up to join the rear of the fast-moving hit team. The Cadillac's engine gunned to life, and Blancanales made out the muzzle of an assault rifle as the vehicle raced under a streetlight.

Then the world seemed to blow up directly across the street, Russian shooters piling out of their vehicles and cutting loose with assault rifles as two warheads slammed into a couple of the waiting FBI vehicles.

At the same instant, Blancanales and Schwarz cut loose with their M-16s on anything that moved with an AK-47.

LYONS WAS HALFWAY down the sidewalk, marching Mosnivoc toward the Ford, door open to receive the cuffed crime boss, when the sky seemed to fall on the FBI men. Somehow Lyons spotted the shadows on the rooftop where Schwarz and Blancanales were watching from below. A glimpse of a cone-shaped warhead, and Lyons shouted, "Incoming! Hit the deck!"

One, then two vehicles were blasted into flaming scrap. Lyons was hurling Mosnivoc to the ground when the real shooting started. It had all happened with such lightning ferocity, Lyons briefly wondered if this would end before it even began. Already at least three, no, four FBI men, despite body armor, were dropping, dead before they hit the ground.

Head shots.

On his belly, as wreckage blew over his head, the SPAS-12 sweeping up and booming a round at the first Russian shooter who made the scene, Lyons tapped the button to his com link. The roar of autofire was deafening and Lyons was forced to shout, "Pol! Gadgets! Someone get up on that roof and take care of our rocket problem before all of us are diced and sliced!"

WHILE SCHWARZ BLAZED away on the vehicles that had, in effect, cut off the FBI convoy from making a hasty escape, Blancanales copied Lyons's order.

"I'm going up top to nail whoever's playing with the heavy stuff!"

Schwarz nodded, holding back on the trigger of his M-16, sweeping a hellstorm of 5.56 mm lead over the Russian vehicles, taking out windows and scoring three quick kills.

It was total insanity down there, Schwarz thought. The only good news was that Lyons hadn't been taken out during the opening rounds. Ironman had called this setup, wanting it to go down before the sun rose and traffic created a typical New York clusterscrew. Carlington, he suspected, had been spotted going into the brownstone by a roving Russian surveillance team. Or had the State guy led the Russian shooters there?

It didn't matter. If they lived to see the sun rise, questions would be answered, and, no mistake, heads would roll.

Then yet another RPG warhead uprooted a black sedan off its wheels in a thundering fireball, spreading a few FBI men all over the street in twisted heaps.

It was a turkey shoot for the Russians, as things stood.

Schwarz could plainly see it looked real bad for the good guys. If they didn't turn the tide here and quick, Schwarz knew Lyons and the rest of the FBI men were dead meat.

BYLOKIV DUCKED as some shooter poked an assault rifle out the window of the apartment building and blew in the window. Kyricik snarling a curse, the wheelman rammed a Ford that was attempting to flee.

They were out the doors, and seeking targets a moment later. Blood trickling down his head from flying glass, Bylokiv was forced to direct a barrage of 7.62 mm lead at the shooter in the window, saw his stream of bullets taking out the glass, the figure pulling back from sight, leaving him to wonder if he'd scored and taken care of that particular problem.

Never mind. Plenty of problems to be solved now stood in his way.

Crouched, weaving ahead, AK-47 chattering, Bylokiv waded right into the smoke and flames of the burning FBI cars. Kyricik had already blown in the windshield of the FBI vehicle with an extended burst of autofire, erasing the stunned looks off the faces of the Americans in red clouds of gore.

He saw a big man with a massive shotgun blowing away his hitters, glimpsed Mosnivoc raising his bulk. He wasn't sure what he saw next, but he believed the boss slammed his cuffed hands over the big man's head, and started to run as the shotgunner was laid out on his belly.

Bylokiv had his hands full at the moment, cut down another FBI man with a burst to the face, aware they were wearing body armor, then began a beeline up the sides of the FBI vehicles, firing on the run.

One way or another, he alone would take care of the Mosnivoc problem.

THE DOUBLE WHAMMY caught him by surprise. Before he knew it, Lyons was falling to the sidewalk, bullets snapping the air all around, another FBI man spinning and dropping dead ahead as blood gouted out the side of his skull. He was gathering himself, hauling Little Bulldozer out of his war bag, when two hardmen came running through the swirling smoke and dancing fire, tracking him with their AK-47s.

He put Mosnivoc out of mind and gave the hardmen more than they could ever bargain for, tapping out one 40 mm round that blew up real estate two feet in front of them and sent them sailing for the street.

The FBI agents were holding their own, but no one seemed aware that Mosnivoc was escaping. It was understandable, given the raw suicidal fury of the Russian charge, their minds racing and hearts pumping with adrenaline, everyone aware it was pretty much every man for himself.

Lyons glimpsed the Russian boss, heading toward Flatbush Avenue, and gave chase.

BURSTING THROUGH the door, Blancanales caught the trio of rocket men as they were in the act of attaching warheads to their RPG-7s. He had to have made some racket with his kick to the door, since two of the rocket men wheeled his way. One Russian was grabbing an AK-47 when Blancanales opened up with M-16 autofire that nailed the guy before he even got off a shot.

That left two, and they were already armed with AKs and splitting up. Another quick burst on the run, and Blancanales caught a hardman in the chest, kicking him over the edge of the roof, the Russian gone for a swan dive to the waiting street.

He dodged the hasty return fire as lead zipped over the open door, drilling holes through flimsy wood.

There was no cover except for a large satellite dish. The Russian dropped to the ground behind the dish, stuck his AK-47 around the edge and cut loose.

Blancanales sent a 40 mm round chugging over the rooftop. The sat dish vanished in a thunderclap of smoky fire, the roaring explosion putting out the shooter's lights, as debris and bits and pieces of the Russian were strewed over the rooftop.

It was wrapped up here, but judging from the sounds of autofire and shouts and screams on the street below he knew it was just heating up for Lyons and the FBI.

Blancanales hugged the edge of the roof and began selecting targets.

FINDING MASTERSON was one of the casualties, Lyons cursed, brushed the FBI SAC's eyes shut, then got his bearings. Curbside and crouched behind a Ford four-door, he counted maybe ten Russian shooters taking up positions around their vehicles in the middle of the street, twenty yards or so out. They gave cover fire for the suicide chargers, throwing another shooter here and there into the foray behind long, raking fusillades of AK-47 autofire. A hardman was breaking cover, made it all of three feet when half of his skull vanished in a pink halo. A glance down the street revealed a mushroom cloud of smoke hovering along the rooftop, and Lyons figured either Schwarz or Blancanales had waxed the rocket team, taking back control of the fight from above.

It was Lyons's turn to crank up the heat.

Little Bulldozer was up and chugging out the hell-bombs, the first series of fireballs blowing through the vehicles, when Lyons saw an AK-47-toting hardman intercept Mosnivoc just before they hit Flatbush Avenue. The hardman placed the muzzle of his AK-47 on the links of Mosnivoc's cuff, tapped out a burst and freed the don.

A dip into his war bag and Lyons pulled out the spherical reloader, dumped another set of HE rounds into the squat rocket launcher with a quick tap of the release button. There were still Russian shooters across the street, holding back on the triggers of their Kalashnikovs from alleyways, stairwells or behind trash cans. Lyons laid waste to the remaining shooters hunkered down behind one intact Cadillac, blowing them all to hell with three HE fireballs.

Soon enough, he knew the blue-and-whites would come screaming onto the scene. This sort of urban warfare would have NYPD edged out, trigger fingers nervous. He could only hope they were aware enough to separate FBI from Russian hit men.

Either way, he wasn't about to lose Mosnivoc to a mere sucker punch.

BLANCANALES and Schwarz rolled out onto the sidewalk. Side by side they hit the blind side of three Russians blazing away from a stairwell, M-16s stammering in unison. Blancanales wasted no time in taking them out, then searched the fiery wreckage, finally peering down the street to make out the familiar bulk of Lyons. His team leader, he knew, was on the hunt for runners.

Just as Lyons vanished around the corner, Blancanales saw the blue-and-whites flying onto the scene. Russian shooters turned their guns on the cops as the law burst out the doors with pistols and shotguns adding to the deafening racket of weapons fire.

"Come on, Pol, let's link up with the good guys," Schwarz said, and led Blancanales on an angle for the few intact FBI wheels. The FBI had suffered heavy losses, as Schwarz took in the sprawled bodies down the sidewalk. An FBI man swung their way, his M-16 coming up, when Schwarz shouted, "We're with Agent Lemon!"

"Then help us finish these bastards!" the FBI man yelled back.

Hitting crouches at the back end of the vehicle, Schwarz and Blancanales decided to waste no more time. Between the FBI and NYPD the Russians were pinched off in several pockets in alleyways.

"Let's put Cowboy's hardware to the test, Pol!"

Brandishing their Little Bulldozers, Schwarz and Blancanales cranked out enough 40 mm rounds to nail the surviving hardmen. With each smoky thunderclap, mangled bodies sailed away, or were launched into the street or against the sides of buildings that would need some serious repair work when the smoke cleared. Two Russian shooters were making a run for a vehicle when the double blast from the Able Team warriors all but obliterated man and machine.

THE FLYING SQUAD CARS somehow missed him. Lyons figured they had their attention fixed solely on the urban warfare that was eating up a whole block of Brooklyn. SPAS-12 reloaded and in hand, and Little Bulldozer bouncing from its sling around his shoulder, Lyons put the flashing light show and the sound and fury of all-out battle behind. He could be sure his teammates, with some help from the FBI and NYPD, could mop it up.

Mosnivoc was being hustled along by a tall man in a black leather trench coat. They were heading south on the avenue, sticking to the shadows blanketing the bodegas, shops and other places of business. If they made it four, maybe five blocks on the run, Lyons feared losing them in Prospect Park.

Already the city had come alive with early-morning commuters on the move to beat rush hour. Faces of fear rolling past Lyons, he weaved through the traffic, the sound of explosions and autofire losing their steam.

"Mosnivoc!"

Trench Coat wheeled and directed a long spray of autofire. The back window and windshield of a parked Lexus absorbed the brunt of lead, shattered in a gale force of flying glass that forced Lyons to duck, cover his face. He broke cover, saw them running and triggered a peal of thunder from the SPAS. Half of Trench Coat's upper thigh was sheared off by the 12-gauge frangible buckshot rounds. Somehow the Russian made it a few more steps before toppling sideways into what looked like the mouth of an alley.

Lyons could smell blood, his heart pounding with cold rage over the loss of still more good men. Men whose families would wake up that morning with no husband, no father.

Mosnivoc, as far as he was concerned, would never stand trial.

Crouching at the corner, Lyons spotted Mosnivoc charging in his half waddle, half run down the narrow alley. Trench Coat was crawling along, dragging his leg, throwing a strange fit of laughter back at Lyons. One blast of the SPAS-12 to the Russian's back pinned him there, nearly sawing him in two.

A large garbage bin provided temporary haven for Mosnivoc, who flew behind the container, came around low, firing the AK-47. Darting to the side, the line of 7.62 mm rounds whizzing past, Lyons unslung the compact launcher. Running ahead, he loosed a 40 mm hellbomb. The blast most likely wouldn't finish off Mosnivoc, as the Russian was shielded on the other side of ground zero. The garbage bin was knocked down the alley on a ball of fire, kicking Mosnivoc out into the open.

"You!" Mosnivoc shouted, standing, holding his arms up. "No more! I give up. I have rights. Take me then to your court."

Lyons slowed his strides, let the launcher slip from his grasp and lifted the massive autoshotgun. In the shadows of the alley, he couldn't quite make out the expression on Mosnivoc's face, didn't trust the moment.

Something smelled, and a second later Lyons saw Mosnivoc reaching behind his back to reveal the stink. The Makarov pistol, stripped off Trench Coat, was swinging around when Lyons tapped the autoshotgun's trigger. No Kevlar was wrapped around the don, and when he took the full impact in the chest he was blown off his feet in a cloud of blood, sheared cloth and bone fragments.

Lyons turned and walked away.

IT WAS SOMETHING supposed to only happen in Beirut, or maybe Tel Aviv, but certainly not Brooklyn.

Lyons took in the carnage, rolling right down the middle of the battle zone. Dead men littered the street, curbs, sidewalks and alleyways, a few moans from the wounded raking the air. Wreckage was burning and smoking, with more squad cars, ambulances and fire trucks roaring onto the scene, sirens wailing. Lyons made out Schwarz and Blancanales flashing their phony Justice Department credentials at the uniforms.

This was one mess that wouldn't get cleaned up soon.

Schwarz and Blancanales broke the blue line and marched toward Lyons.

"Mosnivoc? We saw you give chase," Blancanales said.

"Let's just say the don was judged and sentenced on the spot."

"So, the don is dead," Schwarz said, still holding his compact rocket launcher. "I don't think Carlington's pals over at State are going to exactly toast the occasion."

"They can kiss my ass," Lyons growled. "This thing is not over. Carlington's dirty, and he has friends over at State and Langley who know something we don't." Lyons scanned the slaughter, saw a uniform heading his way. Flashing his own credentials at the cop, he said, "Special Agent Lemon. Any FBI man holding on by a thread is to receive the best care this city can deliver. We clear, Officer?"

A nod, the cop saying, "We're on it. I have three of your men down, but they might make it."

"No might about it." He read the name tag. "MacPherson, you just became personally responsible for seeing to their immediate evacuation to the nearest hospital.''

Lyons saw the cops checking for survivors beyond a drifting wall of black smoke. By then plenty of curious onlookers were craning faces out the windows of apartment buildings or standing watch in the doors of brownstones.

''I've got a live one over here.''

A cop was kneeling by one of the Russian shooters. ''My people first!'' Lyons shouted.

''Understood.''

''Damn right,'' Lyons said.

CHAPTER THIRTEEN

Along the Saudi Arabian–Iraqi Border

Forty-three satellite images of the Syrian compound in question were spread out on the large metal table. David McCarter had the enhancements of every building on each of four quadrants of the site marked off and laid out to the compass. The leader of Phoenix Force used his Fairbairn-Sykes commando knife to go over the critical areas he'd already circled in red and lettered in accordance to their importance.

Important, he was stating in his final brief, was relative to the threat they would encounter when hitting the perimeter. Looking approvingly at the grim determination on the faces of James, Hawkins, Encizo and Manning, he raised his voice some as a fighter jet screamed overhead the large tent Phoenix Force was housed in, courtesy of the commander of the American air base along the Saudi-Iraqi border.

"Without question, Jack has to take out the MiGs, the antiaircraft batteries in the southeast and northeast quadrants here, hopefully some of the APCs on the way, too. With any luck and all the skill he and the blacksuit crew can muster, the first strafing will also hit what we believe to be the command-and-control center, as you can see," he said, stabbing Circle C, "with its radar dishes and banks of antennas. Blow up these two buildings, D and E, which are the troop barracks and probably double likewise as quarters for the men with the brains building the bomb. We'll be dropping here," he said, turning and indicating an area due west of the Anti-Lebanon Mountains, the maps of Syria, Jordan and Saudi looming on a tripod-stand mounting.

"The way Jack and I have by the numbers, by the time we land from thirty-five thousand feet up, sailing in as close to this wadi as possible, he'll have circled back, timed our landing and our jaunt in, he'll raise me to give me an ETA when he can let it rip. NVD goggles on the way in, weather conditions are good according to our report from the Farm. We've HALOed many times, mates, into enemy territory. But this time our LZ is going to be cutting it close to the guns. It will come down to timing our run to Jack's flight back south and around and hoping their radar does not pick him up and scramble their MiGs to have an up-close and personal look at the Spectre."

"And those spacesuits you mentioned, David?" Manning asked. "Have you reconsidered that particular burden?"

"I have. I know Barbara won't like it, since, as always, she wants us out and back in Saudi in one piece to a man. The problem is lugging our gear and weapons and fifty pounds of C-4 per man through this wadi along with the spacesuits in their nylon rucksacks. Too much weight. When T.J. and you, Gary, make the entrance to the reprocessing site, go down and set the charges, I need top speed the whole way in and out. If it hits the radioactive fan, I can have Jack order one of the crew to drop our NBC suits somewhere over the compound. We'll crate them up, rig up a chute before we head out. Either way, I don't much care for having to make an evac, probably under enemy fire, while lumbering around in one of those alien contraptions.''

A pause, McCarter looking at each Phoenix Force warrior in turn, giving the opening for any questions.

"You say the head honcho in charge is one Colonel Ali Sandi," James said. "Heads up the Twenty-fourth Brigade of the Syrian army. Brigade means a bunch of bad guys with guns and tanks, David. Anything more from the Farm about numbers?"

"The biggest problem, according to my understanding, is that there isn't a CIA operative in Syria. My guess is no intel on the inside is why this site could be built and go unknown up to this point. Meaning we have no clear fix on numbers other than what the sats have picked out. Ten Soviet T-62 tanks head out for some sneak-and-peek into the Bekaa Valley on a daily basis. I'm figuring anywhere from fifty to a hundred troops, could be closer to one-fifty. The Farm's holding its breath that the tank crews don't return before we've blown up and burned down the place, hurled up enough radioactive waste to make the entire site uninhabitable for a long time to come."

"Any suspicions about this Nabaj and his Islamic cronies being housed and given the golden jihad treatment by this Colonel Sandi?" Encizo asked.

"If he's on-site, we're looking at maybe anywhere from another twenty to thirty fanatics. In the event they turn up, well, they'll receive anything but that golden 'jihad' treatment you mention, Rafe. That's why the Spectre has to lay waste to at least fifty percent of the compound before we make our grand entrance felt. In all the confusion, once the bombs are dropping and the bullets are flying, we should be able to move in, with the two teams I've already designated, and pinch them off before we link up at the entrance to the reprocessing site. Long odds, granted, but I'm counting on Jack and company to pave the way.''

Hawkins grunted, showed the troops a wry grin. "Well, fellas, it isn't like we haven't rolled the dice before and waited to see if we were gonna crap out. What the hell, huh, is life without a little adventure?''

"It will definitely be balls to the wall, mates,'' McCarter said.

"Irradiated balls,'' Encizo said, cutting a grim smile, "if we blow a bunch of nuclear waste over our heads. Or if the Israelis drop in for a surprise visit and start hurling nukes our way.''

"Speaking of that,'' Manning asked, "any word from Katz on the Israeli situation?''

"All's quiet on the Israeli front,'' McCarter answered. "Katz, I'm told, managed to reach a couple of cooler heads in the Mossad and IDF upper echelons, but the Israelis are getting antsy, to understate the situation.''

Grimaldi, in black leather bomber jacket and dark aviator shades, swept inside the tent on a blaze of sunlight. Even though the sun was going down, the opening faced out to the western edges of the Saudi Arabian desert. Just the same, McCarter knew darkness was on the way, the onslaught of night fueling their precombat jitters and adrenaline to get the show on the road.

"How's our bird?" McCarter asked.

"She's shipshape."

McCarter, sensing Grimaldi was about to elaborate, held up a hand. Knowing that the Spectre would get them there and back and do the dirty work from above was all he needed to know. "That's good enough for me," he said. "Let's cover a few more things, especially what we know about these sort of fly-by-night, primitive nuclear reactor sites. Then I want us to double-check our weapons, gear, chutes, the works. The sun will be going down by the time we're wheels up and over Jordanian airspace. Oh, by the way, Jack, I hope you don't mind, but we'll have three F-16s and three Thunderbolts escorting us in case that antiradar jammer hasn't been fixed one hundred percent and we suddenly find some MiGs up our rear ends."

Grimaldi grinned. "Oh, it's working, all right. But something tells me, David, before this is over we're going to need a little help from wherever we can get it."

Calvin James grunted and spoke what was on the minds of all the troops. "I hope to hell not. If we find ourselves needing a handout, we are all in a major world of hurt."

Stony Man Farm, Virginia

"YEAH, THE THREE of us came out the other side on this one. Some nicks and gashes that needed stitching. Funny how you never know you're banged up until after the bullets stop flying and the adrenaline stops racing.''

Brognola and the others in the Computer Room were listening to the grim update by Lyons over the sat link. The anger in Lyons's voice, when he informed them yet another seven FBI men had been killed by Russian gangsters, with three other agents clinging to life, came through loud and clear. There was a moment of silence on both sides as everyone tried to digest the enormous and tragic cost of life.

"Hal, I was thinking maybe we should bring Carlington back to the Farm for some extended Q and A,'' Lyons suggested.

"That would require some rather ugly arm-twisting with the FBI in New York,'' Brognola said.

"It might be a good idea,'' Price said. "We've already run down a few other State Department officials who have numbered accounts.''

"And who would appear to have some close ties with the SVR in Russia,'' Wethers added.

"I have a feeling,'' Kurtzman put in, "that Carlington knows a lot more than he's willing to tell. Unless, of course, we put the fear of God into him.''

"I'll work on it, Carl,'' Brognola said. "With the FBI losing so many agents, I don't think they'll be in the mood to just hand over to me what looks like a link from our side to the Russian Mafia. Especially since it'll take a call from the President for them to give him up to me.''

"That's all I can ask for, Hal,'' Lyons said. "Just one more crack at this weasel.''

Brognola took a moment to fathom the madness Able Team and the FBI had faced down. Urban war-

fare had erupted in the early morning out of nowhere
in Brooklyn. The good guys didn't even get off the
street, or even make their vehicles with Mosnivoc
when the shooting began. Well, the don was dead,
and there was no telling how the Russian diplomatic
front would react to the news. For a suicide squad of
Russian hit men to charge in, blasting away, with no
concern for their own lives, much less clearing the
scene or the country, told Brognola there were shadows hiding over at the State Department or the CIA.
Even, he believed, major power players in Moscow
who'd given the orders to the hit squads to die on
their feet, if necessary, to make sure the don was either whisked back to the motherland or left for dead
so that whatever truth he knew would never see the
light of a sweetheart deal in the Witness Protection
Program. What little Lyons had already informed
them about a connection between Mosnivoc shipping
nuclear waste and component parts for a light-water
reactor to Syria, spelled out conspiracy to Brognola.
And with Striker flushing out the Russian Mafia in
Hawaii, a traitor who ran the classified military base
in Molokai where the prototype nuke-armed UFO was
built and maybe parts of it about to be shipped out to
Russia...

Brognola was beginning to see a vast conspiracy,
pieces to the puzzle scattered all over the globe.

"Anything else, Carl?" Brognola asked.

"Just grant me that one request to be alone in a
room at the Farm with the State's fair-haired weasel.
I'll get you all the answers you want. It's already been
pledged in the blood of those dead FBI agents."

"Don't I know it," Brognola said in a quiet but pained voice.

Hawaii

THE FORBIDDEN ISLE struck Bolan as the perfect landing spot for whatever mystery or treachery awaited him. Also known as the Friendly Isle in recent decades, it was Hawaii's least-populated island, perhaps because it was once the exiled refuge for legions of lepers more than a hundred years ago, and before that home to the powerful kahunas, priests whose lives were shrouded in mystery and who were claimed to have been slayers of some great lizard dragons that once roamed the island. A little too much bad history and mysticism, Bolan figured, didn't place the island high up on anyone's tourist agenda.

Fantastic folklore and tales of sorrow and suffering aside, the Executioner had a date to keep with grim reality.

Hunched in the open fuselage doorway of the Bell JetRanger, taking the rotor wash in the face, the soldier peered through the infrared binoculars, searching the dense canopy of the tropical vegetation as the chopper soared past the rocky cliffs along the northwest end of the island. The Executioner felt himself standing on the clock, racing against time.

Critical hours had been consumed once the soldier had put the Golden Palace behind, barely riding off in his rental car before an armada of squad cars had pulled up and barreled through the doorways to find the slaughter that waited for them. After touching back with the Farm and updating the command-and-control center troops, Bolan paid Rivers a brief visit. Fortunately, the fallen agent had some rough idea where the UFO base was situated. Just what Bolan needed to get him on the way and on-site, since the Farm couldn't get hold of any sat pics of the classified base, and it would be hours before any satellite made a passover of the island. Sensing Rivers was holding something back, Bolan used a little persuasion with some choice cold words of warning, since the fallen agent had neglected to mention the Russian Mafia sightings. It turned out Rivers had even taken a little chopper ride, out of curiosity, if nothing else, to scope out the mysterious compound.

The fallen angel had come through.

A mile inland, and Bolan saw the blinking red lights on the control tower of a large airfield. South of the airfield he made out three large white buildings that were framed in soft white light shining from klieg lights mounted on poles. There didn't appear to be any human activity around the buildings, no roving security force he could see, but he clearly made out a C-130 at the north end of the runway. Four executive-type jets and two choppers were grounded near a series of hangars to the east. Nothing going on that way, but they were busy loading up something in the cargo hold of the C-130. A forklift was rolling up the ramp, a massive crate held out, vanishing inside the transport plane.

They were moving something out, and Bolan had a strong suspicion what it was that was about to be flown off the base.

The Executioner was ready to make his move. Once he penetrated the grounds, he could expect armed company trying to intercept him. He didn't care for the idea of shooting down American soldiers assigned to guard the compound, but there were traitors among their ranks. If he was forced to, he would go for nonlethal but incapacitating shots.

Now, he thought, scanning the perimeter, how to make his move? It looked like some dense vegetation was snugged up against the razor-topped cyclone fence, the small remote area of tropical jungle reaching out for the C-130.

Looked as good as it would get.

Bolan knew the crew was about to fly off with what he suspected were parts of, or even the entire shell, the prototype aircraft and whatever other component parts were being shipped back to Russia. The crew was about to find they would be taking along an unexpected and very unwelcomed passenger.

The Executioner marched into the cockpit to give the Justice Department pilot his orders.

SERGEI KAKOV WAS becoming suspicious. So far everything looked and felt too easy, too simple. His manufactured security clearance had seen them through the front gate. The SVR contact back in Russia had already seen to it that his laminated card with photo ID and magnetic strip matched the same one as the CIA agent who worked out of Area 51 in Nevada. Punching in the codes on his laptop during the chopper ride to Molokai, Kakov had his clearance, the card rolling out just as the SVR man said it would. A long stint next, once they landed, in the admiral's office where some calls were made around the base, Howard having to issue threats to certain personnel to get them moving. Finally, he reached the airfield, where Howard got busy on a handheld radio, barking out the orders and the forklifts were rolling and loading up the cargo hold of the C-130.

Kakov was an experienced pilot, had flown for the SVR when they fielded crack Spetsnaz teams to quell some unrest or had to terminate some terrorist faction in one of the more unstable republics. He'd flown transports, even fighter jets before, logging thousands of hours in the air and boned up on foreign aircraft in his spare time. A man never knew what manner of duty would call. He had to figure the American Hercules C-130 wasn't much different, with an exception here and there, to an Antonov AN-22. Usually, it took a crew of five to get the C-130 from A to B. A loadmaster wasn't necessary, since three armed men in black overalls were already filling up the cargo hold. Radio operator? Who did he need to speak to, other than the control tower at Vladivostok, where he was already set to land and refuel. Flight engineer, two pilots? Well, he'd just have to pull triple duty. All the high-tech goods were fixed to the console in the cockpit, attached to his monitor that would double as radar screen and radar-jamming transmitter. That task alone had eaten up two hours, figuring out the instrument panel, where to attach what to where. With some reluctant guidance from the admiral, who was also an experienced pilot in his own right—so stated the SVR background intel on Howard—Kakov got it all rigged and working.

Kakov touched the bulge beneath his jacket, aware of the weight of the Makarov pistol stowed in the shoulder rigging. Maybe it was all simply taking too long to get in the air, his nerves jangled and talking to him as his mind boiled with any number of worst-case scenarios. From the chopper ride to the island, where the pilot had thrown him a few curious glances...

What the hell was Howard looking at?

Kakov was marching down the ramp, following Howard's worried gaze, when the admiral growled, "We've got company. A chopper just dropped off someone—I'm sure of it. And he's headed this way."

"Dammit!" Kakov saw they had just finished dropping off the last crate. All three cargo handlers were armed with 9 mm Berettas. "Order these men to go intercept whoever it is. He is trespassing, and he's to be shot on sight. While they are doing that, we will be flying away."

Kakov looked at the stygian darkness that shrouded the dense vegetation in the direction from which the intruder had landed. He couldn't have been there that long, as Kakov spotted the vanishing black dot that was the chopper soaring out to the channel. In the next moment Kakov saw only two of the cargo handlers bounding off the ramp to go greet the trespasser with deadly force. Turning, he saw Howard engaged in some dispute with the remaining man. Something about Kakov's clearance being questioned. Something about a fingerprint check being required before the C-130 could leave the grounds.

Not good.

Somehow the SVR contact had overlooked the not so little matter of a simple fingerprint clearance.

Kakov wheeled, reaching inside his jacket for the

Makarov, prepared to end the discussion if it went on much longer.

THE EXECUTIONER gave silent gratitude to the gods of war for putting him in the right place at the right time. Because his intent going in was to put himself on board for whatever the C-130's destination, Bolan was armed with an M-16/M-203 combo to tackle any large numbers of armed men. Combat harness was in place, spare clips and grenades already fixed. He was outfitted with all combat necessities from the stash he left behind at Fort DeRussy, with backup war bag now slung around his shoulder, stowing his sat link among other tools he'd need to take on whatever was coming next.

Briefly, Bolan wondered why this stretch of the compound would be left thick with a small jungle of trees and tangled wild shrubbery and brush, where anyone so inclined could cut through the cyclone fence. His question was answered when one of the shadows lifted something that looked like a remote-control box, aimed it his way and turned on the lights hidden in the trees.

Bolan was framed in the blinding glare. He was already dodging the opening rounds as the two black-clad figures started cracking off 9 mm Parabellum slugs from their Berettas. Tree bark was shaved off near Bolan's face, huge leaves that looked like some dinosaur's clawed feet blown to pieces beside his head.

On the run, Bolan held back the trigger on his M-16. Two pistols and two guys out in the open were no match for the full-auto barrage of 5.56 mm lead that Bolan ripped out. No sooner were they spinning and falling than the soldier was charging on. Getting a fix on the sprawling grounds beyond the massive transport, the Executioner didn't find any armed guards breaking from the distant buildings. If he didn't know better, Bolan would've sworn the compound was nothing more than a series of abandoned buildings. Maybe it was the hour of the morning, all hands asleep.

No matter.

He was making the ramp when two shots rang out. Bolan was charging ahead when a beefy dark-haired figure spotted the M-16 pointed his way, suddenly pitched away the pistol he'd just used to shoot two men down in cold blood. One of the corpses was the tall man who had made this hijacking possible.

"We can make deal. What is in these crates is far more important than any one man's life."

Bolan never made a deal with a savage. His plan, though, coming in, was to board this plane and take the ride to its final destination. Whatever was crated up, Bolan could venture a good guess, but it was all the source of a conspiracy for which the soldier wanted answers to.

The Executioner, training the assault rifle on the Russian, hit the button to start closing the ramp. The Russian smiled.

"I see. You are flying with me?"

"All the way. I wouldn't want to disappoint whoever is waiting on the other end. I take it whatever is in these crates has been bought and paid for."

"In much money and blood," the Russian answered.

"I also take it you can fly."

"I am experienced pilot for SVR covert operations against terrorism in Russia. It would be—how do you Americans say—no problem."

"Sounds like you've got it all figured out."

"Indeed."

Bolan patted down Mr. Know-It-All, found him clean of weapons, then confiscated the Makarov. The Executioner indicated with his M-16 for his pilot-hostage to move for the cockpit. In a graveyard voice, the soldier told the Russian, "You can fill me in once we're in the air."

CHAPTER FOURTEEN

Syria

Muhmad Nabaj scowled at his men. They were feasting on lamb, eggplant, chicken and bulgur, the cracked wheat of the region, all of his freedom fighters sipping strong Turkish coffee. They were living it up, celebrating their Bekaa victory against the infidels, while he was dying inside from fear and uncertainty.

His stomach churning with anxiety, Nabaj felt his insides knotted up all the way into his bowels, and silently cursed this terrible clutching of dread. Since their flight across the border to the colonel's compound, he hadn't eaten, but had somehow forced himself to swallow a few gulps of tepid water from his canteen during the day. He desperately wanted to sleep, tired to the bone, but knew sleeping that night was a fool's dream. He envied their appetites for a moment, then looked away and gazed at the burlap sack by his feet. Perhaps it was the stone tube inside the sack and the story from a now dead man that so troubled him.

But why?

"Saladin," Nabaj quietly said to the man who had heard the incredible tale told to him before the archaeologists were shot. "Come with me."

The short, heavily bearded Saladin stood and followed Nabaj away from the long metal table to a far corner in the room of their barracks.

Nabaj nearly whispered as he said, "Tell me again what was said about the scroll inside the tube."

"The old one, he was raving about the end of the world, insane he was with fear, I have to believe. Do you really care about the ramblings from some crazy man?"

"Tell me!"

Saladin blinked at the sudden ferocity in his leader's eyes. "He said their John the Divine had been told the exact date on the infidel calendar of when the world would end. The old one said it was written on the scroll inside the tube. It also names certain catastrophic events that will bring about the end of the world. Before I shot him, I listened, for I, too, found it all incredible."

"But he seemed sincere, a believer?"

Saladin shrugged. "Facing certain death can do strange things to a man's mind. Who can say? The Christians claim some apocalypse will engulf the world in fire and death, famine and plague. The Jews believe their messiah is coming to save mankind from itself. Then there is our own Mahdi, who is believed by imams to come soon someday and give back to Islam our rightful place of glory in the world. The infidels have all manner of lunatics and cults who say the world will end any day, but how or when none of them knows. Who can say? Why care?"

"Let me be the judge of what to care about. What else did he tell you?"

"I have told you already."

"Yes, I know. Tell me again."

"The old one claimed if the scroll is looked upon by human eyes, that man will burst into...he said something about spontaneous human combustion."

"A human fireball," Nabaj muttered, and stared back at the sack.

"It is not my place to tell you what to do. But if it troubles you that much, why not just open it?"

Nabaj glared at Saladin for implying he was afraid of superstitious nonsense. "Perhaps I will."

"May I go?"

"Yes, yes, go eat. I would not want you to starve to death."

Standing alone, Nabaj began hearing two voices in his head. One voice told him to go ahead and open the scroll, reveal to himself and the others that it was a mad hoax, scribbling on a piece of papyrus naming the time and place of the end of the world nothing more than fantasy drummed up by a feeble mind. Then the other voice whispered from some dark corner in his head, warning him to leave it alone. Nabaj didn't know what to do. One look at the colonel and he knew he was set for what, he believed, they called in the military another dressing-down.

The door opened and Nabaj found the colonel's sun-burnished, hawkish face aimed at him.

"A moment with you," the colonel said. "Outside."

Nabaj strode out the door, aware already the colonel was displeased with their recent trouble in the

Bekaa. While the colonel clasped his hands behind his back, Nabaj found himself unable to meet the man's penetrating stare, took a moment instead to let his eyes wander around the compound, then followed the beams of searchlights mounted above the razor-topped wire strung along the fence. The glaring fingers of white light quickly petered out, swallowed by the darkness shrouding the valley and the hills to the east beyond the chain-link fence. Nabaj felt the night world out there so quiet and still the silence only stoked yet more unease, coiling his guts even tighter. What was he so afraid of? And why? The antiaircraft batteries and the racks of Soviet surface-to-air missiles seemed unreal to him right then. Worse, he knew what they were doing belowground, Syria's best minds hard at work creating an intermediate-range nuclear missile, but they were having problems with the delivery system.

He didn't know much about nuclear weapons, but he'd heard enough to know they were delicate, intricate, perhaps even temperamental things. They were dependent on elaborately involved delivery and detonation systems. One glitch, and all that would be left was a hunk of useless uranium or plutonium in a scrap shell. The Russians, he knew, had sown the seeds here to put his country on the map as a world power to be feared. The rumor was that very soon Syria would have two, perhaps even three nuclear-armed missiles that could vaporize Israel.

"I feed your men," Colonel Sandi began. "I give you shelter and safe haven. I personally receive the funds from Damascus to sponsor our jihad against the Israelis. My point, you ask? What you did in the Bekaa was reckless to the point where I may now be in jeopardy of an Israeli attack, if my source in Beirut is correct. I believe him. My point is I do not like holding my hand out to you and having it bitten at a most critical time. Look over there,'' the colonel said, pointing to the vacant area where the Soviet tanks were usually parked. ''No T-62s. My soldiers, sixty strong, have not returned from the Bekaa. My radar is suddenly malfunctioning. I have heard no report from my commander in the Bekaa, no word why my tanks have not returned.''

''What, exactly, are you saying, Colonel?''

''I am saying it is always most quiet before the storm. I am saying your slaughtering the Israeli-American archaeologists could haunt me, could destroy everything the Russians have helped us get so close to attaining.''

''I told you. I had no choice. They would have found our main weapons cache in those ruins. I would have lost—''

The colonel waved a hand. ''I have heard this already. Your forays into Lebanon were meant to recruit martyrs who would go to glory in attacks on Israeli soldiers. Not massacre well-known Israelis and Americans who would be missed and whose blood would cry out for vengeance.''

''There are no innocent infidels in my mind, Colonel.''

''Nor mine. But from now on choose your victims more carefully.'' He let the warning sink in, then said, ''Since you returned here safely, with the obvious blessing of God, and with your Russian weapons in the trucks, I would suggest you be alert for any show of force that may strike our compound. I have a patrol out there now, prepared to alert me, in the event some Israeli commandos attempt to move in and destroy all my work here. Put the food and the coffee down, and have your men arm themselves.''

Wheeling, the colonel marched off for his command-and-control center. Alone again, Nabaj searched the darkness beyond the compound, and felt the fear gnawing on his stomach so bad he thought he might throw up.

Stony Man Farm, Virginia

''WHAT THE HELL is going on?'' Brognola growled.

Price had long since received word Phoenix Force had jumped. The team in the Computer Room was now braced and on the edge of their seats for the opportunity to watch Phoenix Force in combat, live and in color. Now the giant monitor was a wavy haze of static. Brognola nearly bit his cigar in two. Price was on the sat link, trying to raise McCarter while Kurtzman and Tokaido were pounding on the keyboards hooked to the TV monitor.

''Nothing wrong with the satellite linkup,'' Kurtzman announced.

''Check the monitor. It could be something as simple as a freaking picture tube.''

''I doubt it,'' Kurtzman said.

''I don't like this one bit,'' Brognola said.

The bad news got worse a moment later as Price said, ''It seems the minicams were blown off during the jump. David says they're down and all in one piece. No cams.''

"I thought they were supposed to fix those when they landed," Kurtzman said.

"I guess they didn't," Price replied. "Between the fall and the freezing cold air, the adhesive cracked."

"And now we just lost five very expensive mini-cams to the Syrian desert," Kurtzman grumbled.

"Well, so much for watching our troops in action," Akira groused.

"With the numbers they may be facing," Wethers stated, "it would have been useful for us to have monitored the action, front and back, alert Phoenix if they missed something on their sixes."

"That's not the worst of it, people," Price said, as grim as hell.

"Now what?" Brognola growled.

"David signed off in a hurry," Price answered. "They nearly dropped right into the lap of a Syrian patrol."

"Don't tell me they're already under fire before they even get into position and before Grimaldi can fire away?" Brognola wanted to know.

"Not yet. They're moving in as we speak to take care of the problem," Price announced.

Brognola cursed. Another snafu.

"It gets worse," Carmen Delahunt said.

"How can it get any worse?" Brognola asked.

"I'm monitoring NRO sat recon of the region. There's a lot of air traffic over Lebanon."

"Let me guess. Coming from Israel," Brognola said.

"Yes," Delahunt answered.

"I've confirmed it with my Mossad source," Katz added. "As of now, the Israelis are officially in the hunt. The good news is their F-16s are blowing up a bunch of Syrian tanks in the Bekaa. If they stay tied up in a protracted fight in Lebanon, it might give Phoenix just enough time to get in, do the dirty work and get the hell out.''

"People, do we understand what we might be saying here?'' Brognola raked a solemn look over the team. "We might be looking at the start of a major war in the Middle East. A war that could have a ripple effect all the way to Iran, Russia, God knows where it will end. Do I need to elaborate on what could happen if the Israelis start lobbing around a few nukes?''

The extended silence spoke grim volumes.

And Hal Brognola once again saw a world on fire flaming up from the darkest cavern of his mind.

Russia

MAJOR ZHERKOVSKY watched as they hauled the parachute out of the sludge.

"He is on the run, this American pilot,'' the SVR agent said.

"There are two sets of footprints, comrade.''

"Two?''

Zherkovsky pointed at the ground where the glare of the Mi-8 Hip's lights washed over the area in front of them.

"Very well. We have two Americans who piloted the craft and are somewhere, moving east.''

Zherkovsky stood like a piece of stone in the rotor wash, his eyelids slitted against the blast of whirling snow, searching the darkness of the woods beyond the transport choppers. Yet another mystery, and perhaps another set of problems. And, incredibly enough, as he watched his soldiers roaming the woods with their Geiger counters, there wasn't the first hint of radiation in the area.

"There should be high levels of radiation still, given the size of the explosion," Zherkovsky commented.

"I do not understand, either," Denkov said. "Perhaps, once our scientists discover what they tell me already is some type of element they have never seen before, we will learn that the Americans have developed some advanced form of nuclear energy."

"Perhaps."

"You sound doubtful, comrade. Speak up."

Zherkovsky grunted. "It is not important."

"Let me guess. You are disturbed because I informed you there are certain important men coming here from Moscow to oversee the compound."

"Oversee? Or take it over? And precisely who are these men?"

"Let us just say they are former KGB agents who are now important businessmen with much political influence in Moscow."

"Gangsters, you mean."

"If you prefer to call them that, but I would not, at least not to their faces."

"I am getting a very bad feeling about where this is all headed, Comrade Denkov. I am beginning to suspect there has been some renegade operation involving this craft. I am beginning to feel the SVR has a few wild cards who are holding hands with the Russian Mafia. Maybe even a CIA agent or two who have sold their country out, who knew about this craft, its origins.''

Denkov attempted to chuckle it off. ''You make it sound as if it is all some great conspiracy. You are seeing bogeymen, comrade, that is all.''

Zherkovsky turned his head, peered at the SVR man, but said nothing. Bogeymen? Corruption had become something like a formalized institution in Russia. The bogeymen were those few with all the money, primarily the Russian Mafia, who could buy and sell entire legions of politicians, officers in the military, even SVR agents. Nothing about Russia surprised Zherkovsky these days. His country was a vast out-of-control mess, and he feared the worst days were just over the horizon.

''I suggest you have a large search party strike out to the east,'' Denkov said. ''I will scramble a few more helicopters to help in the search. We will find these pilots. We will learn how this craft works and how to fly it.''

''I hear an 'or else.'''

''What you hear is the sound of Mother Russia prepared to take a giant leap ahead on the evolutionary scale of technology.''

Zherkovsky looked away from the sudden fanaticism he saw burning in the SVR man's eyes. This was not good, he thought. Whether he liked it or not, the major suspected he was going to be forced into a conspiracy that may or may not end up taking his life. There were decisions he would have to make in the coming hours. Did he just step aside and let the Russian Mafia run roughshod over him? Or did he stand up and assert his authority?

Either way, in time Zherkovsky knew he would be forced into a life-or-death struggle. The hour of truth was just around the corner.

Syria

SOMETIMES UNFORESEEN events popped up way beyond the control of even the most experienced combat veteran. In short, shit happened and a warrior, McCarter knew, had to take charge on the spot without even blinking and turn the fan around.

Like now.

McCarter was cradling his HK MP-5 subgun when he tapped his com link, whispering to each of the four Phoenix Force warriors in turn, getting a read on their positions, handing out the orders.

He was short and to the point. They were to kill the bastards, quick, somebody making sure they found and took down the one with the radio pack in the opening rounds.

Crouched in a narrow gulley, he watched the APC rolling his way. He counted a full squad, with two figures in the cab framed in his NVD goggles. McCarter couldn't figure why the Syrians would march an armed patrol their way, unless their radar had picked up the Spectre, which presented another series of potential fiascos. Judging the manner in which the Syrian soldiers were casually marching along the steppe, looking east, McCarter was sure he and his men could make quick work of the enemy here. The Syrians obviously didn't know their positions, if they even had a clue to begin with that there were a few armed shadows scoping them out and ready to drop the hammer. Maybe it was just a routine patrol, McCarter thought.

No matter. They had to go.

Since he was the last one out the door of the Spectre, McCarter had landed the farthest east, with the other commandos making the deep yawn of the wadi their touchdown point. The ex-SAS commando searched the darkness of the lunar landscape to the west and spotted several hunched shadows heading his way. He was counting off their pace, gauging his own distance to the Syrian squad.

Phoenix Force cut the gap to less than fifty yards.

McCarter tapped his com link, eyeballing the marching troops dead ahead, thirty yards and angling off to the west. His webbing, like the rest of the team's, was loaded down with fragmentation, flash-stun and incendiary grenades, spare clips for his SMG. Standard Beretta 93-R in hip holster, commando daggers in ankle sheathing all around. The fifty pounds of C-4 was an added burden, but with racing adrenaline McCarter knew he'd feel light on his feet once the shooting started and he was charging ahead.

The Phoenix Force leader tapped the button on his com link. "On my say-so, then let it rip. Keep on moving in, mates. You have their rear, and I'll hit them from the port side."

McCarter rose, edged ahead, sighted down on three figures clearly framed in the headlights of the APC. Lady Luck smiled a moment later as he made out the radio backpack. Of course, there could be another operative in the transport hold, but with speed of move-ment...

McCarter hit the com link and gave the word to attack.

"Go!"

James, Hawkins, Encizo and Manning opened fire at the same instant. Breaking cover, fanning out and surging ahead, they blazed away, three HK MP-5 SMGs, with Hawkins the designated M-60 man-eater. The big shadow that was McCarter boiled out of the gulley, spraying the pointmen with a long raking burst of 9 mm Parabellum shockers. The radioman went first, his line of communication to the compound sparking into mangled ruins as he toppled for hard-packed earth soaking up his blood.

James raced up the port side of the APC. The driver gave the big Soviet-made transport rig some gas, gunning the engine in an attempt to break free of the ring of lead doom. By now, AK-47s were returning fire, but the Syrians had been caught off guard, signaling to the Phoenix Force warriors the patrol was more of a routine matter than a search-and-destroy hunting party.

Holding back on the trigger of his SMG, James blew in the driver's-side window, exploding the wheelman's skull in a burst of dark flying gore.

Manning, Encizo and Hawkins rolled up on the passenger side, their barrage of lead cutting down more Syrians as they scrambled away from the APC.

"I've got the back!" Encizo shouted over the roar of autofire.

Crouched, the stocky Cuban thrust the muzzle of his SMG into the darkness of the troop hold. Empty.

The shooting ended when Hawkins mowed down

two Syrian soldiers who danced away from the front end of the APC. A quick check of the dead by the Stony Man team to make sure no possums rose up, and they gathered, all eyes searching the darkness beyond the edge of the hills to the south.

"It's what, three miles through that wadi?" James wanted to know.

"We may have cut the odds some," Hawkins said, "but if there's another patrol out here we better hope Jack's on top of his game."

"Could be the radar jammer is still fouled up," Manning stated. "Could be the tangos already know we're here. What the hell, we've seen snafus before."

"I don't think so," James said. "If Jack says our bird's fit to fly, you can take that to the bank."

"Gary, you ride with me, take the wheel," McCarter said. "We ride in through that wadi, get as close as possible, then leg it in. We stick to the plan. I'll raise Jack and rearrange the numbers. Let's roll!"

Phoenix Force boarded the APC.

CHAPTER FIFTEEN

Above the Pacific Ocean

He was no Jack Grimaldi, by any stretch, and would never even pretend to put himself in ace-pilot ranks. But Bolan had flown in enough C-130s, even copiloted a time or two, to see the Russian could handle the big transport plane like a seasoned pilot.

The soldier checked the vast darkness beyond the glazing of the flight deck, then to his flanks, peering through the "eyebrow" windows. No light show of unidentified flying objects of any kind, of the earth or beyond, had made their appearance when they'd put Molokai behind, finally climbing to a ceiling of thirty-five thousand feet, where they were now coasting along at top speed over the clouds. It was an endless expanse of blackness out there, but the soldier knew daylight would break soon from the east. They were flying blind, lights off except for the soft glow burning off the instrument panel. In the ghoulish-looking green bask shining off the monitor of the Russian's radar receiver-jammer, Bolan caught the man sporting a grin that didn't exactly inspire trust in the soldier.

"Will be long flight. Suggest you sit back and enjoy the bus ride."

"What's your name?" Bolan asked in Russian, just to let the guy know any sudden radio transmissions he might have to make to set up their landing would be understood. And just in case he had any notions to alert somebody on the other end about his unwelcomed passenger and the soldier found a few AK-47s there and waiting on the ground.

The Russian turned and blinked at Bolan. "Ah, very good. We will not have some failure to communicate should the need arise where we must speak in Russian. I am Kakov. Sergei. And you are?"

"Comrade Badasski. What's the story?"

"Story?"

Bolan kept his M-16 by his side as he pinned Kakov with an icy look from the copilot's seat. "Everything from *A* to *Z*. Who, what, when, where and why. First you tell me about our refueling stop."

"We fly nearly straight due northwest, my good Comrade Badasski. There is an island, about seven hours away in the Pacific. It is under control of SVR. They own the island under the name of an oil company out of Ukraine. Of course, there is no such oil company."

"How many on the ground?"

Kakov shrugged. "I am not sure. Why? You going to start some war, take this war with you into Mother Russia? One man?"

"Don't make me repeat myself. And I'll ask the questions."

"You have the gun."

"Don't forget it."

"We land on island. On my maps, everything has been outlined and detailed. I have outlined all American military bases around Japan. We skirt by Japan, fly past Sakhalin Island, then down for Vladivostok. One more fuel stop. Then we are off to Siberia. It is military installation near the Ural Mountains. Top secret nuclear facility. Compound ZX545. It houses many of my country's nuclear missiles. It is also where the American UFO was shot down. And its shell is being kept there, I understand."

"Are you SVR or Russian Mafia?"

"I worked for Yuri Mosnivoc. Many former KGB agents are part of Mosnivoc's organization. I am former SVR. When Comrade Yuri was falsely accused and arrested—"

"I know all about the FBI sitting on him in Brooklyn. And skip the speech on Comrade Yuri's sterling character."

The Russian grinned. "Maybe if you tell me what you don't know, this will go much easier."

"One other thing—I don't like smartasses. What's Mosnivoc's connection to Fugasami and why the hijacking of a prototype U.S. aircraft?"

"SVR has known about your Area 51 for many years. You would be surprised how easy money will make even those sworn to secrecy and under the threat of death even by your own speak the truth and reveal secrets. Even the KGB, the SVR's predecessor, was engineering an attempt to steal one of these flying disks several years back out of Nevada. Mosnivoc still has much influence on what happens in Russia. There are even several CIA agents who were aware of Centurion X who were convinced, again by money, to lead us to Molokai, where we made contact with the late Admiral Howard, who ran the classified base we just left behind. Howard fell to Fugasami's geisha. Blackmail pictures.''

''Benny's finished. Forget him.''

''What do you mean?''

''He's dead. I shot him. Your Yakuza connection has been chopped off at the head. I see you're not smiling now.''

''It does not matter. The SVR and its—what you call Russian Mafia—allies will have what they want.''

''Why steal it?''

''Because it was there? How should I know? We learn now the thing was perhaps even capable of delivery of nuclear missiles. It is simply our way of keeping up with the other side. And make no mistake, many in my country still consider America the enemy.''

And likewise Bolan, ever the grim realist, knew Russia was still crawling with plenty of bad guys, from top to bottom, despite the smiling face of democracy a few naive or deceitful political types wanted to show the West. In fact, Bolan knew Russia was on shakier ground now than before the so-called fall of communism.

''So, what is the plan, Stan?'' the Russian wanted to know, once more showing Bolan the grin that would have done a used-car salesman proud.

''For you to keep talking and filling in the blanks. Then I'm going back there to take a look at what your SVR and Mafia buddies want so bad. A little word of advice. While I'm gone, if you try to phone home and have a few shooters attempt to storm this plane when we land to fuel up—''

"Yes, yes, I know. I will be the first one you shoot."

Now it was Bolan's turn to smile. "You're right, Sergei. I think we've gotten beyond any failure to communicate."

Syria

PHOENIX FORCE WAS in place and ready to move thirty minutes after taking out the Syrian patrol. They had ridden in, slow and with the lights out, the APC now parked deep in the wadi to the east. After quickly touching base with Grimaldi, McCarter adjusted the game plan.

It was just about time to start the fireworks.

McCarter, Encizo and James were hunkered down in an off-shooting spine of the wadi, hidden a hundred yards directly across from the southeast end of the compound. Manning and Hawkins were long gone, having skirted the base of some foothills to secure their attack point to the northeast. The three Phoenix Force warriors took in the illuminated compound.

"These places always look huge compared to the sat imagery when you're ready to hammer down," Encizo whispered to McCarter.

Until the attack was launched, McCarter had ordered radio silence between the five of them, even buzzing the Farm to warn them not to attempt a call on his com link. He would have preferred no talking right then, even in low voices, but he knew the adrenaline was charging them up.

"The camo netting wasn't there on the pics," James said. "Tells me they suddenly want to hide from some eyes in the sky."

"A little late for that," McCarter stated.

"The way I'm seeing those soldiers roaming around, something tells me we—or somebody—is expected," James said. "I'm seeing a lot of bad nerves over there."

McCarter checked the illuminated dial of his chronometer, then searched the black skies to the south. Grimaldi had stated the Spectre's ETA was an agonizing fifteen minutes and counting once they had disgorged from the commandeered APC to move in on foot.

McCarter gave the sprawling grounds a long surveillance. Four MiGs were grounded midway up the east quadrant of the compound. As James had observed, at least twelve AK-47-toting Syrians in uniform were marching in what McCarter read as nervous steps around the barracks. A figure walked outside the building.

"I don't see a uniform on that one," James said, taking a closer look through his binoculars. "Bingo. That's our number-one tango, Nabaj, in the flesh."

"We can kill the proverbial two vultures with one stone," Encizo said. "The night's shaping up."

McCarter knew the night would be a long and bloody mess, even if they launched the attack by the numbers. At the deep northwest end of the compound, he made out the entrance to the reprocessing plant, which had been dug into the foothills of the Anti-Lebanon Mountains. Five Syrian soldiers were guarding the entrance. Some excavation had to have still been going on, since McCarter noted the half-dozen massive hydraulic digging machines. If it was a typical plant inside, there would be an enrichment area, fabrication plant, and the breeder reactors, with hermetically sealed doors, decon area, the works, primitive as they might find once they penetrated the entrance. Hawkins and Manning would have to sweep on the move with their Geiger counters for any areas that were hot. Enough C-4 planted and spread around, going primarily for the breeder reactor, the seals of fuel rods, and the Syrian's labor of war here would be crippled.

"This waiting's going to get my last nerve. Come on, Jack, let's get this show started," Encizo urged quietly.

"No tanks I can find," James said. "If they're out and about, that cuts the odds some in our favor."

McCarter read the grim expressions on their faces, even spotted the sheen of sweat on the brows of Encizo and James. Since they'd donned the standard thermal insulation beneath their combat blacksuits, warding against the freezing cold air when jumping to begin their HALO, they were now all perfectly comfortable in the chilly night air on the ground. Racing adrenaline fueled the warrior fire in their hearts, adding to the heat trapped by the second layer of clothing, and even McCarter tasted the sweat beading up on his lips.

Another look at the compound beyond the fence, McCarter aware part of the Spectre's initial strafe would see whole sections of the fence blown away for easy penetration, and the Phoenix Force leader took in the motor pool beyond the buildings he figured as the troop and terrorist quarters. There were a dozen jeeps, maybe half of them fitted with machine guns. Antiaircraft batteries were unmanned at the moment, outfitted with what looked like a Russian ZSU-23-4 cannon, some SAMs aimed skyward. Four guard towers were strategically placed around the compass. Suddenly, lights flared on in each of the four towers. Search beams began raking the steppe, gliding up the massive black wall of the mountains. The south light began hitting the sky, wandering around the dark heavens.

The Phoenix Force warriors crouched lower in the gulley.

"That's not good," Encizo rasped.

"Don't tell me their radar maybe picked up the Spectre," James said.

"If the base commander tried to radio that patrol, then these blokes are on high alert."

McCarter saw the lights weren't reaching out their way, figured their presence remained undetected. He checked his chronometer. Three minutes and counting until the Spectre showed and let it rip.

That much time could prove an eternity, McCarter knew.

Stony Man Farm, Virginia

BROGNOLA FIGURED they'd caught a lucky break when Katz finally raised Colonel Meissel. He listened, his heart pounding away in his ears, as Katz urged the colonel to hold off hitting the Syrian compound from his radio console.

"Colonel, our men are in place. From my understanding of your situation, you are in the process of mopping up things on your end in the Bekaa. I kindly ask you to not send in your fighter jets. We have a gunship en route as we speak to clear the way for our people to penetrate and take out the plant.''

''I understand your predicament. Understand I am breaking orders now from my superiors to even speak with you. Unfortunately, it is not my call whether the F-16s and F-15s fly on to attack the compound.''

Katz cursed. ''The major, right?''

''He is in charge.''

''Where is he? I want a word with him.''

''He is in his transport plane, directing the battle from the air while I am prepared to move in and capture any Syrian ground troops or help my own men should the Syrians not give up. Since the major has made it clear this is his operation, he has effectively cut me off from any communications with him. I do not even have his radio frequency.''

''Are you still going nuclear?''

''Given this new set of circumstances, where the lives of your people are on the line, I believe, should I be able to somehow contact the major, we can cancel any nuclear strike.''

''Just make it happen, Colonel.''

''Call me back in, let us say, twenty minutes.''

Brognola stood there, feeling the grim looks aimed his way by the Farm's best.

''It's touch and go, Hal,'' Katz said.

''We'd better damn well hope the colonel can talk some sense in that gung-ho idiot of a major,'' Brognola growled.

Kurtzman wondered aloud if Lyons was having any

better luck with his interrogation of Carlington in the War Room.

"We'll know soon enough, provided, of course," Brognola said, "Lyons doesn't get too carried away and kill the guy by accident."

THE STATE DEPARTMENT man became a human missile as soon as Lyons marched him into the War Room. Lyons sent Carlington airborne on a running throw, one hand clawed into the seat of his pants, another fist taking up space between the shoulder blades of the man's suit jacket. Sailing down the length of the conference table, Carlington bowled through Brognola's wingback and hit the floor with a thud.

"You can't do this!" Carlington roared, tried to gather himself to stand when Lyons rolled over him and belted a backhand off his sputtering mouth.

"Take a look at me," Lyons growled. "I got lucky. Twenty-something stitches while dodging a thousand or so bullets and flying shrapnel when your Russian hitters came at us out of nowhere. I could start counting up the unlucky, meaning all the good FBI agents who won't be going home for dinner with their families. Do you know where you are? But of course not. You were blindfolded the whole way in, which should tell you you're somewhere you're not supposed to be or know about. You're somewhere where if I don't get some answers from you, I can march you outside, dig a shallow grave and eighty-six your carcass."

Carlington held up his hands. "All right, but if I talk, what's in it for me?"

"How about you keep on breathing?"

"That's it? I'm prepared to spill my guts about a Russian Mafia-SVR-CIA connection and you're offering me, what, a long stay in a federal prison?"

"I won't make any promises, but if you give me something I can run with, I'll put in a good word for you. That's as good as it gets."

Carlington showed Lyons a withering look of despair and seemed to ponder his options, which were next to zero.

"There's a chain of command over at State," Carlington began. "Several of them are former CIA operatives who worked with me over in Russia. Two are former NSA ops."

"I'm listening."

"It's going to get ugly."

"It's already ugly."

And Lyons listened as the State man began to spill his guts about a conspiracy that reached all the way across the Atlantic. By the time Carlington was finished some twenty minutes later, Lyons had key names and an address where the State man claimed the person in charge had set up a meeting. Lyons got the time from Carlington for the get-together and told him he was going to put in a call to his buddy.

If nothing else, Lyons knew Able Team could tie up some loose ends. There was still some butcher's work to be done. And after what he'd just heard, it would be good to get back out there and nail a few more traitors who waved the Stars and Stripes for show while spitting on it behind everybody's back.

CHAPTER SIXTEEN

Aboard the C-130

The Executioner almost decided to leave the unknown for someone else's viewing privilege. Answers to all the mystery and hoopla, all the backstabbing by renegade SVR and CIA types and a conspiracy to steal the flying disk and tales of its origins—all would be waiting at the end of the ride anyway, a Russian nuclear-missile silo called Compound ZX545 in the Ural Mountains of Siberia.

If nothing else, the soldier could at least be certain of encountering the earthly touch, at any rate, bad men with guns, with dark schemes and hearts seething with lust for money and power and knowledge of something they had no business knowing about, but in the final analysis only sought leverage to control, dominate, manipulate. And he was prepared to take on all comers involved in the vast shadow scheme to steal something from his own country. Whether shades of Roswell or Area 51 or a dozen other tales of close encounters would reveal the truth in Mother Russia when he reached the final destination, Bolan wasn't sure, pretty much didn't even care.

Whatever, the Executioner dealt in reality, what he could see and deal with in his face, especially now more than ever on this current agenda that had begun as a campaign that had dropped in his lap as a favor to a friend. Little gray men with heads and eyes like grasshoppers and whopping tales of spacecraft from another world or dimension were the stuff and trappings of fantasy.

Or was it all fantasy?

Curiosity finally got the better of Bolan to know what all the flak was about, why so many had sold out their souls, their country and even their own lives. Whether for a quick buck or to keep pace with the other side, everyone prepared to hurl a litany of excuses and rationalizations for murder his way, it didn't matter to the soldier. A traitor was a traitor in Bolan's mind.

Kakov left in the cockpit, the soldier took his stroll to have a look, perhaps, into tomorrow's technology. He needed to alert the Farm about his intentions anyway, his sat link in a nylon satchel around one shoulder. With the maps detailing the flight of the hijacked C-130, aware of its final resting place, he knew that at some point he would require intel from the Farm, perhaps even need help getting in and out of Russia. From what he suspected, after his grilling of Kakov, he was facing a renegade SVR-Russian Mafia operation involving the American UFO, with, it seemed, some help from a few of the so-called good guys on the home team.

Bolan suspected his problems had only just begun.

Taking a titanium-tipped crowbar from a workbench amidships, the soldier walked on through the soft glow of the overhead lights, the M-16 slung around the other shoulder, the thrum of the four turbo-prop engines in his ears. He went to the first of the largest of the crates and worked the lid off with a few good twists of the crowbar.

And stared down at the fantastic.

One look at its size, squeezed into the cargo hold and taking up space from port to starboard, and he figured the disk didn't take up much more space than maybe two M-2 Bradley tanks parked side by side. He ran a hand over the glassy-smooth dark gray surface. The skin on the craft felt like hardened wax to his touch. No nuts, no bolts or even the hint of the edges of parts that had been even been melded together for assembly. It was just one round piece.

A shell.

He struck it with the butt of his M-16 to see if it was hollow and found he could have been striking granite as the blow jarred him to the bone. The shell was just large enough to hold two men. Pilots, right. But how did they get into the thing? Bolan wondered. No windows, no doors, no hatch he could find.

Opening two smaller crates, Bolan found what appeared to be a series of amplifiers. Again, no outlets, plugs or wiring. It could have dropped out of the sky in one big piece. When he picked one up, it felt lighter than air in his hands.

He'd seen enough, but opened the other two big crates just to look. Inside he found two more shells of disks.

The Executioner hauled out his sat link to let the Farm know he was bound for Russia.

A whole lot of death, a bunch of killing of the bad

guys on the other end may or may not solve the UFO mystery.

Whatever waited, the Executioner was taking this bus ride to the end of the line, to the ends of earth, if need be.

Someone needed to answer up.

Syria

THE AIR OF PANIC around him nearly struck Nabaj as slapstick. The colonel was bellowing at his men to take up positions around the perimeter of the compound. Give him two squads full strength inside the plant, he shouted at the assembled soldiers. Then he chose the ones he wanted to man the antiaircraft batteries, even though Nabaj knew it would be long agonizing minutes before the SAMs were cranked up and ready to fly.

Perhaps it was because Nabaj was so strung out on fear, exhaustion and worry that the scene he now witnessed wanted to make him laugh. Out of nowhere, the colonel was charging around, roaring how he hadn't heard from his patrol or his tank commander in Lebanon. Radar was jammed. Radio communication to Damascus was buzzing with nothing but static. But apparently one of the colonel's contacts in the Bekaa had gotten through to alert him his tanks were under fire by Israeli fighter jets.

Would the Israelis then veer their F-16s east and bomb the compound off the map? he wondered.

"I need your men to fall in with my soldiers!" the colonel shouted.

"But, of course," Nabaj answered, an AK-47 in

one hand. He held his ground in front of the door to their quarters. The tube was wedged behind the sash around his waist. If they were going to be attacked, perhaps now was the time to look at the scroll. If he was going to die, what would it matter if he burst into a spontaneous fireball or was blown off the face of the earth by Israeli fighter jets?

Nabaj turned to go through the doorway when he heard what sounded like distant rolling thunder. He froze, looked south and made out some mammoth flying machine about the size of a cruise ship descending for the compound.

The Syrian laughed. Even as he charged through the doorway, looking for cover, he knew it was wasted effort. But he had to try to save himself. Maybe if he got lucky…

The sky opened up on deafening peals of thunder, a sound that shook Nabaj to the bone. It sounded to him like the end of the world, that apocalypse he'd heard mentioned back in the Bekaa.

"WHOA!"

Hawkins and Manning wanted to watch the show, but as the Spectre unloaded the works on the compound, so many explosions hurled so much debris for hundreds of yards in every direction that they were forced to duck as rubble flew their way.

Hawkins had heard Grimaldi boast enough about the Spectre to know what the gun crew could dish out: a 105 mm howitzer thundering away on its hydraulic mount just ahead of the rear cargo ramp; twin 20 mm Vulcan Gatling cannons and one Bofors

40 mm .70-caliber cannon, the triple army slayers mounted and speaking hellish volumes.

Hawkins couldn't resist risking a long look at hell on earth down there.

The MiGs were turned to flaming scrap. The anti-aircraft batteries went next. The fuel depot erupted in a volcano of screaming fire.

Grimaldi had come in low, nap of the earth, the gun crew banging it out as soon as the Spectre closed on the southern end of the compound. Cutting back the speed so that the massive war bird seemed to creep along, some chugging ocean liner but with guns, Hawkins thought, Grimaldi and company had more than half the compound boiling in fireballs and flying wreckage by the time they were midway along the strafe.

The guard towers went up in brilliant flashes of fire. The motor pool vanished in vomiting lines of thundering fireballs. Every building out in the open took hits from the Bofors cannon, which, if handled by two seasoned pros, could pump out one hundred rounds per minute.

Grimaldi and company were going for the gold.

"HOLY…"

McCarter had to silently echo Encizo's awe. It was some show Grimaldi and mates were putting on. The Phoenix Force leader could see through all the smoke and fire and flying body parts that long sections of the fence had been blown up.

Easy access, but whatever damage the gunship did, McCarter knew it was up to the ground troops to nail it down.

With the Spectre flying directly above and right behind them, grimly aware of what they were seconds away from charging into, McCarter knew he'd feel lucky to walk away from this with little more than some ear damage. It looked and sounded as if the end of the world had come falling straight out of the stars above. Cannons kept thundering on as the Spectre sailed along the east edge, letting them have it with hundreds of rounds in the time it took to blink once or twice.

Tapping the button on his com link, McCarter shouted through to Hawkins and Manning. "T.J.! Gary! Let's move in!"

The order was copied. McCarter rose to the sound and fury of men dying fast and hard, and led his team down into the swirling fires of death.

IT HAD TO HAVE been God's will that saw him safely through the opening rounds, Nabaj believed.

Thinking he had to have been chosen then to live and carry on the jihad, no matter how many of his own men died, he crabbed through the rubble of the barracks, sliding through pools of blood, kicking through a severed leg or arm here and there.

The tube!

Turning as he heard the screams of men in agony and the earsplitting roar of explosions outside, he searched the heaped stone and strewed bodies. He found that, incredibly, despite whatever was leveling the compound out there, at least three-quarters of the barracks remained standing. He could hide perhaps, he figured, long enough until the flying beast moved on, then escape into the desert. He had contacts, friends all over the Syrian desert who would give him shelter, food, drink. He would rather live to fight another day.

In the wavering firelight beyond the smoking maw where the building had taken a direct hit, his gaze fell on the jagged shards of the tube. The papyrus scroll was partially open.

Did he dare?

He stood, took a step toward it, heard the awful moaning of his men in pain but left them where they had fallen.

He hesitated, then decided, why not?

Aboard the C-130

"IF I DIDN'T KNOW you better, Striker, I'd say you were stark raving mad."

Bolan allowed a tight grin over Brognola's consternation. Updates all around, and the Executioner knew the big Fed and the team at the Farm had their hands full with three separate crisis points, and the fires were a long way from being put out. Bolan knew the last thing they needed was this latest headache. It would be no small feat to pull off what he intended to do, but the soldier saw no other way but to fly into Russia and go for broke against the conspirators who'd engineered the hijacking of the prototype U.S. aircraft.

"From what Carl learned from the State guy he grilled," Kurtzman told him over the sat link, "some loose ends are starting to tie together. That's the good news. Able Team is moving in soon to cut the head off the Hydra on our end. The bad news is that you'll be hung out to be skinned alive once you touch down near this Russian compound.''

''I've given that some thought,'' Bolan said. ''When the time comes, I'll have my flyboy do a quick aerial recon, get the lay of the land and move in on foot. I was actually counting on a little help from Phoenix.''

''They'll be lucky if they walk away from Syria in one piece,'' Brognola said. ''But if they do come out the other side…dammit, Striker, we're talking about creating our own private little war and on Russian turf.''

''It's a renegade operation, Hal. From what you've told me Carl learned, there's some shadows on both sides of the Atlantic who helped get Syria as far along on its nuclear program as it has. Now we know this same renegade faction is linked to the late Mosnivoc, whose organization is still pretty much intact. They came for our flying disk, they have it and I don't think they're going to let it come back to us without a fight.''

''I have to concur,'' Brognola said. ''But what you're proposing, and if I even get the Man to sanction Phoenix for a clandestine operation in Russia…it will take some serious convincing to get him to give them the thumbs-up.''

''You might want to try a diplomatic channel. Use your contacts in the Company, have them arrange something with anybody in the SVR they think they can trust. We're jumping the gun a little, but if anyone can make quick work of the Syrian problem, it's Phoenix Force. I will need the guys and Jack on this one.''

"All we can tell you, Striker," Barbara Price said, "is we have to wait and see what happens in Syria."

"Understood. I know you'll do your best to make it happen. A few more items about my flight plans and Russian itinerary, then I need to go check on my Russian pilot."

The Executioner knew he had the undivided attention of all hands in the Computer Room as he went on and laid out his plans to unleash his clandestine war in Russia.

CHAPTER SEVENTEEN

Syria

McCarter slipped between the gnarled steel fingers where the Spectre had so rudely blasted a hole in a section of the fence at the southeast end. The Briton and James took point, their SMGs leading the way, while Encizo palmed the squat stainless-steel rocket launcher that had been stowed among the latest shipment of gear from the Farm. One glance over his shoulder, and McCarter caught the grim smile on Encizo's lips as he began chugging out the 40 mm rounds, blowing up six shadows that came staggering out of some wreckage from the west. McCarter didn't have time to admire the minidoomsday piece John Kissinger had created.

There were problems dead ahead, all around actually, and they were armed with AK-47s, looking angry and wondering what the hell had just hit the compound from the dark skies over their own turf.

Their HK MP-5s drawing target acquisition on the first line of enemy traffic, McCarter and James squeezed off several concentrated bursts, hitting a group of mangled survivors near what used to be the base MiGs. As the enemy danced and dropped into the fiery wreckage, the ex-SAS commando and the former Navy SEAL peeled off, searching for fresh prey.

"Flyboy to Phoenix One, come in!"

McCarter didn't like the tone of urgency in Grimaldi's voice. He hit the trigger of his SMG, sent a bloody stick figure at two o'clock reeling with a zip of 9 mm Parabellum shockers across the chest. The Briton took cover behind a pile of rubble as Encizo and James leapfrogged ahead, laying waste to anything that moved, the ex-SEAL rolling over a mauled form on the ground, drilling the shadow with a 3-round burst to the back. Wreckage was still raining to the compound, and there were still plenty of survivors, armed runners darting pell-mell all over the compound.

An amputee weaved, McCarter saw, like some Saturday-night drunk from a pall of black smoke, the AK-47 bouncing around and flaming away in the grip of the one-armed hardman. Without missing a beat, James let him have it with a lightning zip from his SMG, moved on.

McCarter keyed his com link. "Phoenix One here. Nice work, Flyboy. Hats off to the gun crew likewise."

"I'll be sure to pass on the congrats if our own party doesn't get crashed and burned to hell."

"What's the problem?"

Beyond the barrage of weapons fire, the Briton made out the distant sound of rolling thunder that was their flying death ship, knew Grimaldi was swinging around to come back and lend a hand.

"The Farm just raised me, Phoenix One. We've got serious problems headed this way. I just picked them up on the screen. Looks like the Israelis are bulling their way into this one. I was just informed by Katz and Barbara that they're going straight for the plant. They intend to bring the mountain down on the place."

McCarter cursed. "Are they going nuclear?"

"Katz said he had the solemn pledge of the second-in-command that they will not go nuclear."

"Second-in-command? Somehow knowing that doesn't exactly fill me with confidence. What's their ETA?"

"Less than three minutes. Keep T.J. and Gary well away from that plant. My understanding is twelve, count 'em, twelve F-15s are going to drop the sky on that place and bring the whole damn mountain down on it."

"Roger that. But, hell, does anyone on their team know or care if they pull off that stunt, they could create a radioactive wasteland in our faces, and maybe see all of us down here eaten up by leukemia or cancer two weeks or so down the road?"

"My hunch is they know something about the place we don't. Or maybe if they drop the mountain on the entrance, they figure they'll seal up the plant and keep the hot zone buried.

"Yeah. Well, I find myself in a hospital bed, tubed up and bedpan stuck between my cheeks, I hope this second-in-command is a decent enough chap to send a get-well card and smuggle in some good food while we're all waiting to croak. Fly back and give us a hand here, but keep in mind we're on the eastern side.''

"I copy. Flyboy on the way.''

McCarter saw Encizo and James angling for the barracks where they'd seen the terrorists quartered. There was still some activity beyond the doorway, some flapping of arms, an assault rifle or two outlined from the dancing flames of nearby wreckage. Only partial destruction had claimed maybe a third of the building, with something like half the roof gone. The damn place, he knew, still housed plenty of bad guys.

The Briton keyed his com link. "T.J., Gary! Move south and link up with us. We've got some trigger-happy Israeli top guns flying in. I'm told they're going straight for the plant but supposedly they're not going nuclear!''

"What the hell we supposed to do with all this C-4?'' Manning growled, the demolitions man sounding annoyed that he wouldn't get the chance to show off his stuff.

"Save it for later. Who knows, maybe there'll still be something left later to blow up. But make your way toward us. Copy that.''

Hawkins and Manning rogered the order.

McCarter then heard and saw a massive roiling fireball shooting for the sky just beyond the terrorist quarters. He believed the delayed explosion erupted from the fuel depot. He was stunned by the sheer force and eye-searing flash of the explosion, then was blinded by the screaming wave of ignited fuel that he believed came from the depot. Squeezing the stars out of his eyes, he looked back and saw what he thought was a curtain of fire dropping straight into the terrorist quarters.

CALVIN JAMES WAS blinded for a dangerous second by a white light that seemed to fall over the barracks from out of the sky. He'd heard the explosion from the mauled depot, the ground quaking beneath his feet. He'd been angling for the barracks, ready to arm a frag grenade and go in with Encizo when it happened.

Now they were screaming like the damned from inside the barracks. It lasted all of maybe two seconds, then James caught the sickly sweet stink of roasted flesh, heard total silence from beyond.

James got it together, hit a crouch beside the doorway, across from Encizo.

"What the hell happened in there?" the Cuban commando wanted to know.

"The fuel depot went up. Delayed blast. A whole damn wave of fire caught and hit these tangos, that's what."

A look inside with Encizo and James found the blackened mummies of corpses still smoking. But no fire.

Weird, the ex-SEAL thought. He'd seen plenty of explosions in his day, but nothing with the kind of sudden fury like he'd just witnessed. It all struck him as if the fire itself had been a living entity, which he knew was impossible. But how could he explain, much less fathom what he'd just seen?

"Let's roll, mates," McCarter said. "We've got runners headed Gary and T.J.'s way. The show's over inside there!"

The Phoenix Force trio rolled ahead, fanned out and scoured the flaming slaughter zone for new prey.

GARY MANNING never liked having the rug pulled out from under him during a mission. The plant was their designated target, and he'd been eager and all too grimly willing to penetrate the entrance, mine the works, blow it all to hell and back.

Now some gung-ho Israeli flyboys were going to steal their thunder.

What could he do? he thought, and decided he could at least direct his frustration at the bad guys. With Hawkins hitting a group of Syrian soldiers near the entrance with a pounding sweep of 7.62 mm NATO slugs from his M-60 man-eater, the big Canadian helped tear into that group with a long fusillade of bullets stuttering from his HK MP-5 subgun.

They were finished down there, the hard-packed soil of the compound pooling with fresh blood, so Manning and Hawkins forged on, weaving through the rubble, grim eyes surveying the destruction and lakes of fire on all points.

The Spectre rumbled back, hugging the face of the Anti-Lebanon Mountains. No matter how much damage the massive war bird had inflicted on the compound, Manning spotted runners in flight for two intact jeeps at the shadowy edge of the west quadrant. He was about to make a beeline for the runners when some Bofors and Vulcan thunder from the Spectre took out that particular problem.

Manning and Hawkins caught some return fire, hit the deck as bullets snapped over their heads from out of nowhere. Slugs whined off stone and slapped off jagged sheets of smoking debris. The pencil-tip flames from AK-47s stabbed through the smoke and gloom of a mountain of rubble, dead ahead.

Six, maybe seven Syrians, Manning figured.

Frag time, and he told Hawkins to arm a grenade.

Together, the big Canadian and ex-Ranger let the steel eggs fly. There were shouts of alarm from that direction as a few pairs of alert eyes spotted the flying grenades and beat a hasty path away from ground zero.

As the twin thunderclaps sent lethal steel bits razoring all around and screams rent the air, Manning and Hawkins broke cover, firing on the run. The three Syrians who beat death twice before struck out the third time around. A double dose of lead manglers from Manning and Hawkins dropped them as they flew from the boiling smoke.

Somewhere off to the west, Manning heard the Spectre tearing it up in round two, eating up whatever few buildings were left standing to the west.

Rounding the corner of the leveled command-and-control center, Manning spotted McCarter, James and Encizo hard at work mopping up. Encizo plugged up the holes in scattered mounds of rubble for the Phoenix Force trio, blasting away with his rocket launcher on entrenched Syrians. The explosions flushed a few of the enemy into the open.

On the fly, Manning, filling his SMG with a fresh clip, came in from the blind side of some runners. Hawkins mowed down three of the shadows, empty shell casings twirling around his grim visage as he swept the man-eater left to right. Seven figures shuffled and wobbled around on his right flank, and Manning was forced to burn up his clip to drop them to a man.

Then a new set of problems rushed out of the gaping maw that led to the plant, as Manning got his bearings. Some were armed, while others were tripping along in their white lab coats.

"We've got one minute to clean this up," McCarter said, and led his men to the west to intercept the latest wave of runners.

Aboard the C-130

THIRTY POUNDS of C-4 he'd brought with him in the war bag should do the trick. The instrument panel, the flight deck and the crates were mined, det cord hooked up, all of it good to go with one touch of his thumb to the button on the hellbox, the works tied in to one radio frequency.

Kakov wasn't smiling now when he said, "I say I cooperate, I cooperate. Is this necessary? You intend to turn this plane into a suicide ship?"

M-16 cradled in his hands, Bolan reclaimed the copilot's seat. "Only as a last resort. When we land you won't leave your seat. You'll tell the ground crew you are alone. Give whoever you talk to that disarming charm of yours, and get me a rough fix on numbers. Whatever it takes, whatever you have to say. Make it happen. Tell them they should come onboard and take a look at our UFO. Remember, I know Russian."

Kakov gave a shake of his head. "And if there is trouble?"

"You'd better hope there isn't, at least not for me."

What Bolan neglected to tell his Russian pilot was that once he had a read on their numbers, he would allow them to venture into the cargo hold, thinking they might just want to have a look at the special delivery destined for Russia. He still had a few hours yet to mentally iron out the details, nail down the game plan.

But he was looking to ante up.

The Executioner intended to clean up any problems as he went along. He could be sure when the time came, curiosity would indeed kill a few Russian cats.

Syria

THE SLAUGHTER WAS a rush job, since McCarter knew the cavalry was less than a minute away from bringing down the sky. Still, he figured they'd come this far, risked their necks to not see the job done right, and by their own hands.

They were rounding the corner, firing on the run, when the Phoenix Force warriors nailed the first wave of runners. Armed or not, McCarter and company intended to see them all taken out. If these were Syria's best nuclear physicist brains, he didn't need them hanging on beyond here to help build another bomb tomorrow.

Encizo had just filled Little Bulldozer's chambers, and the other commandos had their SMGs fitted with fresh mags, while Hawkins had fed a fresh belt link into his M-60. Phoenix Force, spread out and moving toward the overturned flaming wreckage of the motor pool, doused the runners with a long barrage of lead and HE rounds. Some return fire sought them out, but it was over in about ten seconds. Soldiers were chopped to bloody ribbons, their screams mingling with the shrill cries of terror from the physicists. Lab coats turned red as gaping holes punched through them, crotch to sternum. A line of three HE fireballs marched across another clustered group that found a sudden urge to run the other way.

When the last of them had fallen, McCarter said, "Let's move the hell out of here on the double."

The Phoenix Force leader didn't have to tell any of the troops to stay alert.

A possum rose from a litter of smoking debris, but was crucified by a triple burst of subgun fire from McCarter, James and Manning.

Alert and jogging east, they surveyed the devastation, the stink of burning fuel, torched flesh and emptied bowels hitting them in the face the whole way toward the eastern quadrant.

McCarter heard the roar of turbofan engines before he looked up and saw the staggered formation of fighter jets. They came in low from the south, two at a time, and started unleashing the works.

Phoenix Force picked up the pace before their own world blew up in some radioactive apocalypse. McCarter was looking toward the far northwest, unable to resist watching the fireworks, when the first missiles flamed over the compound, streaked on, seemed to vanish into the huge yawn in the side of the mountain. Even as the first series of explosions lit up the entrance, more Sidewinders and Sparrows were on the way.

So far all of them were still standing and running,

not vaporized by a nuclear fireball, telling McCarter the second-in-command had kept his word.

It was an amazing sight, just the same, McCarter decided, watching as the fighter jets hurled their missiles with such pinpoint accuracy through the boiling fireclouds that an avalanche was created by the force of the impacts.

A good part of the mountain was already sliding down, set to seal the plant.

McCarter led them through the hole in the fence. The deafening peals of the explosions shattered the air around Phoenix Force, all but drowning the shriek of still more fighter jets racing overhead to further lower the boom. God help anyone left behind in the plant, McCarter figured, thinking if they were caught inside the mountain with what he saw erupting and coming down on their heads...

Their dead Syrian comrades may just end up being the lucky ones.

CHAPTER EIGHTEEN

Stony Man Farm, Virginia

Brognola hung up the red line to the Oval Office, heaved a breath, massaged a face that felt as if the jowls were weighted down by lead. Even if he tried, he couldn't remember the last time he'd slept, changed clothes, took a shower, talked to his wife.

And why bother? he thought.

Everyone at the Farm was under the gun, slammed up against the ticking doomsday clock. Not to mention what the troops in the field had endured and tackled, kicking the enemy in the teeth on three different crisis points. And they were going to keep on marching into the eye of yet another storm or two. Another day, two tops, and Brognola may or may not see daylight on this one. Just the same, the big Fed felt as if he'd aged ten years in a few short days.

"Well?" Barbara Price prompted.

Brognola, Price and Katzenelenbogen were alone in the War Room. The only good news so far was that Phoenix Force was still on the ground in Syria, in one piece to a man. Syria's play to go nuclear was history, and no nukes had been used by the Israelis to level the compound or destroy the reprocessing plant. Of course, it would hit the diplomatic, political and religious fans over there soon enough, Brognola knew, with Syria and a few other radical Islamic countries railing at the world about a criminal attack against a sovereign nation. That was down the road still, and Brognola had a full plate of his own problems to tend to in the present. Continuing any grand designs for peace in the Middle East was someone else's headache.

"The Man is not happy that Striker took the initiative to go marching into Russia and take matters into his own hands," Brognola began. "But he understands that national security is at risk if the prototype aircraft is allowed to fall into the hands of the Russians, or if they keep what parts they already have or somehow bag the pilot. And given what happened in Brooklyn, the Russian president and several of his top generals and members of his cabinet have even stated to the Man they are embarrassed that some of their own gangsters are involved in what appears a mass conspiracy between a few renegade SVR agents acting on their own in collusion with the Russian Mafia. The FBI blood that was spilled by their own criminals is a—and I quote the Man quoting the Russian end of their hierarchy—'terrible and shameful thing to all good Russian people.' It seems the Russian president wants to put out any more fires before they start. Now according to Striker, this Compound ZX545 has been somehow taken over by a renegade faction of SVR-Russian Mafia gangsters. It's been confirmed over at Langley. Embarrassment aside, the Russian president actually gave his blessing for Striker to act and will turn a blind eye for any limited covert foray into Siberia to retrieve the wreckage of our UFO."

"Limited foray?" Katz said. "Meaning what exactly?"

"And our guys will just sail in, then on out of the country, just like that?"

Brognola read the suspicion all over Price's face, the dark concern in Katz's stare. "Not exactly. If we can get Phoenix back to Saudi and on the way, the Russian president says an MiG escort will be waiting for our people when they cross their border with Iran in the Republic of Turkmenistan. I have a radio frequency with which to contact the commander of the base in question."

"I know we're all aware here," Price said, "that we could well be marching Phoenix Force into a trap. That the Russians have no intention of simply handing back what they blew out of the sky."

"It's not the mainstream power structure we have to worry about, Barbara," Brognola said. "What Striker and Phoenix will be looking at is apparently a small but powerful shadow government inside the real government over in Moscow."

"And they want our side to clean house for them?" Katz posed.

Brognola nodded. "That's about the size of it."

Arlington, Virginia

"AND WHAT ABOUT me when this is over?"

"Stop whining! Just shut up and do what I told you to do," Lyons growled.

Hunched behind the driver's seat, Lyons couldn't

believe the only person Carlington was looking out for was number one. Not that it surprised him, but this was the worst time possible for any hint to some watching eyes up there that the State Department traitor wasn't alone in the van.

Lyons peered between the seats, bit down the curse when he spotted the mounted swivel camera on the gate post nailing Carlington right in the face. This was supposed to be a swift and deadly takedown, or so Lyons had planned it. He was going in with the SPAS-12, while Blancanales, who was crouched behind the passenger seat of the black Chevy van with its U.S. government plates, seemed to have developed a kinship with Cowboy's Little Bulldozer. Schwarz, nearly breathing down Lyons's neck, was bringing an M-16/M-203 combo to this particular party.

Lyons gave the split-level, brick-facaded, million-dollar home in Arlington a hard look. Lights were on, top to bottom, with four luxury vehicles parked in the semicircular drive. Carlington had just announced himself, and whoever was on the other end opened the wrought-iron gates with the flick of an electronic switch from somewhere inside the mansion.

Lyons didn't like the setup—three against however many gunmen—but there was little Able Team could do other than bulldoze and blaze away at this point.

The State guy's superior was some hotshot diplomat liaison to Russia named Beasley. According to Carlington, Beasley was ex-NSA with all kinds of clout and connections to the worst element in Russia. Beasley also apparently damn near ran the State Department. Lyons didn't care how the political machinations in downtown Wonderland worked, aware to the extent it was a circle jerk of who knew who and how much ass was kissed or who bought dinner at the right time for the right person, but Beasley was right then prepared to jump ship.

Early retirement with no letter of resignation, if Carlington was telling the whole story and hadn't neglected to fill in all the blanks.

This particular sinking ship, though, was prepared to be rescued by some Russian Mafia types on-site. Again, according to Carlington, this meet in an isolated stretch of north Arlington, in the thick woods near Chain Bridge, had been engineered some time ago. If Mosnivoc was not 'reseized' by his fellow Russian gangsters, Lyons thought, recalling Carlington's spiel, then the bad guys on the American front would meet here at Beasley's seven figure estate, pull up stakes and bail the country.

The mother lode of intel was also allegedly on-site. And Lyons intended to take the gold home to the Farm. Beasley, in the event it went south on him, had detailed the nuclear shadow game between the former KGB, the CIA, the Russian Mafia and a few other big shots in the Russian power structure. Supposedly, there was a hard disk inside the mansion, in Beasley's possession. Supposedly, it came complete with names, dates and flight corridors through Russia to Syria, the whole nine yards for all the shipments of U-235, U-238, P-239 and all essential component parts that had nearly launched a terrorist state into a nuclear power.

Thanks to Phoenix Force and a few Israeli F-15s, that was no longer a reality.

Able Team was rolling in, as Carlington headed the

van up the drive, to clean up another mess on the home front. Lyons had made the call back at the Farm for the three of them to take no prisoners, but get the disk, no matter what it took or how much pain they needed to inflict to get their hands on it.

"Someone's coming out," Carlington said.

Lyons shook his head. The guy just wouldn't listen about not flapping his gums.

"He's got a machine gun! Oh, my God! The bastard's aiming it..."

Lyons was raising his head a few inches to take a look when Carlington braked the van, a stutter of subgun fire sounded and the windshield blew in all over his face.

Or what was left of it anyway, as autofire blasted half of Carlington's head away in chunks of flying blood and brains.

The State guy's troubles were over, but Lyons knew the three of them had just been dropped face first into the fire.

Syria

MCCARTER STEPPED away from the Spectre. He found his Phoenix Force mates, Grimaldi and the blacksuit gun crew assembled on the steppe where their ace pilot had found a suitable strip of LZ to give the big war bird a well-deserved breather.

The Briton had just come from the belly of the Spectre where he'd been on the sat link to the Farm for the past twenty minutes.

A tall lean figure in black camos and matching beret stepped up to McCarter.

"I am Colonel Avi Meissel." He offered his hand and McCarter took it. "You and your men are to be congratulated."

Nodding, releasing the man's firm grip, McCarter looked past the Israeli colonel at the flaming hellzone, a half mile to the north. It could have been a vision of the end of the world, scaled down, of course, but there was nothing left in that direction other than raging firestorms and rising walls of black smoke in all directions. The compound had been utterly destroyed. Overhead, the Briton heard the shriek of fighter jets as both the Israelis and their own flying escort from Saudi Arabia patrolled the area, searching for any Syrian tanks that might want to bark about what had happened here in their backyard.

"Just call me Mac, Colonel," McCarter said. "This was a damn close shave all around, sir. But I'm taking it you're the man I should thank for calling off the nuclear hound dogs."

"Yes. Had it been up to me, I would have simply let you and your men gone ahead and taken out the plant. It wasn't my call."

"No need to explain, Colonel."

There were several black gunships similar to Hueys grounded near the Spectre. A full squad of Israeli commandos in black camo with Galil assault rifles was standing by outside the rotor wash.

"The Syrians have a sorry track record when it comes to air combat," the Israeli colonel said. "But should they scramble some MiGs, I could have some of our own F-15s give you an escort out of the country just to be on the absolute safe side."

"Appreciate the thought, Colonel. But we have our own flying guard to see us out and on our way."

"In that case, good luck to you and your men, wherever you land and whatever may be up next for you."

The colonel threw McCarter a salute, which the ex-SAS commando returned. When he marched off, McCarter felt as if he was suddenly missing a good friend he'd never get the chance to know. Meissel, whatever and however he'd done it, had somehow seen to it Phoenix Force hadn't been reduced to shadows burned into the earth by a few nuclear fireclouds.

"There goes a stand-up act," McCarter said, more to himself than anybody else. He wheeled, looked at his gathered force. "Listen up, mates. We're going back to Saudi where we've got some new wheels waiting and where Jack and company will be flying us to Siberia."

That got their solemn attention.

"Anything special on the menu?" Hawkins asked, cutting a grin. "Or is this the Farm's way of shipping all of us off for some R and R?"

"I was kind of lookin' forward to getting out of these thermals," Calvin James said, a wry twist to his lips. "Only so much itching and sweating even a SEAL used to a life of discomfort and deprivation can take."

"No R and R, mates. We're going in with two things in mind. One, we're taking back a UFO the Russian Mafia stole from our side. Two, we're flying in because Striker has hijacked a C-130 with said UFO aboard and is en route to Siberia as we speak to give the bad guys a loud piece of his mind. So saddle up.''

Arlington, Virginia

IF THE BEST DEFENSE was a good offense, then Able Team went for the quick score.

When the firing died from the front steps of the columned entranceway, Lyons caught the sound of footsteps pounding on the pavement around the van, coming up the passenger side. Gesturing with his hand for Blancanales to throw back the door and get out of the way, Schwarz was already bursting out the back doors of the van.

Lyons lifted the massive autoshotgun as Blancanales flung the door wide and two shadows rolled up into the opening. They started triggering their HK MP-5 subguns when Lyons let them have it with the SPAS-12. An angry hornet's nest of enemy 9 mm Parabellum slugs whining around the van's interior, a slug hacking off a chunk of skin on Lyons's bicep, he sawed the first shadow in two with a blast of 12-gauge frangible buckshot. Lyons tracked on, tapped the trigger and blew the second shadow a dozen feet across the driveway on a dark cloud of his own blood and shredded innards.

He followed Blancanales out the door. On the other side, Lyons made out the familiar stammering music of the M-16 going off in Schwarz's capable hands.

Blancanales then lit up the night, pumping three HE rounds through the massive double doors leading to the foyer. Swinging his aim, Blancanales used Little Bulldozer to blow in the huge bay window, peppering the living room beyond with an explosive light show that more than likely pulped everything to ruins, Lyons figured.

It was only just heating up, Lyons saw, as he led Able Team's charge up the steps.

Another shadow with an HK MP-5 wobbled out of the smoke cloud of the foyer.

Lyons and Schwarz triggered their respective weapons on the fly and blew the shadow off his feet.

Now the tough part, Lyons figured.

He'd been a cop long enough in the past to know that going through the front door of an enemy's lair was usually the most dangerous part of a raid.

Only Able Team wasn't looking to cuff any suspects here.

This was slaughter, pure and simple.

Lyons and Schwarz hit the front door as bullets started snapping over their heads.

Island in the Pacific

BOLAN WATCHED through the eyebrow windows, counted four dark-garbed men jogging from the thick tropical jungle just off the dirt runway. Their heads were bent as they shouldered into the heated air blown at them by the turboprop engines. The soldier noted the holstered side arms, the universal AK-47 wielded by the Russians. Before they could get a close look, he ducked from their view.

The play was set.

While descending for the remote island that sat in the Pacific Ocean by itself, Kakov had put in the call. In Russian the pilot had launched himself into a pretty good act, hurling excitement at the ground crew about what he had in the cargo hold. He told them to fuel him up as soon as he landed, then he'd let them come onboard to have a closer look at the American UFO.

Four gunmen, Bolan thought. One more Russian by the giant fuel bladder, getting the hose out and ready to fill her up.

When Kakov had the big transport bird braked, the engines shut down and the ground crew began pumping in the fuel, Bolan took the plastic cuffs.

''Tell them you're going back to lower the ramp and let them in.''

Once the message was relayed, Bolan ordered Kakov to stand, move back from the windows, turn and put his hands behind his back. That order complied with, Bolan fastened the cuffs on his pilot, then shoved him for the doorway leading from the flight deck.

CHAPTER NINETEEN

Arlington, Virginia

"Stand aside!"

Lyons caught them barking and snarling in a mixed bag of Russian and American from somewhere beyond the choking clouds of raining plaster and cordite as the enemy sprayed and prayed with their SMGs at this trio of home invaders. The best course of action, Lyons decided, was to let Pol do his Little Bulldozer thing.

While Lyons and Schwarz crouched low and directed some covering fire, Blancanales whipped himself into the opening and brought some more of the house down. Whether he was going for it or not, a chandelier the size of some apartments took a direct hit from an HE round. Now they were screaming and cursing in Russian under the glass avalanche, dancing away from the raining shrapnel, arms flapping in what struck Lyons as a bad chorus-line number.

Their pain and jig stepping was short-lived as Blancanales sent them sailing back on another flashing ball of fire.

Schwarz nailed the stragglers with a sweeping line

of 5.56 mm send-offs, kicking them in a nosedive over something that could have once been a couch, one of those horseshoe jobs, Lyons figured, that could field an entire orgy.

"Up the steps!"

Lyons looked up as soon as Blancanales shouted his warning. Able Team was climbing the steps for the second story, Schwarz pounding out a wave of lead, while Lyons thundered out the remaining rounds in his SPAS-12. Two hardmen appeared to partially disintegrate under the roaring onslaught, then were lost altogether in another HE blast, courtesy of Little Bulldozer.

But it was the limping figure that quickly snared Lyons's full grim attention. The Farm's intel sheet on Beasley filed away, Lyons recalled the ex-NSA man's photo.

Able Team charged up the stairs, Blancanales covering the rear, searching the ruins below in the living room for live ones. Nothing rising, nothing groaning from that direction of their demolition job.

Lyons cursed as Beasley made the second-floor landing, turned and began winging around shots from a Glock 17. Schwarz and Lyons ducked as the slugs chewed off strips of the banister.

"Hold your fire," Lyons told Schwarz. "We need him alive to get that disk."

Capping off a few more rounds, Beasley then vanished from Able Team's sight as he flew through a doorway.

Lyons picked up the pace, unleathered his .357 Magnum Colt Python. The ex-NSA traitor, Lyons suspected, was making one last run, hoping to pull a quick delete job on the golden intel they'd crashed the doors down and blown half the house up to get.

If he pulled it off, Lyons knew it was little more than a Pyrrhic victory, a slap in the faces of Able Team. Lyons didn't intend to go back to the Farm empty-handed.

Island in the Pacific

BOLAN AND KAKOV were hidden from sight behind the crate nearest the ramp.

The C-130 was topped off with fuel. Before leaving the cockpit deck, one of the Russians had radioed to inform Kakov he'd also topped out the auxiliary fuel tanks.

Well, thank you very much, the soldier had thought, recalling the deflated look Kakov had thrown him before the soldier made him copy the response.

Gotcha.

The way Bolan now had it figured they were far from any max payload in the hold that would eat up more fuel. He would have to take a look at Kakov's maps, factor in the distance to the Urals, with top cruising speed. Figure maximum fuel would see them the whole 4,894 miles, and with an auxiliary tank that Mr. Forgetful had somehow neglected to mention, even though Bolan could have read the instrument panel and asked that particular question.

Could be, he hoped, from here on this was a nonstop flight.

"I can fly this thing by myself if I have to," Bolan

warned Kakov in a tight whisper, the ice in his voice and eyes telling the Russian he'd better not sound the alarm when his comrades came up the ramp.

The soldier listened as moments later the Russians started marching up the ramp, talking between themselves in excited tones about seeing with their own eyes a UFO. If they weren't lugging AK-47s, Bolan could figure them for a bunch of schoolkids on a day trip to the Smithsonian, viewing the fossilized remains of some great lizard they'd been dying to see all their lives.

"Kakov! Where are you, comrade? You said you'd be in here. Radio him, Dmitri! He knows they are anxious for him to get this thing into their hands. Now let us find a crowbar and have a look at this UFO."

Bolan stood and rolled out into the open. Four eyes bugged at the unidentified gunman with the M-16. Before they could grab the AK-47s off their shoulders and arm themselves, the Executioner let it rip, holding back the trigger for a full-auto barrage. The M-16 flamed and stammered as he hosed them down, left to right. Right away, he saw his next problem in the immediate future, even as they were cut down, twirling and dancing back down the ramp on his long burst of scything lead.

Number Five had stayed outside.

The Executioner charged down the ramp, putting behind the gloom of the cargo hold for the bright light of this isolated tropical paradise. Bolan was rounding the corner when autofire flung a lead storm his way. Bullets sparking off the hull of the starboard rear, the soldier was forced to hurl himself back onto the ramp.

Arlington, Virginia

LYONS FLANKED one side of the doorway, Blancanales and Schwarz taking up positions directly across
the way. Beasley had gone berserk, firing his Glock
as if it would hold off the end of the world, drilling
bullets all up and down the jamb, cursing the invaders
and calling them every name under the sun.

"Give it up, Beasley!" Lyons shouted into what
looked like some sort of office-bedroom combo. Daring a peek inside, he found the ex-NSA traitor hunkering down behind a partition of some workstation,
a light flaring on, the sound of a fresh clip being
slapped into the guy's weapon. "Your Russian Mafia
pals are history! We just want the disk!"

"You assholes just killed Americans! Don't give
me that patriotic garbage!"

"You mean we just waxed a bunch of your CIA
and NSA traitor buddies. Hey, we can do this the hard
way or we can do it the easy way!"

"Carl," Schwarz rasped, "he's going to erase that
disc!"

"Chop him off at the knees," Lyons told Schwarz,
nodding at the M-16. "I want this jerk breathing and
strung up by his package."

Lyons bulled into the room. The .357 Colt Python
leading the way, the Able Team leader angled across
the room, glimpsed a shadow falling his way, knew
the light was hitting Beasley at his desk. Lyons aimed
high, blasting off chunks of the partition with three
cannon peals from his .357 Magnum. Beasley was
flinching, cursing, standing and wheeling around with

his Glock when Schwarz tapped off a 3-round burst from his M-16.

Beasley screamed as his legs were blown out from under him, but he tried to swing his Glock toward the monitor even as he fell. Lyons left his feet, one hand out like a claw. Knowing he was an eye blink away from losing what the Farm needed, it felt as if he were suspended in the air for a full minute.

Then he hammered down on Beasley, knocked the gun away just as it cracked out a round. Looking up, pinning Beasley with a forearm across the throat, Lyons let a long breath go rasping out of his mouth. The bullet had drilled a neat hole through the drywall just above the computer's monitor screen. Roughly Lyons patted Beasley down but came up empty on any backup weapons.

Standing, Lyons looked at what was on the screen. "What the hell is that?"

"Sat imagery of Russia. From Moscow on down through the Ukraine," Schwarz answered. "The way these particular grids are marked off, indicating what appear military bases, I'd say these are flight corridors. Safe passage, in other words, for the smuggling of nuclear contraband."

"We can't just pull it out and boot it up again, can we?" Lyons asked.

"Not without an access code," Schwarz answered. "I'm sure he has one."

Lyons looked down at Beasley. "How about it?"

Through gritted teeth, Beasley said, "Kiss off."

"There's a laser printer fixed to his computer," Schwarz said. "If nothing else, I can print out what's on the disk. They've cracked tough codes before back home in the Computer Room.''

"Do it and be quick about it," Lyons said. "With all the racket we made, I can be sure Arlington County's finest has been alerted by some civic-minded neighbor by now."

"Who are you bastards?" Beasley snarled, his teeth gnashed as waves of pain washed over him.

"Housecleaning," Lyons said.

Island in the Pacific

A STALEMATE WAS the last thing Bolan needed. One gunman wasn't about to keep him from taking off, sounding the alarm and scrambling the MiGs to intercept, maybe blow the transport plane out of the sky. Of course, Kakov could have lied about the numbers, which meant the soldier could get tied up in a protracted running hunt.

Not on his watch, not today.

Judging the direction from which the AK-47 autofire slashed the air, Bolan gauged the shooter was the fuel man, had already rolled the bladder back on to the four-wheel-drive truck. That would put enough distance for any margin of error from the fuel bladder to the transport plane. Just to make sure he padded that margin, Bolan filled the M-203 with an armor-piercing HE round.

He caught a break in the return fire, rolled off the ramp and let the HE round fly for the fuel bladder. One glance was all he got at the lone shooter crouched beside the massive fuel tank on wheels. The HE round streaked on its zigzag course, the shooter capping off a few rounds, before the world blew up in his face. The fuel bladder obviously held enough flammable liquid meant to top off a few more big planes, as Bolan judged the size of the mushrooming fire mountain that all but vaporized the shooter.

It would eat up valuable time, but Bolan had to check the area around the runway and beyond for any survivors.

The soldier marched off, knowing Kakov would stay put with his hands cuffed behind his back. Unless he was the Russian version of Houdini, Kakov wasn't going anywhere.

Arlington, Virginia

BLANCANALES USED his commando dagger to shred Beasley's jacket and make strips for tourniquets. By the time he was sure the traitor wouldn't bleed to death, Schwarz had a small stack of printouts from the disk ready to go, the hard drive falling into his pants pocket.

"Let's roll," Lyons said.

"I can't walk! I need medical attention!"

Blancanales scooped Beasley up as if he weighed no more than an infant and hefted him over his shoulders in a fireman's carry.

Once they cleared the premises, Beasley would become another headache for the Justice Department. In the event Able Team left someone breathing here, Brognola had already given Lyons the number to contact a special agent who would be on hand on the other side of Chain Bridge to take Beasley into custody.

Lyons was leading the way onto the landing, marching for the top of the steps, when he saw the light show beyond the front doors. Before he even set foot on the steps an army of cops was storming inside, pistols and shotguns fanning the carnage.

"You up there!" the first uniform inside yelled. "Drop your weapons!"

"We're with the Justice Department!" Lyons shouted back down.

"I said drop your weapons now! And put that man down! I want to see your hands! Now!"

"You heard him, guys," Schwarz said. "It looks like another long night for the boss back home."

"How long you think before the Man can cut us loose and have us on our way?" Blancanales asked Lyons.

Lyons pitched the SPAS and .357 Magnum pistol away, then said, "This kind of mess? It will take a lot more than a little bit of sweet talk."

"I won't ask you again! Put that man down and grab some air!"

"This is going to hurt you more than me," Blancanales told Beasley, and dumped him off his shoulders like a sack of grain.

Beasley lashed the air with a sharp cry of pain, hitting the landing with a loud thud, then cursed as Able Team raised their hands to the army of advancing uniforms.

Island in the Pacific

THE SVR TEAM on the island had created a primitive fly-by-night operation. Just the same, the setup came complete with all the high-tech goodies they would need to keep this transshipment point hidden and running. Unless, of course, someone with the proper authority and curious enough about what was really going on here wanted to venture onto the island.

One main HQ, a quarter mile down the trail, it was made of thatch, bamboo and hardwood base. It possessed a trio of satellite dishes, with radio console, radar and sat link. A four-wheel-drive jeep was parked outside, and an executive-style jet, the Russian equivalent of the VIP Gulfstream, sat on the other side of the island. A cabin cruiser was moored to an ancient dock on the east side of the island. There wasn't the first sign anywhere this was an oil excavation outpost. Finding a cache of weapons in the floor beneath the hut merely confirmed this was some SVR link between the Russian mainland and the Hawaiian Islands, the main transshipment point for Moscow's gangsters and the moving of contraband.

All in all, it took the Executioner forty-five minutes to recon the island, find that, yes, a mere five SVR agents had maintained this lonely way station in the Pacific.

Bolan was bounding back up the ramp when instinct warned him all was not right. Moments later, as he rolled up the cargo hold, Kakov confirmed his suspicions. The Russian flew out from behind the main UFO crate, lashing out with a sweeping hook kick meant to break his American captor's face. Perhaps if his hands were free, he might have mustered the strength, leverage and speed to drop Bolan like his worst habit. The Executioner dropped at the knees, the kick sailing over his head. Kakov caught a foot full of crate, yelping as the end result jarred him to the bone.

One straight right, and Bolan smashed the Russian in the mouth, put him hard on his back.

"Easy, easy, comrade! I was merely afraid! I did not know what happened! The explosion, I thought you were dead! I believed one of my comrades was thinking I betrayed them and was coming to shoot me down!"

"Uh-huh. On your feet."

The Russian spit blood from his split lip, wobbled to stand up. "You are very quick. I would never stand chance against you."

The salesman was back to life in Kakov, the Russian grinning and cranked up to send Bolan's bullcrap meter off the gauge. The Executioner turned, moved back and hit the button to bring up the ramp.

"So, we are all alone once again, Comrade Badasski?"

"Just the two of us. And, by the way, I might be making some adjustments in our flight schedule."

"Such as?"

"We'll walk and talk and I'll tell you all about it."

The soldier took Kakov by the arm and marched him down the belly of their bird.

Stony Man Farm, Virginia

THE TEAM GREW MORE grim by the agonizing eternal hour. Brognola knew they had a slew of questions, a litany of worst-case scenarios they wanted to spell out. The cyber wizards were hard at it, poring over sat imagery and detailed grid maps of the most likely flight path both Bolan and Phoenix Force would have to take before they linked up in Siberia.

Kurtzman was the first to begin laying out his fears. "Do you realize, Hal, this is a one-of-a-kind situation? A clandestine shooting war between Russian soldiers, SVR agents, the Russian Mafia and our people."

"Maybe."

"Do you know how many things can go wrong once Striker and Phoenix land on or anywhere near this compound? What I'm getting from NRO has this nuclear installation about as big in area, soldiers, aircraft as maybe anything the Russians have. I've got more MiGs, more Hinds and Hips, control towers, tanks—let's just say if Stalin had been backed up by this kind of equipment, men and matériel at his disposal, not to mention we believe they have maybe over a thousand ICBMs, intermediate range, short-range nukes housed in silos belowground—World War II would have been wrapped up in a day."

"I understand all the concerns, the problems, the logistical nightmare, people," Brognola said. "The way we have it laid out, Phoenix stays grounded for now. We've already factored in the maximum speed of the C-141 Starlifter Jack and crew will man as opposed to the C-130's max speed."

"Part of the problem," Wethers pointed out, "is that Striker said his Russian pilot has some elaborate prototype radar-blocking system hooked into the instrument panel. Even the transponder has been shut down so we cannot even track them by satellite."

"Striker says he'll touch base every two to three hours depending on the situation," Price said. "With his maps and his being aware of the hours they've been in the air, he should be able to narrow it down for us to get Phoenix a timetable that can have them land within at least an hour of each other.''

''There's not much more we can do except monitor the action and put Striker and Phoenix in touch with each other,'' Tokaido said.

Brognola knew they were right. Their hands were always tied in certain situations, meaning a good part of the time they could only stand by and wait while the Stony Man warriors took the burden of the action in the field on their shoulders.

And now Brognola was dealing with a red-tape snafu involving Able Team. He was a minute or so away from using his presidential authority to see the Arlington police send the men of Able Team on their way, along with their weapons and the intel they'd confiscated from Beasley.

''We need to take a look at what Able took from Beasley ASAP,'' Kurtzman said. ''It could help us avert any unforeseen problems for our guys once they penetrate Russian airspace.''

''I'm working on it,'' Brognola said. ''If what we think they have turns out to be the smuggling routes, complete with key names of all CIA, NSA and SVR and other Russian politicos and top brass involved in this nuclear-smuggling operation, we can effectively shut down the pipeline on our end.''

''As soon as Striker calls back,'' Price told Brognola, ''we can get a fix on when to get Phoenix in the air.''

The ensuing silence said it all, Brognola knew. In the coming hours, the team would be pretty much forced to ride out the waiting game. They were pros, would iron out the logistical headaches, do all they could to get Striker and Phoenix Force in and out of Russia and back home.

Beyond that, Brognola knew it was all up to Striker and Phoenix Force to pull off the impossible. They'd done if before, only this time they were set to take on a shadow force inside Russia. That alone was troublesome enough for the big Fed. Brognola knew the Russians often spoke out of both sides of their mouths, saying one thing but meaning something else altogether.

In the hours ahead, Brognola knew his anxiety would only mount. In reality all he could do was hold hard and fast to a hope that the entire weight of the Russian military didn't go gunning for his people once they landed. If that happened...

He shook any doom and gloom out of his head and marched out of there to free Able Team.

CHAPTER TWENTY

Siberia

He was so sick and weak he couldn't get out of Ubizka Yblastsi's bed even if the cabin were burning down.

Arkastk Tamalsty desperately wanted some of the cabbage stew and boiled potatoes his longtime friend and the former coal miner had prepared, but he knew he couldn't keep it down. Several attempts to eat had already seen him vomit the food back up into the bucket by his bed. Somehow, though, he managed to choke down the lemon-flavored vodka that was Yblastsi's homemade brew. Enough vodka kept him floating along through this hellish nightmare of sickness and agony, dulled a pain that seemed to throb through the very marrow of his bones.

"You must try and eat again, Arkastk. Please."

"I cannot."

Sometimes he was hot. Other long stretches he shivered in his own pool of sweat beneath the thick wool blanket. His friend seemed a million miles away in his fevered brain as Tamalsty tried to focus on the white-bearded, stoop-shouldered figure who was sitting beside the bed in a chair.

"You are a good friend, Ubizka. Thank you and God bless you for all you have done. But I am dying. I know I will die soon. I pray for death, do you understand? I will be with my family again. So, you see, food is no longer a necessity for one who is surely dying. Your vodka and your friendship is more than comfort enough."

The old man nodded. "Igor and Fyodor have not returned since yesterday."

"I fear the worst for them."

"As I do."

"How long have I...?"

Tamalsty heard how many days he'd been on the run, then in hiding with the American spaceman, but he was drifting off, didn't quite catch the number. It could have been two days or two years since he'd seen the soldiers murder his family and slaughter the entire village anyway. Time was irrelevant, he decided. Death and freedom from this sick shell of a body were all that mattered any longer.

Tamalsty felt the cold rag on his forehead. Revived, he looked around the room, focused on the shelves of the wooden hand-carved dolls. It was Ubizka's passion since his wife had died many years ago from some strange disease. Since then, Ubizka had spent many lonely years, carving then painting the dolls for the children of the villages in the region. He had a talent that deserved recognition, Tamalsty thought. He should be in the city, earning good money, making the children happy with his gift. And it was terrible, he thought, about his wife. Since there were no doc-

tors for hundreds of miles in any direction, even poor
Ubizka, he knew, was never certain what had claimed
the life of Yvanta. Now he endured this quiet, lonely
existence creating joy in the middle of nowhere, but
now for no one who would ever have the pleasure of
holding his gift, since the soldiers had murdered
everyone in the region and thrown them into mass
graves, according to Ubizka.

Life was little more than a cruel joke these days.

But Ubizka seemed happy to Tamalsty, oddly at
peace with life even in these terrible times when death
was standing at everyone's doorstep. There was a distant but grateful resolve in his old eyes to see it all
through no matter what, no complaints or regrets. Perhaps a life lived with pure selflessness was blessing
enough, he decided, gave a man all the strength inside
and hope he would ever need to face disappointment,
horror, tragedy. Whatever money he had saved over
the long years in the coal mine, well, Tamalsty had
heard from another villager how Ubizka had given it
to his two children to help them leave the loneliness
of the tundra, see them safely to Moscow to seek a
better tomorrow for themselves.

"Your children? They are well?"

"Yes. Thank you for asking. Gregorvka has become an expert automobile mechanic. Martina married a doctor and they have their own family. It is
expensive to get mail from Moscow, but they were
paying a pilot out of their own pockets to deliver
letters once every six months."

Were.

Tamalsty felt the vomit wanting to rise and lodge
like a clenched fist in his throat.

"I see in your eyes you are remembering what the soldiers did to your family and your village...they did the same thing to the good people of Unastka. I can only reason they have not found me yet because I live here alone, deep in the woods."

"But they will find us. We...must leave here. We must run."

The old man shook his head. "There is no saving our lives no matter where we run or how far if bad men want to take them that much. If the soldiers come here to kill, they will kill us all. I will die on my feet and ask for no mercy. I, too, miss my wife and long to be with her again. Understand something. I believe there is a divine being, one who is angry about all the injustice and senseless violence of men in the world. I believe the butchers here in this part of Siberia will meet the wrath of a cosmic justice meted out at some point. The blood of the innocent will not go unavenged." He shrugged. "Maybe that is only the foolish hope of an old man."

Tamalsty felt the wet fire build behind his eyes. "My American friend?"

"He is still here."

"How is he?"

Tamalsty found the American spaceman standing in the doorway. Not even twenty minutes after they'd encountered each other, Tamalsty recalled how he had watched as the American shed his spacesuit, buried it by hand with snow and mud. From that point on, he had marched them east wearing only thermal underwear and his boots. The strange American spaceman's stamina and endurance—not to mention his iron willingness to suffer against the freezing air in only a thin layer of thermals—had amazed Tamalsty, and he found himself encouraged by the American's bravery alone to keep moving. At times the American had kept him going even when he wanted to drop and be left behind. As he grew sicker by the hour, the space-man would put an arm around him, practically car-rying him along through the deep snow. It was more by accident than design that they had stumbled to the cabin here. Or was it destiny? Whatever, Ubizka had not asked the first question about their sudden ap-pearance, not even hesitated to give the both of them safe haven, food and comfort from the elements.

"Not good," Ubizka answered.

Tamalsty saw Ubizka had given the American clothing. The pistol he wore in a holster around his waist didn't escape his eye, either.

"One pistol," Tamalsty said. "Against a small army of soldiers."

The American's lean, bristled face hardened. "It's not for them. And fear not. The weapon is not to use on either of you."

"Why would you commit suicide?" Tamalsty wanted to know.

"Because of what happened. Because if they cap-ture me, they'll want to know how what they shot down flies. How it is built...and so on."

"You took off your spacesuit out in the open," Tamalsty said. "What about this radioactive fallout?"

"I will put it to you in terms that the both of you can understand. It is a form of nuclear energy that exploded when their rockets slammed into my craft. An element was in the nuclear energy inside the re-actor that propelled my craft that releases radiation if exposed, but dies as quickly as it disperses. I can only tell you it is an element unknown—''

Ubizka nodded. ''To Earth? To humans?''

''It doesn't matter what it is anymore,'' the American said, and left them to wonder.

''So there would have been no sickness?'' Tamalsty asked. ''They did not have to kill everyone?''

''They would have killed them anyway.''

''Because the soldiers believed we saw an alien spaceship?'' Ubizka asked.

''Among other reasons.''

''I do not even know your name.''

Tamalsty saw a sad, tired smile on the American's lips. ''It is not important.''

''I would feel better if I knew the name of the man who cared enough to see me out of the cold and not leave me to die.''

He nodded. ''Jim. You can call me Jim.''

Tamalsty smiled. ''It will be a good thing to die in the presence of brave and honorable men.''

''Rest, Arkastk,'' Ubizka quietly urged, and flipped the rag over, laying the damp side on burning flesh.

Then Tamalsty saw the American go to the window, pull back the drape and peer through the frosted glass.

''Problem?''

''Nothing,'' the American said.

Only Tamalsty suspected trouble was headed their way. It could have been a minute or an hour later, but he heard the door in the living room burst open, heard them shouting, ''Stop!''

He saw the American fill the doorway, unholster his pistol. Someone was screaming at the soldiers not to shoot him. As calmly as if he might be sitting down for dinner, the American placed the muzzle of the pistol against his temple and squeezed the trigger. That act alone, as the American crumpled at the knees, seemed to infuriate the screamer even more.

It was over, Tamalsty knew, as he saw the soldiers barging into the room, AK-47s aimed at them. Before they began firing, Tamalsty smiled, knew he would be with his family in a few short moments. It didn't even hurt when he felt the first few rounds tearing into his dying body.

ZHERKOVSKY FELT sick to his stomach over yet more mindless murdering ordered by the SVR man. He stood in the lengthening shadows of the clearing in front of the log cabin, listening to the chatter of AK-47 autofire as they executed the occupants. And the American pilot, judging the bellowed orders from Denkov, had been the first casualty. It didn't take X-ray vision for him to know the American had shot himself, rather than allowing himself to be captured and put under the SVR man's interrogation techniques to discover the truth about the UFO.

He could see the end coming, even if the SVR agent believed he was in control. A small army of gangsters was already on the premises of the compound. They had left them behind, these former KGB agents and Spetsnaz commandos and other assorted high-ranking officers in what used to be the Soviet high command. Back there, he knew, they were busy gaping and gawking, touching the wreckage like little children enthralled by the sight of new toys. Fools. Barbarians.

The Americans were en route to retrieve their craft. A presidential directive had already been issued that the Americans were to take back the thing that belonged to them, fly off from the compound, unmolested. Apparently, this was all to be done in the interest of reshaping and re-forming good relations with the West. Zherkovsky could read between the lines on that score. First, America dumped billions of dollars of aid into the floundering Russian economy every year, only most of the funds, he knew, were siphoned off by the gangsters and the corrupt politicians. Second, he had heard reports from his own sources in Moscow monitoring the situation in America. Mosnivoc was dead, but a number of FBI agents had also been killed by Russian gangsters. The real and bona fide powers in Moscow were embarrassed, afraid American money would no longer find its way into their hands. Letting the Americans reclaim what had been shot down was supposed to even the scorecard.

The following day it would all go back to business as usual, but the future looked as bleak as ever, Zherkovsky feared. Given what Denkov had already said, he knew the barbarians back at the compound were under orders by their own people to turn the Americans away. Even if that meant opening fire on them as soon as they landed.

Zherkovsky braced himself for another tirade as the SVR man stormed outside.

"He shot himself!"

"So I would gather, Comrade Denkov."

"I needed him alive! I needed to know how the craft is flown! What makes it fly!"

Zherkovsky suppressed a fit of laughter as the SVR man stomped around, kicking at the snow.

Denkov had to have caught the look and figured it out for what it was. "You find this amusing, Major?"

"Hardly. Quite the opposite."

"Explain yourself."

"What is there to explain? Whoever you work for has somehow corrupted others into allowing a bunch of gangsters to take over and occupy one of the most classified military compounds in Russia."

"And you disapprove."

Zherkovsky shrugged. "What am I to do?"

"Precisely. Nothing. You will obey my orders from here on. I have already told you what is about to happen at the compound."

"Yes. The president and members in the upper echelons of our military have given an American commando team permission to fly in and take back the wreckage. I wonder how they will react when they discover we forced their pilot into a panic and made him blow his brains out."

"I do not care how they react. I receive my orders from men who care about where Russia is headed, not a bunch of simpering old fools who believe it is better to dance with the Americans, take their money and allow our own country to starve to death while we fall behind in the arms race and the advancement of our own technology. We must return our country to a position of strength, or we will perish. We must weed out the weak and the defiant, or all will be lost to the savage and ignorant hordes."

The fire of the fanatic lit Denkov's eyes, and Zherkovsky found himself momentarily taken aback.

"The republics are nothing these days but breeding grounds for terrorists who come to Moscow and blow up apartment buildings," Denkov raged. "The Pakistanis and the Indians both have nuclear weapons and are as unstable as any of the rebels in our backyard. The Chinese occupy our border and sharpen their knives, waiting for the day they can roll their tanks across the border while threatening us with nuclear annihilation. Are you blind to what is going on in your own country, Major? Can you not understand why it is imperative we do not capitulate to these Americans and simply hand them back what is the leading edge of a new technology?"

Zherkovsky took a moment to steel himself, find his voice and the courage to proceed, aware he was about to tread in waters that could well drown him. "These so-called patriots you mention, comrade. Should you examine it all closely, you would know they are the ones responsible perhaps for the sorry mess that has consumed our country in widespread starvation, mass unemployment, rampant alcoholism and suicide rates that have become an epidemic."

"Hold your tongue, Major! You are close to insubordination."

"I merely call it as I see it."

"What exactly are you saying, Major? That you intend to just let these Americans fly in and take back parts of a craft that apparently was designed as a cross between a spy plane and an aircraft capable perhaps of launching nuclear missiles?"

"I say nothing."

Denkov peered at Zherkovsky. "I would be very

careful, Comrade Major, how you proceed when these Americans arrive.''

"It is my understanding they are being sanctioned by our own president. I understand they will be given an escort by our own MiGs."

"Your understanding of the situation does not amount to little more than a child's view of the world."

Zherkovsky felt the cold anger in his belly. He watched Denkov storm off for the waiting choppers at the edge of the woods. He wanted right then to chase the man down, wrap his hands around the throat of what he believed was a corrupt SVR agent in league with the Moscow gangsters and choke the life out of him before it was too late. Denkov was dangerous, perhaps even insane.

And perhaps, he thought, it was already too late anyway.

Standing alone, Zherkovsky felt very old, tired, afraid. The sick feeling deepened when he saw the soldiers unleash their own version of a funeral pyre on the cabin. The major turned and walked away from the angry whoosh of the flamethrowers.

CHAPTER TWENTY-ONE

Stony Man Farm, Virginia

Brognola eyed the bank of wall clocks, got his bearings on time zones, then looked at the situation map for the sixth or maybe seventh time in the past hour. His nerves were so raw he imagined a butter knife alone could shave the skin off his hide, even believed he could feel himself aging by the hour.

"It will be the dead of night over there when they land." The big Fed started pacing around the Computer Room. Bolan, he knew, was still three hours away from touchdown. According to Price, the C-141 Starlifter would beat the C-130 to landing by maybe thirty minutes. It was something close to a miracle that the timing and the logistics to link up Striker and Phoenix Force that close had been pulled off. Near constant communication with both McCarter and Bolan had seen to it that Price and Katz paved the way to get them this far.

Brognola felt the taut nerves all around, everyone on edge, locked in his or her own thoughts and worries, all focused on the Stony Man warriors and what they would face next. On the plus side, neither plane had been shot down by MiGs, and Kurtzman was quick to point out that fact. Even with presidential directives issued by the Russian president and his own high command backing him up, Brognola didn't trust the situation, recalled how Striker had already voiced his own concerns.

There would be shooting once his people landed, Brognola suspected. His reliable CIA contact had confirmed the compound near the Ural Mountains was now under the control of a renegade SVR-Russian Mafia faction. How far and how deep the corruption reached its tentacles into Moscow was anybody's guess.

"Once they're airborne," Price said, "I've already used our own presidential authority to clear them to fly and land at our air base at Incirlik."

Again Brognola checked the wall map, gauging the distance from the Ural Mountains to Turkey. He appreciated any voice of optimism he heard right then. Their fingers were all crossed, for damn sure, but the pucker factor had them all wound tight, all of them aware it could go either way.

That Striker and Phoenix Force may not be coming home.

"You're still talking about a good jaunt until they're home free."

"But it's a hell of a lot closer than having them fly back to Saudi."

As usual, Brognola knew the Farm's mission controller had a good point.

The team at the Farm had done all they could. From there on, all any of them could do was ride out the wait, chew on their nerves. It would either be good news...

Brognola unwrapped a cigar.

Above Siberia

"FLYBOY to Mac."

McCarter keyed his com link, ran a look over the faces of his teammates. They'd been briefed three times already, knew the drill, even if they didn't quite know the score. Hawkins, Encizo, James and Manning were grouped tight together, sitting on the metal bench in the aft belly of the massive C-141 Starlifter. They were all armed with the same weapons they'd used to drop the hammer on the Syrian compound. To a man they looked tired, grim and more than a little concerned. No matter what they felt or thought, McCarter knew they were good to go to pull off the impossible or die on their feet trying.

"Mac here, Flyboy."

"Sitrep. I've got the compound in sight. Three minutes to touchdown. Fasten your seat belts, gentlemen."

"And your fix on Striker?"

"Striker's still twenty-five minutes out. But he's been cleared to land."

"Who's in charge down there?"

"It was a Major Zherkovsky."

"Was?"

"Someone identifying himself as Denkov of the SVR informed me, none too kindly, I may add, that he's now in charge. I'm hearing attitude from this guy, David. So be ready for it to all go south."

"If I get attitude from any of them, you can be sure we'll cure all that with a little basic testicular fortitude and some flying lead."

"I copy. Anyway, we'll be landing on the far northwest runway. Comrade SVR told me we'd better come out unarmed, but I pretty much told him to stick it where the sun doesn't shine."

Problems already, and they hadn't even deplaned, McCarter thought. The Briton perused the sat pictures spread out on the metal table. "Near the hangar where the wreckage of our craft in question is supposedly housed?"

"That's the one. Like you wanted, I'll keep the engines running."

"We wait for Striker to land before we set foot outside this bird."

"Roger that."

"I've got T.J. on the forklift here, and he'll load up Striker's mother lode before we advance on the hangar."

"I copy."

"Jack, when it hits the fan, I may need you to back our play."

"No 'if'?"

"There's plenty of firepower back here in the bin. Take your pick. That includes your flight crew. We're going to need all hands on this one."

"Affirmative."

McCarter signed off, moved for the sat link to touch base with Bolan one last time before touchdown.

"Nothing cute, nothing fancy," Hawkins said.

"Just like I said," McCarter growled, feeling the

precombat jitters rising a notch. "You load up the goods Striker has on board, then sit tight and move in when I need you to hit their asses from behind, T.J."

"And if the MiGs decide to blow up our ride to Turkey?" Calvin James posed. "They might take exception to us shooting up their comrades."

"We've already discussed that, Cal. It's balls-to-the-wall time."

"No sweat," James said, and cut a mean grin. "We take this ride to the end."

To a man they knew how volatile the situation was, aware they might not leave this compound alive.

"If it hits the fan, mates, then we Wild Bunch our way the hell out and start walking toward Turkey."

Aboard the C-130

"YOU MUST BE VERY proud of yourself. You must be very important man back in U.S. to have our own president and our military high command give the green light to just let you fly in and take what we shot down. And then there is the not so little matter of the UFOs and the particle reactors and the lead crates with the element 116 on board this bus. You get to keep it all. Must be very big moment for you when you go back to your country, a hero."

Bolan ignored him. The sprawling fenced-in compound at the foot of the black granite wall of the Ural Mountains was as large a military complex as Bolan had ever seen. He couldn't even begin to count all the MiGs, assault and transport choppers, all the tanks, APCs, not to mention all the other aircraft grounded in front of dozens of hangars. Then there were at least two dozen large, gray squat buildings spread all along the perimeter on all points of the compass, each structure as long from south to north and east to west as two football fields. Everything down there was so brightly illuminated that the compound glared out into the surrounding darkness like some LZ beacon ready to accept the mothership.

According to the Farm, which had taken its information from a supposedly legitimate SVR source funneling intel through the CIA and the DIA, the wreckage was stored in a hangar at the northwest edge of the farthest runway. There appeared a large group of dark figures standing near the hangar in question. In the dark skies above the mountains, Bolan looked at the flashing taillights on the MiGs patrolling the compound. The soldier then spotted the Starlifter parked at the end of the northwest runway. There was tension building already down there, as McCarter had raised him for an update and a final briefing. It sounded as if Denkov of the SVR was getting an itchy trigger finger. McCarter, Bolan knew, had warned the SVR man to not approach their aircraft. Fine, the SVR man had responded, they'd do it McCarter's way.

They would wait for their American 'counterparts' near the hangar.

Every instinct told Bolan they were set to march for a showdown with the SVR agent and his gangster cronies. And the Executioner had every last clip for his M-16 and every grenade at his disposal fixed to combat webbing.

It was going to get ugly, he knew, but how it all played out was up for grabs. They were looking at odds of two, maybe three hundred or more to one if he factored in the Russian soldiers and other personnel at the compound.

"I go with you as gesture of goodwill, comrade?"

"You'll go with me, all right."

"And if there is shooting? Do I need to hear you say it? That I will be the first one shot?"

"Took the words right out of my mouth."

ZHERKOVSKY FELT the tension rising around him the longer Denkov and his gangster comrades were forced to stand in front of the hangar and wait for the Americans to deplane. He knew the SVR man had no intention of letting the Americans leave the compound alive. In fact, Denkov had only minutes ago told him as much.

Which was one reason why Zherkovsky had taken an AK-47 assault rifle from the armory belowground.

"Six men, they say," Denkov said to no one in particular. "They should not prove much of a problem. Once they are in the hangar, I will give the word, Major. I hope you have no problem with what I am prepared to do."

"None at all. It is—how would the Americans say?—your show."

"I believe that is correct. Yes, it is my show. Should this work out properly, Major, I can put in a good word for you back in Moscow. You could be promoted."

Zherkovsky kept the sarcasm out of his voice. "Then I am looking forward to a successful conclusion to your show."

"I am glad that for once we are in agreement."

"It must have been what you said back in the clearing that set me straight."

"You mean my speech about how we must save our country?"

"That would be the one. How we must save Mother Russia from the barbarians."

"There it is."

Zherkovsky followed Denkov's skyward gaze. The thunder sounded before he made out the dark and giant bulk of the C-130. The rest of the American commandos were still inside the Starlifter. Zherkovsky had also gathered from Denkov that they were waiting until the C-130 had safely landed. Overhead Zherkovsky heard the American commandos' MiG escort screaming back and forth as they monitored the compound. Denkov had been unsuccessful in his attempts to raise any of those pilots, but the word had been passed on by the Russian president himself. The MiGs wouldn't fire on either American plane under any circumstances.

Zherkovsky watched the breath pluming out of Denkov's nostrils, suspected the SVR man was riding an adrenaline rush as he probably began envisioning dead American commandos strewed before him. The major then counted thirty-three gangsters, lining up beside Denkov, all of them armed with AK-47s and looking anxious to shed some American commando blood.

Zherkovsky had other ideas. When the SVR man had been busy an hour ago laying out his intended slaughter plan, Zherkovsky had marched off and passed the order through Colonel Milatovka to be passed down to every soldier on the compound.

None of their soldiers was to engage the Americans in a shooting war. In fact, if there was shooting, Zherkovsky's standing order was for his soldiers on the compound to direct any AK-47 weapons fire at Denkov and his gangsters.

Somehow, some way, Zherkovsky intended to take back command and control of the base. There would be plenty of messes to clean up when the shooting stopped, of course, explanations to be handed out to his superiors back in Moscow. But with Denkov out of the way, Zherkovsky perhaps even informing the president himself the man was a traitor and had disobeyed a presidential directive.

The night may not prove a total disaster after all.

Zherkovsky waited, felt his heart hammering in his chest as the C-130 touched down and began its long lumbering taxi toward the Starlifter.

"GENTLEMEN, glad you could make it."

"Wouldn't any of us feel right to let you come here by yourself and have all the fun," Manning told Bolan as the Executioner marched Kakov down the ramp.

"Not to mention I've never seen a flying saucer," Encizo said. "I guess we don't have time to take a look in those crates, do we, Striker?"

"Not the way our Russian friends over there are giving us the evil eye, we don't," James said, nodding at the armed force strung out in front of the hangar.

"Let's get this show under way," McCarter said, keying his com link, raising Hawkins to tell him to fire up the forklift.

"Understand Syria put a few years on you guys," Bolan said.

"If it weren't for one stand-up act," McCarter told Bolan, "name of Meissel, we would have found a few nuke-tipped Sidewinders up our butts."

"Sounds like Katz needs to pass on a fond thank-you," the soldier said.

Bolan and the other Phoenix Force commandos went into the cargo hold to help load the crates onto the forklift when Hawkins rolled in behind them. The soldier was surprised at how light the crate with the main disk was when McCarter and company helped him lift it a few inches before Hawkins slipped the prongs under and backed out.

"What's in there?" Encizo said, puzzled.

"You say the thing's about the size of one of our M-2 Bradleys?" Manning asked Bolan. "Feels like there's nothing but packing foam in there."

"It's real," Bolan said. "What exactly it is, how it flies...even where a pilot may sit, I couldn't begin to tell you."

"So, what's the plan?" James asked.

Bolan ran a grim look over the faces of the four Phoenix Force warriors. "We're going to go have a little talk with this SVR guy and his Russian Mafia cronies. We spread out, and if they make their play we cut loose."

"Jack and crew and T.J.," McCarter said, "are set to cover our backs."

"Then let's finish loading up the goodies in our ride home and get down to business," Bolan said.

CHAPTER TWENTY-TWO

"Gary, Rafe, hang back and slowly fan out to their flanks. Stay outside the hangar when we go in. Let it rip with everything you've got if it comes to that."

"Understood."

"Aye, aye, Striker."

Flanked by James and McCarter, keeping Kakov a few feet in front as a human shield, Bolan gave the order, then kept walking toward the line of gunmen, thirty-plus hardmen in black leather bomber jackets and trench coats. Mean-eyed to a man, all of them were armed with AK-47s.

"Comrades, really, is all this necessary?"

"Who's talking?"

"I am Denkov."

Bolan watched as one of the black trench coats stepped from the middle of the line. Heart pounding as he felt the tension level torqued up a notch, the soldier kept his M-16 angled across his chest. An HE round was up the snout of his M-203, and he'd dump it in the heart of the pack if any of them so much as twitched.

"Is all what necessary, Denkov?"

The smile the SVR agent showed Bolan didn't exactly ease any of the tension coiled in his gut. From the watchtower to their right flank, a klieg light flared on and framed the Stony Man warriors in a glaring shroud. Bolan was hit right between the eyes, but turned his head away from the blinding light. The M-16 was out front and aimed at Denkov.

Snatching Kakov back, the soldier shouted, "Get that light off us! Now!"

HAWKINS SAW Grimaldi and the blacksuit flight crew running down the cargo hold. They were hauling out a mixed assortment of M-16/M-203 combos and HK MP-5 subguns, cracking home clips and chambering the first rounds when Hawkins saw the light bathing his fellow warriors.

"It's gonna blow down there, guys," Hawkins called up the ramp to the backup team. "Hustle up."

Hawkins watched as the SVR agent began flapping his arms at the other gunmen. An order was barked in Russian at the watchtower, the light died and Striker's pilot was quick to point out his flying comrade from Hawaii understood the native tongue. The M-60 man-eater belted, Hawkins checked the immediate vicinity around the Starlifter. No Russian soldiers came running their way, and he found the startling lack of authorized base personnel a curious and troubling problem. The showdown appeared as if it would be confined to an us-and-them scenario at the hangar. Or was the cavalry hanging back until the bullets started flying? he wondered.

Hawkins checked the MiGs streaking overhead, then as Grimaldi and company bounded down the ramp, he asked, "You sure those MiGs aren't going to blow us clear into the Urals?"

"I was assured by the team leader they would not fire on us."

"Yeah. And when was the last time you talked to him?"

"Twenty minutes ago."

"That was before the heat started to rise."

Grimaldi rolled around the corner of the Starlifter, measured the situation downrange. "Striker told us to stay put, T.J., and go in only if the shooting starts."

Hawkins caught Grimaldi reading the look on his face. "I hate this. I really do. I'm looking at thirty-plus thugs down there ready to stick it to our guys."

"Something tells me, Hawk, you're going to get the chance to stick it back. Just hold on."

Hawkins gritted his teeth and watched the air billow out of his mouth as the adrenaline felt like wildfire racing through his blood.

BOLAN WATCHED Denkov raise his hands. More smiling, the light killed, but Bolan wasn't buying the olive-branch routine.

"You come in peace, comrades, I assume?"

"We want the wreckage."

"It is in the hangar. I have even had it roped to a large pallet. It is on wheels attached to a truck. Easy for you to move it to your plane." A tight laugh. "I must say, you Americans are very ingenious. It is so light, it weighs no more than a feather. What is it made of?"

"I couldn't tell you," Bolan said, cutting the gap

to twenty feet, then yanking Kakov to an abrupt stop. "By the way, there was a pilot..."

"Ah, yes, the pilot. Most unfortunate accident. He was apparently running...well, he came to a village, it would seem. The villagers had seen the explosion. They were scared, they panicked. They believed they were being attacked by some strange invaders," he said, chuckling and shrugging, "from outer space."

"You're telling me he's dead."

"Most unfortunate. The savages here in Siberia."

"Where's the body?"

"Again, most unfortunate. These savages, I learned, after interrogating some of them...they dismembered and burned his body."

Bolan heard James snort, McCarter grunt. The more Bolan looked at Denkov and heard his spiel, the more he sensed it was going to blow any second.

"Major," Denkov called down the line, "if you would."

Bolan watched as another AK-47 figure in a black trench coat stepped away from the group, aimed a small black remote-control box at the hangar doors.

Denkov ordered the gunmen to step aside, right down the middle and allow them through.

"After you, comrades."

The hangar doors parted. More white light spilled out onto the grounds. Beneath the umbrella of light, Bolan spotted the transport truck, the wreckage of the disk lashed with rope beyond the rear, deep inside the hangar. It was going to be a long walk, he decided, if it even got that far.

"How about you and your men first, comrade."

Denkov lost his smile, started to bare his teeth. "We go together. At the same time."

"Whatever."

"And those two men and the ones I see with guns at your plane?"

"They stay where they are."

"This is no way to repair relations between our countries."

"I believe it was your guys who shot up a few of our people on our turf first."

Denkov chuckled, but the laughter didn't reach his narrowed gaze. "My guys?"

"Let's go."

"DAMMIT, T.J., stay cool."

"Screw it, Jack. They're going inside. They slam the doors shut and start shooting them up..."

"All right, then, let's walk out. Slow and easy. I've got enough extra HE rounds for this M-203, I should be able to blow the doors down or find another door somewhere on the hangar if they shut us out."

"Yeah, that's if the whole damn thing isn't made of something like titanium."

Hawkins, Grimaldi and the blacksuits moved out.

THE LONG WALK over, Bolan gave the wreckage a quick inspection. It sure didn't look as if it had been blown out of the sky. There wasn't a scratch or a jagged edge that he could see.

"I see you wondering about it, comrade."

Bolan turned and looked back at Denkov. The way the gunmen were slowly fanning out tripped Bolan's alarm. Coming in from the Starlifter, he'd told James and McCarter how to play it. He'd go from left to right, James would strike for the heart and McCarter would work it from the right.

"How's that?"

"It must be made of some element no man has ever seen before now."

Bolan read the change in Denkov's eyes, got his bearings on the tightest pack of hardmen. The SVR agent started to lift his AK-47, was shouting 'Now!' in Russian when Bolan and the Stony Man warriors got the party launched first.

Splitting away from his teammates, Bolan tapped the M-203's trigger on the run, beating it to cover behind the transport truck as the first wave of 7.62 mm scorchers burned the air around him. He heard the explosion downrange, the screams of men in pain. James and McCarter fired their HK SMGs as they sidled for the cover of a large metal bin. Hitting the other side of the truck, Bolan dropped another HE round into the M-203, hit the trigger and blew a group of four hardmen off their feet and sent them flying back on the smoky thunderclap.

A good number of the Russian hardmen were caught out in the open, and Bolan nailed three more with a concentrated burst of M-16 autofire. Two hardmen were scaling a ladder to reach the higher ground of the catwalk when the Executioner zipped a short barrage of lead up their spines and sent them tumbling back to the hangar floor. A glimpse to his side and he found James and McCarter pounding out the lead.

Now, he thought, crouched at the rear of the transport truck and seeking out fresh prey, if they could just hold on until the cavalry arrived.

ENCIZO AND MANNING led the charge. A group of nine hardmen had been ordered to stand guard just outside the hangar's opening. They proved no match for the combined rocket power of Encizo's Little Bulldozer and the blanket of HE rounds streaking past and peppering the hardmen in the opening from Grimaldi and company firing away on the run with their M-203s. Bodies were torn to shreds, flying back into the hangar on a line of thundering fireballs that cleared the way. Striker, James and McCarter, Encizo knew, were deep enough inside the hangar to escape the brunt of that ground-zero detonation.

Encizo and Manning split up as Hawkins, Grimaldi and the blacksuits linked up with them. Even as the smoke boiled and obscured the way in, Hawkins was already picking out AK-47 shooters and letting it rip with the M-60.

THE EXECUTIONER could tell the way they were falling, chopped up to ribbons by flying bullets, that the cavalry had made the party. Not only that, but a few of the Russian hardmen looked surprised by the sudden lightning ferocity of getting hit from behind, spinning this way and that before they were cut down by bullets hitting them from all directions.

High-explosive doomsday had shaved the enemy force down to a skeleton crew.

Bolan rolled out, his M-16 filled with a fresh clip. The din of autofire knifed through the roiling smoke cloud in the hangar's entrance as the cavalry made its presence felt. Just to make sure it was close to being wrapped up, the soldier checked the catwalks, the office up top.

Clear.

A wounded hardman danced into Bolan's line of sight, and the soldier cut him down with a 3-round burst to the chest.

Moving up the side of the transport truck, the soldier found Hawkins sweeping the M-60 back and forth and mowing down a trio of hardmen running for the cover of a forklift. Another pocket of shooters had secured cover behind a stack of crates, and Encizo sent them riding for the ceiling as he obliterated their hiding point with a few HE rounds from his squat rocket launcher.

The Executioner fanned the carnage with his assault rifle. A moaner was put out of his misery by a quick burst from Manning's subgun. The big Canadian was turning his SMG on another figure crabbing through the drifting smoke, when McCarter shouted, "Don't, Gary!"

Manning looked at the Briton as if he'd lost his mind.

"The major there," McCarter explained, "gave us some unexpected help. He took out the SVR bloke, then I glimpsed him drop Striker's pilot when the guy grabbed an AK."

"I will help you…"

Bolan walked up and stood over the major. The Russian's legs were drenched in blood. "Why?"

"I despise traitors of any kind. Denkov was nothing more than a gangster…I have radio in here. I call the pilots…go…take your damn flying disks…you are free to go…."

Encizo knelt by the major, checked his wounds. "I'll get you a tourniquet for that."

"No time..."

Bolan watched as the major took a handheld radio from the pocket of his coat.

"I'll take care of it...please...you must trust me...."

"I don't see where we have a choice," Bolan told the Stony Man warriors. "Let's get what we came here for loaded up. I want us gone in five minutes."

THE EXECUTIONER STEPPED into the cockpit of the Starlifter as Grimaldi held a steady course at the max speed at a thirty-thousand-foot ceiling. The flight deck was more like a sprawling office complex than someplace for a flight crew to navigate an aircraft. With a bird as big and complex as the Starlifter, Bolan knew it housed all the high-tech state-of-the-art goods to keep them sailing along and watching the action, in the air and on the ground. Right then all hands were monitoring radar screens, com banks. In the darkness off to the port and starboard, the soldier spotted their MiG escort.

"My Russian counterpart," Grimaldi said, "doesn't sound too happy about the slaughter show we left behind."

"So far we're still in the air."

"So far. We're still a long ways from Turkey, Striker. I'm just hoping someone back there doesn't get second thoughts and decides to pull the plug on us. We don't have the first piece of ordnance fixed to this baby."

Bolan showed his friend a grim and weary smile. "If it looks hinky, we can just lower the ramp..."

"And what? Strap yourselves in and take potshots at those MiGs with a few SMGs?"

"Just a thought."

Grimaldi chuckled. "What about our UFOs?"

"Barbara's already made arrangements to have the Air Force take the stuff off our hands when we land in Turkey."

"You don't know how glad I'll be to get us there."

"Amen to that. By the way, Rafe and T.J. were telling me you've become quite the chef."

Grimaldi chuckled. "Those guys. By the time we hit Turkey, I'll be so damn tired they'll be lucky I call out for pizza."

"I'll pass that on."

Grimaldi grinned at his friend. "When you break their hearts, tell them to keep the squawking to a minimum."

The Executioner returned the smile, then left the flight deck to go be with the troops.

Stony Man Farm, Virginia

BROGNOLA FELT his heart lurch with relief when Price announced, "They just entered Turkish airspace. Jack just told me our own escort of F-16s has made the scene."

The big Fed felt the collective relief and gratitude around him like a palpable force. Only he knew a few more problems were still on his plate.

Kurtzman and Wethers began sifting through the sheaf of printouts Able Team had brought back to the Farm. So far they'd had no luck cracking the access code, but he knew in time they'd break through. Cyber burglary was what they did as good as anybody in the business.

"Hal," Kurtzman said, "what I'm looking at here is a veritable Who's Who of the CIA, the SVR and an assortment of Russian military and political clout that helped keep Mosnivoc's nuclear-smuggling operation going."

"I'll deal with that later, rest assured. Right now, I need to go call the Man and give him some good news for a change."

Brognola saw Carmen Delahunt staring at her monitor. "What, Carmen?"

"You know, we still don't know it flies."

"I even ran those symbols through my CONTACT program," Kurtzman said, "every language, mathematical or chemical symbols known to man. I even went through archaeological files at the Smithsonian and a few other places on ancient languages. No match."

"Maybe we're not supposed to know."

"But someone does," Akira said.

"That's something else I have to do. Tell you what, folks, make a few copies of that disk, then give one to me. There's someone who might know what to do with it. But we'll hold on to what we have. You never know when we might need some leverage down the road."

And Brognola left them to it to begin the long hours of damage control. Shortly, he'd find out just how bad the state of affairs was between America and what too many out there were calling the new and improved democratic Russia.

EPILOGUE

He saw the lean shadow standing by his Lexus. Brognola walked slowly away from his black sedan. With all that had happened, all the endless hours he'd spent on his feet, feeling his nerves, it seemed like a year ago since he'd put in the call to his contact from the Pentagon to arrange this rendezvous in a parking garage in Rosslyn.

Neutral turf.

Brognola heard the rap of his hard-soled shoes as he moved through the nearly empty garage. The shadow man waited in the gloomy recesses, standing there in his dark Brooks Brothers suit, adjusting the dark sunglasses with an index finger. He knew the man's name, his position inside the fifth ring, but if he bothered to run a background check he could be sure he wouldn't find the first shred of information on the man. Not even a Social Security number.

"I understand our side is looking at quite the mess over in Russia," the shadow said as Brognola pulled up behind the vehicle.

"Nothing that another billion dollars in aid won't cure."

The shadow chuckled. "And so it all marches on. Business as usual."

The shadow held out a hand and Brognola lifted the disk out of his coat pocket and gave it to him.

"I'm sure you made yourself a copy."

"You never know," Brognola said. "I might need to pull an ace out of my sleeve someday."

The shadow cut a smile, dropped the disk into his coat pocket. "It doesn't matter. There's only a few men alive who know how to read what's on it anyway."

"I'm curious about something."

"Ah, my Justice friend, careful. You know what they say about curiosity and the cat."

"It's true, isn't it? Roswell, all the sightings. All the wild tales you hear coming out about Area 51. We've known, haven't we?"

The shadow man seemed to think about something, then nodded. "Yes. In fact, we've known for a little over fifty years now." He turned and opened the door to his car. "We know the truth."

...ney through the dangerous frontier
known as the future...

JAMES AXLER

DEATHLANDS

THE
SKYDARK
CHRONICLES
Book II

Judas Strike

A nuclear endgame played out among the superpowers created
a fiery cataclysm that turned America into a treacherous new
frontier. But an intrepid group of warrior survivalists roams the
wastelands, unlocking the secrets of a pre-dark world.
Ryan Cawdor and his band have become living legends in a
world of madness and death where savagery reigns, but the
human spirit endures....

Available in June 2001 at your favorite retail outlet.